TYRANT

MAIN CORE

L. DOUGLAS HOGAN

DOOMSDAY
PRESS

This book is dedicated to the American that pushes back against tyranny; the oath takers that do their job resisting unconstitutional laws; the American service member and their predecessors, the veterans, both living and the fallen. This book is written as a wake-up call to every American, that there are unconstitutional laws waiting for the right moment to be utilized. There are vain and aspiring men in offices, waiting for the right moment to make their ambitions known and to build them upon the backs of the unfaithful oath taker. Stay vigilant, oath taker, and never assume large government has your back...

If anyone, then, asks me the meaning of our flag, I say to him —it means just what Concord and Lexington meant; what Bunker Hill meant; which was, in short, the rising up of a valiant young people against an old tyranny to establish the most momentous doctrine that the world had ever known— the right of men to their own selves and to their liberties.

—Henry Ward Beecher

BY THE END of the year 2032, America's population had dropped significantly. There was no electricity or running water; all agricultural farmland and equipment, along with transportation and oil supplies, had been seized by a tyrannical organization known as FEMA, an alleged emergency management system devised to control the United States populace in the event of a national emergency.

Of the few American survivors, there remained only the strong and those who had prepared for the fall of the American way of life. Their search for resources dwindled on the hope that they would be able to restore a free nation of commerce, trade, and travel, but wherever there was liberty, there was also tyranny.

Some survivors banded together and pooled their dwindling resources to secure private safe havens and a way of life. Others looted at will—stealing, killing, and raiding from those deemed as weak.

Despite the depravity of some survivors, there was a

common enemy: the United Nations had a growing presence in America. Their ground forces, which were supported primarily by Russia, Iran, and France, had the technological backing of China. They had provided them with ground-breaking technology that could give them an edge against the "resistance"...against the veterans of the former United States military.

CHAPTER 1

The District

December 5, 2032

GENERAL ABDUL MUHAIMIN was well settled into his new position as executive commander of America. Every day that went by, he was hearing less of the patriot resistance against his regime. He had grown tired of the reports of constitutionalists rising up against him and putting a foothold in the territory he was trying so hard to control.

The UN's "Agenda 21" was supposed to be a way for the global community to shrink within "sustainable" limits. The US's Second Amendment proved to be more than a sore spot for the UN, whose sights were set on a global population of no more than five hundred million. Telling a country's populace whose constitution gave them unabridged rights to guns that they must comply or else had been anything but a successful tactic for the UN. For them, it was a miserable failure and a plan B was necessary. If they could not successfully remove the resistance from the American lands, then they would be forced to take less desirable, but necessary steps to ensure the eradication of the population: natural selection through biological interference, a course of action that even the general was not aware of.

"Councilors, I assure you that I am moving ahead and am on schedule with the relocation protocol," General Muhaimin said. He was in the Situation Room and was viewing a projection hologram of the Council of United Nations Emissaries. They met regularly to check on the progress of American restabilization. To the UN, restabilization meant a vacated America, for the purpose of controlled colonization.

"General, you have been selling us the same story for the past couple months. We are looking for progress, not excuses and demagoguery," Ambassador Pao said as he disconnected the signal that linked them to the District.

The United Nations, Beijing, China

Ambassador Pao was a Chinese member of the UN Council. He was deeply involved in the agenda's process to neutralize America, but he knew the president of the People's Republic of China would not commit a single soldier to American soil without absolute certainty it would not fail, and so far, General Muhaimin had proven the patriots' resolve.

Turning towards the other council members, Ambassador Pao said, "We cannot continue to wait on this demagogue. He has been unable to control the Americans. This is why the

Chinese Dynasty cannot commit our people to the cause. We should initiate 'Black State' immediately."

"We cannot and should not, except as an absolute last resort. Our goal is to inhabit those lands, not make them uninhabitable for decades to come," Russian Ambassador Makarovich said. "The Americans are entering into their winter months and are without power. Natural selection will take its course through exposure to the elements."

UN Base, Marion, Illinois, 270 miles south of Chicago

Nathan, Denny, Jess, Cade, and some of the others were enjoying the warmth of a large military generator, compliments of the UN.

The Posse and Buchanan's Marines had fought their way through what remained of Murphysboro and Carbondale to reach Marion, where they met up with a large unit of national guardsmen. With the additional firepower, they engaged a battalion of UN troops and seized all their equipment.

Buchanan and Nathan's group, along with a split of the national guardsmen, had made a previous arrangement to separate for the time being. Nathan, half of the Posse, and some Marines and soldiers were to stay in the Marion, Illinois, area and round up what they could of a resistance force. Buchanan and what was left of his Marines, along with some national guardsmen and the Posse, headed north to collect along the way. Buchanan was to set up a stronghold in the Cook County area and wait for reinforcements.

Every one of them had to change their tactics over the course of the last couple months. The Marines and guardsmen now found themselves flying a US flag over the UN vehicles that they had confiscated from their enemies. They had discovered that retaining UN equipment proved more valuable than destroying it. Loose groups of American survivors had seen the US flags on the equipment. They were finding both hope and strength knowing that their invaders were outmatched and losing their equipment to American patriots.

Each time they ran into a unit of UN troops, it would generally mean the retreat of UN forces and the engagement of UN targets. The Americans just had to be careful that they were not firing upon friendlies that had seized UN equipment, as they had. Likewise, they felt it was smart to keep the UN flags should they need them to cover their identity.

In addition to the seizure of UN equipment and weapons, they also found dissidents like Sergeant First Class Reynolds, who had surrendered himself to Buchanan and his Marines just a couple months prior.

"Has anybody seen any more of these FLIES in the past couple weeks?" Cade asked as he stood over the table and looked at the dissected machine they'd shot down fifteen days ago.

The Chinese piece of technology came flying into their view and was recognized immediately as "E-Tech." E-Tech was the generic name they were using for "enemy technology." In this case, they had some decent intelligence that something called FLIES was being shipped in from the Chinese to the American shores. The patriots didn't know much else about them, other than what the acronym stood for. The forward lasing identification electronic surveillance drones were still somewhat of a mystery to them. They had a damaged one lying on a table in the UN base they were currently occupying.

Nathan joined Cade's side and said, "No, I haven't seen one since. I'm sure they're out there, though. We barely sighted this one."

Cade was wearing a pair of rubber gloves as he carefully moved the FLIES unit around, revealing a pinhole camera.

"Guys, did you happen to notice this tiny camera?"

Nathan stooped down to get a closer look.

"What I wouldn't give for a magnifying glass about now."

Denny walked up to the table and took his backpack off. From one of the inside pouches, Denny pulled out a magnifying glass.

"Really?" Cade said.

"I have it for survival. It's a good alternative for fire starting," Denny answered.

Denny hadn't been the same since the Gorham raid resulting in the death of his sister. He went a month without talking and had just reached the point where he could joke around. Back in October, just before the Southside Raiders attacked Gorham, Pastor Rory Price shared the name of the guy in charge of the raiders. He told the Posse the guy's name was Cade Walker. Denny's state of mind had blocked out many of the details of the Gorham raid.

Nathan took the lens and held it up close to the tiny camera.

"Well, at least you have a good eye," Nathan joked with Cade.

"Probably why I don't need a magnifying lens," Cade joked back.

The FLIES drone resembled a large dragonfly with four round housing units that contained the propeller blades. There were two larger propeller systems on the front of the drone and two smaller ones in the rear. It measured about one foot from the outermost edge of the front propeller to the other front propeller and about seven inches from the outermost edges of the rear propeller to the edge of the other small rear propeller. Each of the propellers could operate independently of one another. They could maneuver in the same fashion as a gyroscope. The bottom of the drone was an off-white color, making it difficult to see against the sky. The drone was covered in tiny circuitry that nobody there could understand and was powered by tiny solar panels covering the upper portions of the drone.

"We need to push on," Nathan said as he walked away from the table. "We still have an objective."

Jess stood up and walked over to the FLIES drone.

"If we can barely see those things flying overhead, then we have a restless trip ahead of us."

Ash joined their side and replied to Jess, "Before I shot that thing down, I didn't even know it was there. It was making a soft buzzing sound, reminiscent of the old sound of humming electricity. I had no idea how long it had been watching or what it was doing."

"Doesn't matter now," Nathan said from across the room.

"We've been on the move for two months, and yeah, we've made progress, but we're still quite a ways from Chicago."

Nathan was packing up his gear and loading his weapons with ammunition.

Everybody was well loaded with ammunition, but sadly, they were having to accustom themselves to the shooting of UN-seized weapons. Not very accurate, but very reliable. Cade felt the most comfortable with AKs. He was loading his AKs when he started to go on another one of his diatribes.

"I remember when the lights went out. Before that day I had no idea I would be shooting these things again. My unit was in Iran and we had just won a major battle against the hajis. We were told to return home immediately, that our services were no longer required. The war wasn't over and we were giving the jihadists a wartime victory by leaving. After that, they continued to flood through the Mexican border and were rallying on US soil and blowing things up. Everything was on fire after the Flip. It was impossible to tell which were acts of terrorism and which were caused by looters and rioters. I guess when it came down to it, they were one and the same."

Ash shared a similar story as he was packing his gear.

"When the Flip went down, I was in the front room. I remember the sounds of low-flying jets overhead. There were dozens of them. They were moving so fast and creating so much noise that the chinaware in our home was vibrating. I went outside to take a look and about that time, the village sirens began to wail. Nobody knew why. We all thought that we were under some kind of attack. Little did we know, we were under attack alright, it just wasn't the enemy we were expecting."

The group finished their packing and started to load up the equipment. Before Buchanan had left, a month back, TOW platoon reported to Buchanan that their tube-launched, optically guided, wireless (TOW) missile supplies were running low. He had already routed a path on his map to the next TOW cache. He made sure it was in the direction they were already headed and was hoping the cache was still there. If it was, they could also pick up some much-needed ammunition for the 50 cals, M4s, and MK19s. The combined anti-tank assault teams (CAAT) were heavily used before the Flip. Any infantry unit would have a supply cache of the ammunition. The problem would be whether or not they were still there.

"I wonder if Buchanan did well with acquiring his heavy guns equipment," Nathan asked.

"I'm sure he did," Jess said. "His men know what they're doing and they were surviving quite well before we were added to the mix."

Gorham, Illinois

Tori Cunningham was a member of the Southern Illinois Home Guard before the Flip. She lived in Belleville and was also a Marine Corps vet. She was the same age as Nathan and met him on a forum that Nathan had designed when he was a web designer and blogger. He recruited her into the Southern Illinois Home Guard, but when the grid went down, her husband refused to leave town, choosing instead to stay and endure, come what may. In the end, they weren't so lucky. The inner city proved too difficult to survive in. There was mass murder, looting, and violent crimes of every sort.

They had kept their house boarded against break-ins, but eventually they came. A group of men with guns demanding they surrender their home, food, and weapons. Her husband, Richard, refused. They sent Molotov cocktails against their sturdy reinforced doors and windows. They caught fire and burned their home to the ground, killing Richard and their six-year-old daughter Charity. Tori had barely escaped with her life and had almost lost that in the proceeding gun fight. She was unconscious when she was rescue by a group of preppers, only to awaken to the fact that two of her family members were burned alive. Her oldest daughter, Amelia, had escaped the fire, but was caught by the bandits and traded to an old man for whiskey. When Tori was well enough to venture out, she went looking for her daughter Amelia, only to find that she, and other children, had been cannibalized by the old man.

Tori had been on the road for a full day, having just recently traded a Ruger 9mm for a running motorcycle; she was tracking down the SIHG group. She had made her way to Gorham and was devastated at what had become of the place. She had been to Gorham on multiple occasions in the past, for meetings and training sessions with Nathan and Denny. She wasn't prepared for what she was seeing.

Gorham, for the most part, was burnt to the ground. She saw very few residents and very few standing homes.

She was met with indignation from the people within the community. They looked out their windows and dropped the curtains when she looked in their direction. She knocked on doors where she saw movement, but they would not answer. Tori understood why the people were paranoid of her. She had endured such atrocities in Belleville, so was being empathetic toward their behavior.

"Hello? My name is Tori Cunningham," she began to yell. "I'm sorry to disturb you, but I'm looking for some friends of mine. Maybe you know Nathan Roeh, Denny Ackers, or Stephen Gill? Nathan used to live around here, up the road, I think. We were supposed to meet here if martial law was imposed."

It seemed like no one was listening, when a little girl came peeking around the corner of a burned-down trailer.

"Hello there," Tori said as she stooped down. "My name's Tori. Can you help me?"

The little girl just shook her head no and stood there. About that time, Christina came calling.

"Sydni."

The little girl took off running and Tori stood up and walked towards Christina's voice. She saw the little girl run to a tall lady that she assumed was the girl's mother.

"Excuse me," Tori said as she walked towards the lady. "My name's Tori. I'm looking for some friends of mine. Maybe you know them? Nathan Roeh, Denny Ackers, or Stephen Gill?"

"What do you want with them?"

"I'm a friend of theirs. I knew them before the Flip and I've left my home in Belleville to search for them."

Christina took notice of the pistol she had tucked in the front of her pants, the Remington 270 she had slung over her shoulder, and her rugged appearance. She had a black eye and a busted lip that looked to be scabbed over.

Tori took note that Christina was looking at her weapons.

"Oh, I'm sorry," Tori said. "This was a gift"—Tori touched her pistol—"and I captured this from a thug in Chester," she continued, touching the shoulder strap of her rifle. "I don't mean to scare anybody."

"Are you a soldier or something?"

"I was in the Marines with Nathan a few years ago. He got out and I extended."

"Well, they're not here anymore. They've headed north to save some people from the FEMA camps."

"I see. Did they happen to say which route they took?"

"No, I'm sorry. I watched them drive off in that direction."

Christina was pointing east.

"That's not north," Tori said. "I wonder why they headed that way."

"I'm not sure. Would you like to come inside, out of the cold, to warm up a bit before you leave?"

"That won't be necessary, ma'am. I need to keep moving."

"Okay, but stay safe out there. Our boys are with a group of Marines, so keep your eyes open for them. They might be able to help you."

"Thank you very much. Your kindness is appreciated."

"You're welcome."

Christina was not being honest with Tori. She knew that the group were heading to Chicago to overthrow a fortress full of American prisoners.

"Oh, by the way, if you see my husband, Rory, with them,

tell him that we miss him and that his wife and daughters love him."

"I will Mrs..."

Tori hesitated and waited on a name.

"Oh, I'm sorry. Christina Price."

"Alright, Mrs. Price. I'll give him the message."

As Tori was getting back on her bike, Christina was overwhelmed with guilt that she had lied to Tori about the group's destination. It was against her morals as a Christian to lie, and her conscience was now weighing heavily.

"Tori, wait," she yelled, but Tori had already started the motorcycle and couldn't hear Christina over the engine.

Tori left Gorham on her motorcycle and headed towards Murphysboro, not seeing or hearing the FLIES drone overhead.

CHAPTER 2

Springfield, Illinois

IN SPRINGFIELD, a small command post had been set up by the UN and was commanded by Captain Zacharov, a Russian military man with twenty years' experience. He was a tyrant and cared little about America's status in the world. He cared only for Russia and would be a fine example of Russian patriotism, if not for his evil tendencies.

"Captain Zacharov, the Cunningham girl was followed to Gorham, where the suspected southern Illinois resistance was once located," the junior sergeant said in Russian.

"Good, continue to follow her. She is the only remaining RFID-chipped survivor of the Southern Illinois Home Guard. What of the other resistance groups?"

"They are still actively repelling our forces. They know their areas and have the advantage, being their homeland."

"Continue your surveillance and report to me immediately when you have something actionable."

"Yes, sir."

The Main Core program had been a growing conspiracy theory since the 1980s. Originally started as a way to monitor extremist groups, the government ran with it and it grew into a shadow government type of program that placed Americans, specifically veterans, on a watch list for the most simple of reasons. If you were government trained, you were eligible for placement; if you were outspoken and had opposing views to the government, you were placed on the list. Eventually the list became unmanageable and a new high-tech way of storing data on these extremists became necessary. In the two decades following September 11, 2001, the NSA's program grew exponentially and became the melting pot of data collection for everyone the government wanted to watch.

Through spy programs, the Chinese were able to hack the Utah Data Center and collect information on everyone included within the list. Most recently, the Chinese started the FLIES drone program and synched the drones with the data center, essentially giving FEMA and what was left of the federal government unprecedented access to information.

For the last decade leading up to the Flip, the US was including RFID chips as part of the inoculations routine for all government employees, especially the US military. This data was linked directly to the UDC and provided exact whereabouts and whether or not the individual was living or dead. The RFID chip was powered by electrical currents emitted by the human heart. If the chip was somehow removed or the body was deceased, the chip would discontinue to function.

Tori had stayed in the Marines an additional four years

beyond Nathan's time of service. She had the chip imbedded in the fatty tissue of her buttocks, but like most people, she didn't know it was there, even though it had been leaked to the media through government defectors. Most people didn't want to believe shadow government conspiracy theories when they heard them. When these types of leaks were made public, most chucked it off and some listened but didn't let it bother them. Tori was the latter; she listened, but didn't seem to let it bother her.

The Russians had used the Chinese FLIES drone to follow a faint signal to her whereabouts. The RFID chip was like a homing beacon to the FLIES drone once it was in range. They worked in unison once it was on target. It could read heart rates emitted from the electrical signal of the RFID chip, and the UDC could receive visual and audio signals from the drone. The person's location, which was approximate to GPS, combined with the capabilities of the FLIES drone, made triangulation possible and exacted a location.

There were a few thousand of these drones flying autonomously across a vast American country, searching for veterans. When one was located, all they could do was watch and relay data back to the UDC.

Marion, Illinois

The combined forces group had amassed a couple hundred more members from the Illinois National Guard unit in Marion. They had a discussion on which route would be safest to take to the next National Guard armory. Everybody was in agreement that the interstate was just too dangerous. They had agreed to take a state highway, but to get to that road would mean doubling back a ways and then rerouting north towards Mount Vernon.

Nathan had learned quite a bit about tactics from Buchanan. As was now customary for Nathan, he had the Army Rangers and the Force Reconnaissance units ahead of the group. Sending a small group of elites ahead of the bulk of fighters provided them with intelligence of what was ahead of them.

As they had traveled, they ran into small skirmishes of raiding groups and individual fire, but nothing unmanageable by the now seasoned grunts.

Before the scouts had a chance to completely leave Marion's borders behind, they stumbled upon a train that was on the roadway blocking the convoy's route. As FORECON approached the track and looked down the length of it, one of the Marines noticed that it had been knocked off the tracks in an apparent ambush of sorts. Several of the front train cars were smashed and off the tracks.

As the Marines and Rangers approached the train, the group stopped their HMMWVs and exited onto foot patrol, but not without first relaying back to the convoy what was happening.

Back in the convoy, Nathan and the rest of the Posse came to a stop on the state route they were traveling, and waited on the FORECON and the Rangers to relay back some intel.

Meanwhile, at the train wreck, the lead scout threw up a hand signal for *get down* and *column formation*.

Hand signals were a universal type of sign language across the branches of the US military and offered silent communication in wartime.

All the scouts lowered their profiles, went on high alert, and waited on the leader to see what was happening. There was a rifle pointing in every direction as they shifted into a staggered column along the roadway. Tensions were high because the front man had seen something and hadn't communicated to the team what it was yet.

Everybody waited patiently for the signal.

See, one, enemy was signaled by the leader.

He had seen the motion of a running pair of feet on the opposite side of the tracks from where they were positioned. The train was blocking the view, but relaying an enemy was erring on the side of caution for the leader.

The team formed up along one of the train cars and proceeded to cautiously clear all of them. Every car door was open and they could clearly see human shackles attached to the walls of the cars. There were steel bars running the length of the cars from front to rear along the walls, both near the ceiling and low near the floor. The shackles were attached to them. High shackles for hands and low shackles for feet.

Once the team leader knew there were no immediate threats present, he radioed in to Nathan.

"November One, November One, this is Echo Four Juliet. Over."

"This is November One. Go with your traffic. Over."

"November One, we have stumbled upon a block in the

highway. A transportation train, similar to the shipping containers on Big Mike. Over."

"10-4, Echo Four Juliet, secure the perimeter. We're coming in. Over."

Nathan stepped out of his vehicle and out to the side of the convoy and gave the hand signal for *rally on me*.

Every member of the combined forces group rallied on him. Nathan, Denny, and Jess stayed tight together as the crew bunched up around him.

"Okay, listen up. The scouts have stumbled upon a road-block ahead. It's blocking our route, so we'll have to figure a way around it. Apparently, it's not a normal freight train. Evidently, the train was being used for the transport of human beings in shackles. I told them to set up a perimeter and to wait on us. I want us to take a look at this. Your input could be vital. When we get there, stay on guard. We don't know what could be waiting in the wind. Mount up."

After Nathan gave his instructions, everybody started walking back to their vehicles.

"What do you think?" Jess asked Nathan.

"I was about to ask you the same thing. Are you going to be okay with seeing it, since you were... you know...?"

"Taken? Yeah, I'll be fine. You know, not to brag or anything, but I've been taken twice! I've got my guard up."

Cade was eavesdropping on the conversation between Jess and Nathan. His suspicions that this was the Gorham group were already high. Now he was confident that he had the people that had destroyed his organization and pulled the carpet out from underneath his little empire.

Denny was also hearing the conversation, but took a

mental note that Cade was especially attentive to what they were saying. Denny couldn't help it, he was a very blunt man and also tactful, but this time he blurted out what he was thinking.

"Hearing everything okay?" he asked Cade.

"Oh, ha-ha, it's cool. Just being nosey. What happened to Jess?" Cade asked Denny.

"She was taken by a group of bandits a couple months back."

"That stinks. I guess things ended okay, because here she is."

"Yeah, she's a fighter," Denny said. "Killed a man with a pen."

Denny was paying close attention to Cade's replies and interest as he fed him the information. He was suspicious of Cade and, in truth, had always been suspicious of him.

Fortunately for Cade, the one man that could physically identify Cade as *the* Cade Walker from Murphysboro was Pastor Rory Price, who never had a chance to see Cade. He was in the convoy that picked Cade up off of the side of the road, just two months prior. Unfortunately, he was on the opposite side of the convoy, towards the rear, and stayed in the vehicle when the on-the-fly decision to split up was made.

The decision to split was made in October. It was now December and not much had changed with Cade. His way of manipulation was to take as much time as he needed to build trust, cause division, and then take control. Not only was this his modus operandi, but being with a strong group had been his goal all along. The only thing he would change at this point was to be in control. To get there, he would have to take out a number of strong men and women. He had spent the last couple months sizing up everybody in the group, especially Nathan, Denny, and Jess. He was arrogant enough to believe everybody else would just follow along.

There were other strong members in the group, but he had identified the strongest and had made up his mind that he needed to hasten his plan. The group was growing too fast and soon he would lose any window of opportunity.

"Killed a man with a pen? Now you have my curiosity piqued. Please don't leave me hanging."

"You're going to have to talk to her about it. I'm not sharing her business."

Denny wasn't a busybody or a gossiper. He certainly wasn't going to share details of Jess's abduction with a man he was already suspicious of.

Cade was now suspicious that Denny was onto him, and made up his mind that Denny had to be taken out. Cade's ambitions, when combined with his narcissism, provided for a dangerous concoction of overreaction that had led to bad outcomes and, most recently, failure. Realizing that his previous mistakes in Murphysboro and Gorham had cost him everything, he had decided to keep a low profile, with snuffing Denny on the backburner.

The entire group had arrived at the train tracks and were staring intently at the train cars. One of the Rangers rallied on Nathan when he pulled up with the others.

"When we first arrived, we saw movement, so stay on guard. We're not sure who's here or what level of hostility, if any, we might encounter," he told Nathan.

Nathan turned around and said, "Stay in groups of no

less than two. Spread out and examine this train. You're looking for any signs of life or intel that may be able to shine a little light on what we're dealing with here."

They acknowledged and broke up in pairs of two or three. Everybody was on high alert.

Cade looked at Denny and said, "Can I tag along with you?"

"I don't care, but I'm going to be with Nathan."

Cade looked at Jess and asked her, "Hey, you mind if I tag along with you?"

Jess looked at Nathan and saw that he was preoccupied with Denny and whatever they were talking about.

"Sure. No problem."

Jess double-checked her weapon to make sure that she still had a round in the chamber and rounds in the magazine. After that, she looked at Cade and said, "You ready?"

"Let's rock 'n roll," he replied.

The train was huge. They could see where the trains had collided into something, throwing the engine and lead cars off the track. As they looked back down the track towards the rear of the train, they couldn't see the caboose. It seemed like miles of train. There were also about a dozen tracks at this particular space; room enough for several trains to be parked side by side.

The group was now well spread out and headed in opposite directions to examine the find. Denny was at last alone with Nathan.

"I don't trust Cade."

"He's different, but he's given me no reason not to trust him."

"Haven't you seen the way he's constantly studying everybody?"

"Yeah, but we're surviving the apocalypse, man. It's okay to be paranoid."

"He somehow seems familiar to me, but I can't place it. Maybe I'm being *too* paranoid."

"I'm not sure if *too paranoid* is even possible, these days. Although, I'll admit, my sixth sense was tingling when we first picked him up. Not meaning to change the topic, but I wonder how Buchanan's faring?"

CHAPTER 3

Bicentennial Park, Northwest Indiana

Buchanan had amassed a regiment-sized group of veterans, active-duty military, and patriots over the course of the last month. With the UN equipment and radio communications that he had been acquiring, they were able to make contact with large groups and rendezvous at key points. One group in particular had laid siege to most of Kankakee, Illinois, completely ridding it of UN forces through guerilla-type tactics. The urban environment was the battlefield of the times.

When Buchanan found Kankakee and met up with the group, he found that they had an individual they called *the oracle*. The oracle wasn't a prophet, seer or any such thing, but he had survived and escaped from Goose Island, a FEMA stronghold, where they were shipping Americans and exterminating them, according to the oracle.

The oracle had no tongue. He was a hardened farm boy,

once upon a time, but grew into a man that was paranoid of an overreaching government. He was on a list of suspected terrorists, for being associated with patriotism. The list, titled Main Core, was the government's compilation of tens of thousands of America's most patriotic citizens. He was high on the list and was working in Chicago at the time of the Flip, making him easily accessible.

The oracle was housed in a special cell, where he was tortured by UN troops and pressed for intel on the whereabouts of other patriots. When he refused to talk, they cut his tongue out and sent him to Goose Island, where he was to meet *the common good*. According to the oracle, the common good is a catchy phrase the UN uses when they are justifying the genocide of a population, or *invasive species*.

The oracle couldn't speak and didn't know sign language, but he could read and write. He spent his time educating the group on the topic of Goose Island.

Lieutenant Colonel Buchanan, Captain Riley, Sergeant First Class Reynolds, and Gunnery Sergeant Franks had spent the last two months pushing towards Chicago from southern Illinois. With the find of the oracle, it had been anything but uneventful.

The trek northward had cost them both men and supplies, but they had replenished both along the way. Their trip wasn't a straight line, but was a strategic zigzag along the way. They had to reroute when they encountered UN movement that was too big to overtake, force on force. Some of these detours turned out to be a good thing, especially the detours where they met other large survival groups. Each group of locals was able to provide intel that led them from military reserve post to military post. At each post, they managed to accrue assets, if not supplies, then people. The combined forces group had grown to a sizeable regiment of about five thousand armed men.

Along the way, Buchanan found himself dodging UN strongholds, only to meet up with other survivors and head back to the stronghold to overwhelm it. By using this tactic, it pushed their arrival to Chicago back, but it gave them the necessary equipment, ammunition, and weapons to help sustain the effort. Not all of the UN soldiers were foreign. Buchanan had accepted the enlistment of at least a hundred US military men that were previously assigned to the UN Missions Agreement. They were in a situation similar to Sergeant First Class Reynolds and his Rangers before they had joined up with Buchanan.

Among the newly acquired members of the group were Major Scott Andrews, an Indiana national guardsman, and Staff Sergeant Anthony Greene, formerly an Army linguist, who was assigned to the UN Missions Agreement. Andrews and Greene knew each other before the Flip, when the National Guard was still under Title 32 of the United States Code.

When the Flip went down, former president Adalyn Baker activated the National Guard under Title 10 of the United States Code, giving her federal authority over them. She called for all linguists to report to the capital building in Washington, DC, now known as "the District." Upon reporting to the District, the president assigned Greene to his original region, where he would act as a translator for the UN troops from Iran. It wasn't until Buchanan's arrival that he found the courage to defect from the totalitarian control that was over him.

Andrews' story was more similar to Buchanan's. He defected with a company of soldiers at the first mention of martial law. Andrews started preparing his men for the eventualities of such a disaster long before it happened. Andrews would have his senior enlisted men standing in the BEQs (bachelor enlisted quarters) when the news was running and make snide remarks about the president's decisions on foreign affairs and domestic abuse of authority. It was his way of grooming them into knowing he was against tyranny and that he would resist it, should it ever come. Eventually it came, and his men knew who to turn to for direction. He tried to get his seniors involved in the resistance, but they wouldn't have it, choosing instead to report to the District for orders. Andrews left with his men, and his seniors had nobody to command when they returned. Andrews never returned to find out what had happened to them and what orders they had received from the District.

Buchanan not only had a regiment-sized group of fighters, but he had also seized much-needed vehicles from the UN companies that had been posted at random locations. The radios worked well, but the frequencies had to be changed. He assigned Greene to maintain a constant surveillance over a couple different radios that had been confiscated from the invaders, the rest were assigned to squad-sized groups within the combined arms force and given different frequencies. From what Buchanan had discovered, the UN was divided into units of countrymen. One UN unit may be comprised almost entirely of Iranians, and another of Russians. They were almost never exclusive. Many of the units did not speak English, so they had linguists or former US military men assigned to them. In addition to this setup, each unit also had a French, Russian, and Farsi speaking member assigned to it. This allowed loosely educated UN units to communicate with one another and not be so scattered in the orchestration of tactics. It was, however, a weakness that had been exploited a few times by Buchanan. He had learned from Greene that if you hit the UN units hard and fast enough, they lacked the capability to organize a rapid response. The result was chaos for the UN soldiers, who couldn't relay for assistance quick enough.

Greene was surveilling one such radio when he heard some chatter that had piqued his curiosity and caused him to call on Buchanan.

"Bravo One, Bravo One, this is Mike Bravo. Over."

Mike Bravo was the call sign given to Greene. Being the linguist, his area of operations was suitably called the Mother Brain, or, as the military would call it on the radio, Mike Bravo.

"Go for Bravo One," Buchanan responded. The radio discipline had slacked a bit over the course of the last couple months, but there were certain etiquettes Buchanan was willing to sacrifice and others he was not.

"Bravo One, I'm picking up some interesting comm from due east of us. Can you return to Mike Bravo? Over."

"Ten-four, Mike Bravo, I'm en route."

Buchanan dropped what he was doing and reported back to Greene.

"What did you find?" he asked him.

"Sir, I was contacted by a rogue patriot group due east of here who had stumbled upon our frequency."

"What did they say?"

"They were calling for you, sir. I didn't respond."

"Good job, Staff Sergeant. What was their call sign?"

"Three twenty-five marforce?" Greene said inquisitively.

"You've got to be kidding me," Buchanan said shockingly.

"Sir?"

"It's a unit designator; 3/25 Marforres. They're a Marine Force Reserves unit," he replied. "Marines from Brook Park, Ohio. Gimme the mic," Buchanan ordered him.

"Three twenty-five Marforres, this is Bravo One. Over."

Buchanan waited anxiously for the radio traffic to return. There was a pause that made him nervous. He was assuming the call was coming from a Marine unit desiring to rendezvous with his combined armed forces group. The resistance was growing in word and deed. So, it was natural assume this call would be no different than other calls that he had received in the past.

At the end of the long pause between relays, he was more surprised than he had anticipated.

"Bravo One, I know I'm breaking radio protocol, but this matter is urgent and we are past etiquette. This is Joint Chief of Staff and commandant of the Marine Corps, General John James. I am near your location with fellow Joint Chief of Staff Admiral Belt McKanty. We have already dispatched a unit of Marines to a mutually distant waypoint. Rendezvous with these Marines and use their intel to communicate with me further. They will be at MGRS Sixteen Tango Echo Lima Three Five. How do you copy? Over."

Buchanan was shocked and apprehensive about what he had just heard. His initial reaction when he had heard who he was communicating with was excitement. However, he was soon overwhelmed at the possibility of a trap. While Greene was taking good notes from the relay, Buchanan was listening closely and conceiving a plan to meet up with the commandant and still be safe about it.

"Commandant, this is Bravo One. I copy and am dispatching a rendezvous party immediately. Over."

"Loud and clear, Bravo One. We are going radio silent until we hear from you again. Over."

The radio went silent and Buchanan handed the mic back to Greene and put his hand on his shoulder.

"Good catch, Staff Sergeant. We've got work to do."

"Reynolds up," Buchanan yelled.

Fort Wayne, Indiana

General John James and Admiral Belt McKanty had not only survived the execution of the Joint Chiefs of Staff, but had journeyed from the District, in Virginia, through West Virginia, Ohio, and into Indiana.

Their goal had always been to reach South Dakota, where John had a regiment of Marines tucked away with supplies and armaments. Along the way, they had lost several friends, including the cab driver, Joshwa, who had secured their way safely out of the District, Joshwa's wife, Zamora, and their two sons, Aaron and Gideon. Ironically, their route took them to a town called Defiance in Indiana. The general and admiral thought it to be a matter of coincidence when they were met by a band of patriots, national guardsmen, and Marine Corps Reserve units that were actively opposing the occupation. The group had beaten down several UN convoys and overwhelmed UN command posts. For John and Belt, it was a dream come true.

The leader of the group was a National Guard captain by the name of George Clark. He was heading to Fort Wayne when he had stumbled upon the general and admiral, subsequently relinquishing his command to them.

General James and Admiral McKanty had learned from Captain Clark that Fort Wayne was rumored to be a city still operating under the Articles of the Constitution. This was an idea that seemed refreshing to them and reminiscent of a long-lost America. The thought was to move with Clark and his men to Fort Wayne to continue fortifying the city and to help restore the Constitution.

The food supply in Fort Wayne was not ideal, but it was enough to survive on. They had the luxury of local agriculture under its protection and plenty of generators and experts in every field to assist with new ideas for living in such times. America had become so spoiled by its electronic gadgets, electricity, and running water that it had forgotten how to survive without such amenities.

The defenses in Fort Wayne were easy to set up once the lawlessness had abated. There was a short burst of anarchy when the Flip happened, but for the most part, it was crushed early on. The people came to understand that they could survive if they pulled together. Unfortunately, there had to be a certain brand of local law to make it work. Without laws, the people became anarchical and that was unacceptable. The mayor and the governor of Indiana were brothers; that was the biggest asset the city had. They were able to pull resources down from the state level to the city level, utilizing the National Guard and local law enforcement to assist in the security of a free society. Because of these laws, the city was not entirely free. There were curfews and limits on how much food and water were rationed. The people were still free to have firearms for the purpose of resisting tyranny. You were free to leave Fort Wayne at any time, but you could not bring anyone back unless they could be an asset.

The arrival of General James and Admiral McKanty was a welcomed one. It didn't take the city officials long to decide that they had the necessary assets to be allowed into the city.

Governor Jim Williams and Mayor Lawrence Williams had greeted them at the gates and welcomed them in for their accomplishments and sacrifices to the old American way of life.

John and Belt had to explain to the politicians that they were on a more pressing mission: the destruction of FEMA and the removal of all foreign invaders.

Jim and Lawrence concurred with the military men and offered their assistance, essentially allowing them anything they needed to successfully pull their coup.

As they discussed details and tried to develop a strategy on a successful coup, the *roamers* returned with more UN equipment and had stumbled upon a frequency being used by another large group of resistance fighters.

Roamers was a slang term for the groups that patrolled the city perimeter and expanded the territory of Fort Wayne and, ultimately, Indiana. When Michael had arrived with John and Belt, he requested to be a part of the roamers. His new job was primarily maintaining a security net around the city and, secondarily, expanding outward in a spiderweb technique to engulf more territory and safe zones.

In the meantime, John and Belt spent some time with their new allies, listening to radio chatter, and came to a consensus that they were going to make contact with the leader, Bravo One. Volunteers from the local Marine Corps Reserves unit 3rd Battalion, 25th Marines, were sent towards Bravo One with a specific set of instructions from the general, who could tell by the radio traffic that he was dealing with another high-ranking Marine. If he was right, he could solicit the help of a brother and strengthen the cause that much more. Combining the size of Bravo One's force with the Marine regiment on standby in South Dakota could turn the tide.

John was unaware of the intelligence that Bravo One had on Goose Island but had intelligence of his own on the FEMA infrastructure. Being a member of the Joint Chiefs of Staff gave him privy information that would be mutually beneficial to share with Bravo One. For now, John had to be content with waiting for a reply from his would-be connection to the west.

John had given the Marine dispatch a frequency and channel to turn to at a predetermined time. John didn't want to risk transmission interception by enemy forces, so he chose to minimize the possibility by dispatching the channel and frequency manually, rather than over the air. The ball was now in Bravo One's court.

CHAPTER 4

Marion, Illinois

JESS AND CADE had traveled north, up the tracks, leaving Nathan and Denny to travel south, down the tracks. Several of the train cars were toppled off of the rails and lying on their sides, while others were still upright, but smashed between some of the other cars. It was hard for any of them to fathom the amount of force required to cause such a disaster. That was the primary question running through Jess's head as she and Cade walked ever northward, guns at the ready.

"I wonder how fast they were going," Jess said curiously.

"I don't know, but they would have at least been booking it at the sound, by the looks of this wreck," Cade said sarcastically.

He was letting Jess take the lead so he could watch her. While he was actively looking over his shoulder, he would always face back forward and carefully study Jess. He was confident she was the person that had killed Scott, back in

October. His suspicion of her was rapidly taking hold of his thoughts, so that after a few minutes of walking, he wasn't focused on the task at hand, which was searching the train cars for information.

"Hey, Jess."

"Yeah?"

"I was eavesdropping earlier and couldn't help but hear something about you being taken!"

"It was nothing," she said, trying to dodge the topic.

"You know, it's not healthy keeping stuff bottled up. It can create an explosive personality disorder."

"And you're a doctor now?"

"No, just speaking from experience."

"Okay, I'll bite," Jess said. "You tell me what happened to you, and I'll tell you what happened to me."

"Back in my army days, one of the senior noncommissioned officers always had it out for me. He had bullied me for a couple years, only because I was a weak swimmer. Every day was the same thing. When there was a special assignment, I was looked over. When there was monkey matter, I was assigned the duty. Eventually, we were shifted from stateside to the jihadist wars. When I was in Iran, my unit was overcome by hajis. We were running low on ammunition and men. I had watched most of my peers die right before my very eyes. My unit went from several dozen men to five, in the time span of an hour. Air support was tied up on other missions; apparently, we were prioritized. I remember looking over, in the heat of conflict, and seeing my friend Scott bleeding from the neck..."

Cade was telling his story, purposefully mixing truth

with lies, waiting for a response from Jess. He carefully looked over both shoulders one last time to make sure nobody was watching. It was just him and Jess. Nobody could be heard and the only sounds they could make out were the sound of their footsteps and their voices. Cade had one hand behind his back, reaching for the same switchblade that he had used to kill his friend Wayne. He was waiting for Jess to acknowledge the killing of his friend Scott.

Jess was not ignorant of what was being said. What she refused to reveal to Cade was the fact that her senses were now heightened as adrenaline began to flood her veins. She was trained to *act* and to *react*. This training had saved her in the past, and was proving true once again.

"What happened next?" Jess asked, doing her best to play coy.

"I shot the staff sergeant that had been bullying me. I shot him in the head and nobody noticed it happen, because we were all shooting and dropping like flies."

"I'm sure he had it coming. He took you to a bad place," she said, avoiding eye contact.

Jessica played it off as if nothing was going on, but she felt deep down that this guy was somehow tied in with the same Scott she had killed a couple months earlier. She was looking in and around the crashed train cars, as if searching for clues, all along, she was actually buying time to see what Cade's next move was going to be. She thought of her Glock pistol that was tucked into the small of her back, but with Cade behind her, it was too risky of a move. Her rifle was at the ready, but facing in the opposite direction. She could sense something was amiss, but chose to change the topic.

"Look, over there," she said, pointing into a train car. The grotesque scene was one of horror movies. There were corpses still hanging from some of the shackles in the cars. Some of them only had hands and arms hanging from the shackles. The scene didn't faze Cade, who was still pressing to hear her story.

"You said that if I told you my story, you would tell me yours."

Jess decided to risk it.

Her rifle's safety switch was already in the fire position. She had one chambered and she had press-checked it before leaving.

"When I was back at Gorham, I was working with some RNs who had not familiarized themselves with firearms..." she started saying as she prepped herself mentally for an impending fight. She was walking along the tracks, slowing along the way and taking as much time as she needed to prepare herself. With each step, she slowed and looked into a train car. "So I was teaching them how to use them. What I didn't know was that some thug from Murphysboro had snuck into our homestead and decided to have his way with me."

Cade had left his right hand on the rifle trigger. He knew the risk in shooting her. It was one that he wasn't willing to take. His plan was to stick her with his butterfly knife, the same way he did his pal in Murphysboro.

With his left hand, he reached down to lift the tail of his shirt, to reveal the case his knife was resting in. He quietly unbuttoned it as Jess told her story. He slid it out and kept it behind his back. Using his back as a catch to quietly open it, he pushed the button and the blade unfolded just a bit. From there he slowly let the spring do the rest until it was fully unfolded and in the locked position.

Jess didn't hear the click because the rocks they were walking on had drowned out the sound.

"What happened next?" Cade asked, returning his response to Jess in the sick game he was playing with her.

Jess turned around and stared into Cade's eyes.

"I stabbed him in the throat with a pen until I saw arterial spray."

As if on cue, a large pit bull came around from behind Cade, stopped, and began to growl at him. It was Thor. He had been growling at knives since the Southside Raiders' attack on Gorham.

Jess saw Thor and felt at ease, but Cade, not knowing what dog was growling at him, reacted, sloppily turning around to face the dog, revealing he had a knife behind his back. It was all Jess needed. The opportunity was now hers and the ball was in her court to shoot and kill Cade while she had the upper hand. Nobody would question her story or doubt her integrity. She had to act quickly, so she brought her rifle up and pointed it at the back of Cade's head.

Morgan was partnered up with Ash. They were standing inside of a train car going through the pockets of the deceased people that were still shackled when they heard several shots ring out. They briefly stared at each other and then jumped down out of the train car in unison. They couldn't tell which direction the shot came from, so they patiently waited for another sound.

While they stood outside of the train car, they looked at the ground so that they had an ear facing north and south, the direction the tracks were running. Several more shots rang out from the north and both men took off as fast as they could in that direction.

"Wait! Stop here," Morgan said.

"What? Why?" Ash asked.

"We don't know what's going on over there. We need backup."

Both men heard yells coming from the north and south. Shots were ringing out in both directions now.

"We're under attack, Ash. Now we have to pick a direction."

"We can head back south; there's more friends in that direction."

When Morgan heard Ash say that, he remembered that he saw Cade and Jess heading north up the tracks, just the two of them.

"Jess and Cade are alone north ways. I think they need our support."

Ash started running north and Morgan was running right behind him.

The two men only ran a few train-car lengths when they had to drop and take cover. They were now under fire from the north and east side of the tracks. They could not yet make out the location of their attackers, but saw Thor running back towards Ash.

Ash was already leaning up against a train car with his

profile tight against it. He lowered his body to receive Thor, and grabbed him by the collar, pulling him in closer to the train so that he wouldn't get shot.

"What is it, boy? Where are they?" he asked Thor.

Thor turned to face northward and Ash noticed some fresh blood on his ear. Reaching out to touch the blood, he rubbed it off and saw that it wasn't his.

"One of them have been shot," Ash exclaimed to Morgan.

"Well, we're kinda pinned down right here."

Ash was closest to the corner of the car, so he slowly peered around to look for a shooter. He saw several individuals who weren't shooting at them, but seemed to be preoccupied shooting at someone else.

"The people on the east side aren't shooting at us. They're shooting at somebody in that direction and that direction," Ash said, pointing southeast.

"If nothing else, I would say this was a poorly executed ambush," Morgan remarked. "We need to get up there and find Jess and Cade."

Both men and Thor walked with a low profile, moving from cover to cover northward.

Eventually, they came to a spot where they saw Jess running south down the tracks. Morgan and Ash began laying down some cover fire at men shooting from ditches, houses and rooftops.

"Let's go," Jess shouted towards them.

"Where's Cade?" Ash asked.

"He was shot. He's down. Let's get out of here."

"Is he dead, Jess?"

"Yeah, he's dead. We have to leave or we'll be dead, too."

About that time, the convoy came roaring northward, where it stopped to pick up Jess, Ash, Morgan, and Thor. The machine gunners were tearing into the houses and ditches that had assailants in them. Once the four of them were on board, they left, northward.

Nathan was not in the vehicle that Jess had entered, so he spent the next few minutes wondering if she was okay and what had just happened.

When the firefight started, he and the others that were closest to the convoy ran back to it and went to provide cover fire and to rescue members of their crew. From there, he gave the command to head north, past the front of the train.

Eventually, the convoy was able to meet the front end of the train wreckage and cross over to the east side of the tracks. The attackers were now a mile or two behind them.

The convoy came to a stop and Nathan exited the HMMWV on the same side that Jess exited. His heart was relieved to see that she was okay. They began walking towards each other, acting nonchalant, as if to maintain their coolness.

They reached each other and Nathan asked her, "What just happened?"

"I'm not sure, but I shot Cade just before all the shooting started. I think I might have started the whole thing."

"Wait, you shot Cade?"

"Yeah, he was somehow involved in the Gorham attack."

"What makes you think that?"

"The comments he was making."

"Comments?"

"Yeah, he even mentioned the Scott guy that took me and made reference to him being killed by a wound to the neck."

Denny came running up, catching the tail end of what she was saying.

"What's going on?" he asked.

"She shot Cade."

"What? Where is he?"

"I don't know, I shot him and I think that ignited the gun show. I think they were watching us."

"Back to Cade," Nathan said. "You shot him because he made vague references to the Gorham attack?"

"Not just the attack, but the killing of that Scott guy I killed with a pen."

"We have to go back and find him," Denny demanded.

"It's too dangerous," Jess countered. "Nathan, I think he was going to kill me. He was pressing me for information and would have stabbed me if Thor hadn't shown up and growled at him."

"Are you sure he's dead?"

Jess hesitated and Nathan caught the fact that she didn't want to answer the question.

"Denny, round up a crew. We're going back. We can't leave him there."

Denny ran off towards the parked convoy.

Jess was busy trying to talk sense into Nathan, but he wouldn't hear her point of view.

Nathan grabbed Jess by the arm and she pulled away.

"Don't try to rough me up, Nathan."

"I'm not, I'm trying to get your attention. You've shot a

loyal group member based on information that is shady at best."

"I know how it sounds, but you weren't there. You're going to have to trust me on this."

"I do trust you, Jess. But you have to understand two things. First, we need closure. If he's dead, case closed. I'll talk to you more about it later. Secondly, if he's alive, we need his side of the story."

"Fair enough," Jess replied.

Denny returned with a few Marines and Southern Illinois Home Guard veterans.

Nathan told the convoy leader to stay put until they returned.

There were eight of them in the small patrol unit. Each was well armed and had radios.

The group kept a tight formation against the wall of the train cars and trained their weapons towards the houses and ditches where they had seen people shooting from. Aside from the bodies of the men they had killed, they did not see any more people.

Jess led them to the spot where she and Cade were standing when Thor had grabbed Cade's attention.

"I was standing right here and Cade was standing behind me. He pulled his knife out and Thor must have walked up behind him. He growled at Cade, he turned around towards Thor, and I raised my rifle up towards Cade's head and pulled the trigger. At the same time I pulled the trigger, I was being shot at. I jumped in here..."

Jess demonstrated by jumping up into the train car.

"And I took cover. I called for Thor, but he ran back towards you guys in a southward direction."

"So where's Cade?" Denny asked.

Cade was nowhere to be seen.

They did a quick search, looking for signs of Cade or his body, but found nothing but a blood pool where Jess said he was standing at the time she had shot him.

"Alright, head back. He's not here. We can't linger. It's too dangerous."

The patrol started heading back.

Jess was walking behind Nathan, but hurried up to get alongside of him.

"You covered closure if we found his body, and his side of the story if we rescued him. You didn't say what would happen in the event of a missing person," Jess said.

"I guess we had better be watching our backs."

Elsewhere in Marion, Illinois

"He doesn't have any identification on him," Cade heard a man say.

He felt his pockets being searched.

"He had this on him," he heard another voice say.

Cade felt an excruciating pain shooting through his head as he was waking up.

"Lie still, son," a man's voice said as he felt two hands on his shoulders.

Cade was lying on something soft. He reached his right hand out and felt cushions beneath him and realized he was on a couch.

"Where am I?"

"You're in a friend's house, now."

"Am I going to live?"

"Thanks to the quick thinking of some of my men, you will. You'll recover, but you have to rest. You were shot in the head; it seems you have a guardian angel."

"The girl that shot me..."

"Shhh, don't worry about any of that. Those tyrants have left and they're no longer a threat."

"They have others they're going to kill if we don't do something to stop them. I was with them only to stay alive. They have left a trail of blood from Murphysboro to Marion. They are *monsters*," Cade said as he tried his best to manipulate them into believing he was the good guy.

"I have guys following them. They'll collect some information on the monsters and bring it back to me."

"How many of you are there?"

"First things first. My name's Tom Walker, and regarding my men, well, I never share my numbers, but you don't seem like the dangerous type. I can muster a couple hundred fighters."

"Really?"

"Yeah, really. That might seem like a lot, but only a few of them are considered the faithful type."

"No, I mean are you really Tom Walker?"

"Yes. You say that like you've heard of me."

"Were you married to Theresa Walker?"

"Theresa was my wife, a long time ago, yes. Do you know her?"

"She's my mother. I'm Cade Walker, your son."

Murphysboro, Illinois

Tori was kneeling down, with the brass casing of a bullet in one hand and a rifle in the other. Brass casings riddled the ground next to the storefront buildings. Tori had picked one up that appeared to be a 223 or 5.56mm caliber casing. Looking around, she saw more brass, but most of them were 7.62x54R. *Most likely shot from a Russian PKM*, she thought to herself. She was putting the information together that there had been a gunfight here between Russian UN soldiers and/or their equipment and Americans. They were gone now, and there was no further sign that any UN forces were still occupying the immediate area.

Tori had punched her way through Chester with minimal resistance. The cold air had most likely killed off much of the populace or sent them southward towards warmer climates. Regardless of why they weren't there, she was happy that she didn't have to spend much time defending her liberty. The one man she had run into came storming out of a house with a scoped-out Remington 270. He must not have taken notice of the pistol she had in her right hand. Had he been more observant, he might still be alive.

Tori was a survivor, and she had determined that she was not going to be a victim again—not now, not ever. She spent lots of time alone and had all the time in the world to contemplate her existence and the state of America. This was still her home, and regardless of the tyranny that now ran rampant in the District and on the streets of America, she was going to survive for her husband and daughters. The way she saw it, their memory was kept alive in her. She had lost all contact with any other relation the moment the grid went down.

Tori and Nathan had met a few years before the Flip. She never wore her wedding band, for whatever reason, and that led Nathan to believe she was single. She had attended the meetings faithfully for some time, not mentioning the fact that she was married until one day Nathan's flirtations towards her became apparent. Nathan had developed a crush on her, but she had to let him know that she was married and remained apologetic about any confusion for several weeks. Her new quest to search for and locate Nathan had nothing to do with that awkward relationship. It was, in fact, a survival move.

Tori stood up and kept the clues in her head as she moved onward.

It's going to be impossible to track them north of Murphy, she thought to herself. *Murphy* was a slang term the locals called Murphysboro. She knew that if there weren't going to be any witnesses, then her trail would soon run dry.

Tori thought back to what Christina had mentioned about heading north. She followed a trail of UN wreckage from Route 149 east to Route 13 east. She couldn't reconcile Christina's comment about them heading north if all the signs continue to point to a trip that headed east, towards Carbondale, a large town situated between Murphysboro and Marion.

Tori had no desire to drive through Carbondale, but she knew there could be clues in Carbondale that could lead her towards her destination, which, at the moment, appeared to be fluid, rather than a stationary place. She didn't know if Nathan was still alive or if he was dead. All she knew was that the company he kept had pressed from Gorham to the east and, ultimately, according to Christina, to the north.

Her trek to Carbondale was uneventful. Once she arrived, she played with the idea to take back roads around the once large, bustling, college community, but if she did that, she might miss something. Her motorcycle, now stopped, made a soft and soothing humming sound. She was glad she had acquired herself a Harley Davidson. The parts would be more easily attained, since they were made in America, but how many Harley parts would she find lying around if she needed them? She didn't think that far ahead. The bike was loud and that was a problem in large domesticated areas.

With both legs straddling her bike, she strolled along as quietly as she could. The way to keep a Harley quiet was to take it nice and slow. She drove softly along Route 13 east and saw a few people along the way. Most of them were looking from windows, and others were groups of men and women wearing colors that promoted their gang affiliation. They would look at her and watch her ride along, but everybody seemed to be allergic to the highway. They were avoiding it at all costs. The UN didn't sweep through side roads and, in fact, avoided them at all costs. They liked to control the main highways and interstates. So when people saw her on the highway, they did not give chase. This was the rule, the exception was the area around the University Mall. It had been seized by a large group of people that had not only taken control of the mall, but also the shopping centers across the highway.

When Tori's bike came riding into the area, she saw them gathering outside on either side of the highway. They were still several yards from the roadway, but appeared to be a menacing group. Of the weapons she saw them carrying, they had shovels, axes, baseball bats, machetes, and guns. She tried not to panic, but the adrenaline rush flushed her ears and she felt the flow of blood in her veins as it pumped through her face. She maintained her composure and kept a slow steady pace as she moved along.

One person in particular was ahead of the others and moving in her direction. He had a radio strapped to his back with an enormous antenna that stretched towards the heavens. He was the only person heading in her direction. Working against her own instinct, she stopped the bike and waited for the man to arrive.

Overhead, the FLIES drone was maintaining constant surveillance. It hovered silently, monitoring Tori's every move.

Springfield, Illinois

The junior sergeant was eager to contact Captain Zacharov so that he could inform him that Tori had made her way to the site of the UN attack on Murphysboro. He picked up the SATCOM phone and communicated to Zacharov's secretary that Tori Cunningham had found clues on the whereabouts of the SIHG extremist group. Within moments, he received a SATCOM notice from Zacharov's office. "Keep tailing Tori and keep our forces out of her way."

What the young junior sergeant wanted to tell Zacharov next was that the FLIES drone was barely keeping up with the speed of the motorcycle Tori had acquired. The drones were built for maintaining a human-paced run, not the speeds that automobiles can attain. If not for the lock the FLIES drone had on the signal being emitted from her RFID chip, she would have been lost again.

CAPTAIN ALEXANDER ZACHAROV WAS IN A SEPARATE building, apart from the soldiers that were busy securing the streets around the capital, and those working for General Abdul Muhaimin. He didn't know where the Southern Illinois Home Guard was located, but was busy dispatching E-Tech to suspected areas.

There was a suspected SIHG attack on the UN base in Marion, but the nearest FLIES drone was still hours from that location. Captain Zacharov cursed in Russian, then said in his Russian accent, "How are we supposed to maintain surveillance on these extremist groups if we can't find them?"

Zacharov's secretary was a male junior sergeant, not unlike the one monitoring Tori. With the Chinese technology that had recently reached the shores of America came Chinese instructors learned in the ways of spy programs. They had instructed many Russian Army office associates on surveillance using the drones. They had since left America and their Russian counterparts, and returned home. This frustrated Captain Zacharov. He had sent continuous requests to liaison logistic coordinators for better E-Tech or a way to optimize the signal-receiving capabilities of the drones. The way things were going, they wouldn't see much progress in the upcoming months.

"I'm sorry, sir, but I forgot to leave a note out last night. We received an email notification from the Chinese that they plan to ship a new beta program allowing us to maximize the transponders on the FLIES."

"Did they say when they expect to ship the program?"

"Yes, sir. The disc should have been shipped today, according to the message."

"I need details. Anything I can find out about the program can be most useful. It will save time developing an actionable plan if we have details now rather than later. Email them back and request every bit of detail you can securely receive."

The District

Executive Commander Abdul Muhaimin came walking out of the room that was once known as the Oval Office. Walking out directly in front of him was a captain of the IHSF, or Iranian Homeland Security Forces, as it was known. The IHSF was created post-jihadi war for the purpose of monitoring weaknesses in the United States' security systems, whether it be cyber security or national security. The captain traveled to America for one purpose, to reach his supreme commander on earth, General Muhaimin.

"Thank you for stopping by, Captain Kianoush Delwadewala. The information you have provided me is greater than you may know."

"Sir, if ever you need me, please call on me. My plane leaves tomorrow morning; after that, you know how to reach me."

"Indeed, I do, and you have assured yourself a future in my service by proving your loyalty. There may be an opening for you to promote up sooner rather than later."

"Thank you, sir, and good day."

Captain Delwadewala bowed his head to the general and left. He had given Muhaimin information that was beyond valuable.

Apparently, the IHSF had intercepted cyber communications from the UN Council to key members of the UN forces on the ground in America. The information told of an Operation Black State, which was a fallback plan should General Muhaimin fail in securing the Agenda in America. According to Captain Delwadewala, Operation Black State was a biological weapon that would kill enough people to meet Relocation Protocol. Operation Black State was believed to be a weaponized form of the Black Plague pandemic that killed upwards of two hundred million people in the mid-1300s. The operation would make America uninhabitable for some time, so it was slated to be used only in the event of a worst-case scenario. The Russian and, of course, the Iranian representatives were deeply opposed to such a tactic.

Also, according to the captain, Ambassador Pao, of the Peoples Republic of China, had expressed a dislike of General Muhaimin on multiple occasions, sometimes calling him *a demagogue* and denigrating his name in front of other members of the council.

The information brought to the general both gladdened him and angered him. The general had always been a lover of the phrase *knowledge is power*, and being given this information prepared him and gave him the upper hand.

MGRS 16TEL35, Tippecanoe River State Park, Indiana

General John James's Marines arrived at the predetermined rendezvous point hours before Buchanan's men were expected to arrive. They had set up snipers in key positions throughout the park. John had no desire to shoot any of Buchanan's men, but he was smart enough to know the difference between preparedness and unpreparedness. What the general didn't know was Buchanan had Reconnaissance Marines and shared the same tactical readiness, but had better trained Marines. Their ability to locate and neutralize unseen threats through the use of counter-reconnaissance had proven useful. The Reconnaissance Marines had located the snipers and taken them at gunpoint. One of Buchanan's men radioed back and gave a situation report to their commander. The rest lay there quietly, with their fellow Marines tied and gagged, watching the rendezvous point until they received commands to do otherwise.

Within an hour, a platoon-sized group of Buchanan's men arrived and met up with an equal-sized group of James's men. It was Gunnery Sergeant Franks and Sergeant First Class Reynolds that stepped forward first.

"My name is Gunnery Sergeant Franks, Recon, and this is Sergeant First Class Reynolds, Ranger. We are here acting on behalf of our commanding officer. Which one of you represents General John James?"

A Marine Corps sergeant by the name of Rick Hammel stepped forward.

"I'm Sergeant Hammel, Comm."

Franks looked at Reynolds and said, "At least they didn't send a non-rate."

Franks stepped up to Sergeant Hammel and extended his hand.

"Is the general lacking brass that he sends a sergeant?"

"I'm afraid you've called it, Gunny. With all due respect to Sergeant First Class Reynolds, all he has is a Navy admiral and an Army National Guard captain, but we're still gung ho."

"The commandant said he dispatched intel for our commander?"

"Yes, Gunny. I had to memorize a frequency and channel for you to tune to for continued instruction. The commandant didn't want to say it over the radio, knowing the enemy may intercept it. The UHF radios we have mutually confiscated from the enemy can be used to communicate via SATCOM. Unfortunately, if we're not careful, the UN can gain access to our frequencies and receive our transmissions. I understand the science of satellite communications and have been selected to assist you in maintaining tight radio security."

"This is all very interesting, and we definitely could use

your assistance in tightening our radio traffic, but I have a concern that must first be addressed," Franks replied.

"What's that, Gunny?"

"You have yet to prove to me that this isn't bum scoop. How can we trust you?"

"Gunny, the CMC (commandant of the Marine Corps) ordered snipers be placed in random locations around this park. He did this in the event you proved to be a hostile force, but I can see now that you're not and I'm ordering them down now."

Hammel turned and grabbed a mic from the communications Marine behind him.

"Overwatch one, we're secure. Rally on me."

"Roger that," the reply came back.

Gunnery Sergeant Franks already knew there were snipers placed in the park before he had ever arrived. He was playing coy to test the sergeant's truthfulness and mettle. He kept his silence about having secured the snipers to see Hammel's reaction to the fact that he had the upper hand all along, and that was a mutual symbol of his truthfulness, as well.

It wasn't long until several Recon Marines came walking down off of key hilltops with Marine prisoners.

"Sergeant Hammel, you've proven yourself. Let this be my gesture of goodwill."

Franks turned to the Recons and said, "Cut them loose and let them go. We're on the same team now."

Hammel couldn't help but feel small and at the mercy of Franks. He was feeling quite relieved that he had mentioned them being on the same team.

Hammel joined Franks and Reynolds and headed back to Bicentennial Park. Of the remaining group of General John James's men, they did a head count and headed back to Fort Wayne, where they shared everything that had happened to them at Tippecanoe State Park.

Carbondale, Illinois

Tori's Harley was softly rumbling in idle. She had both feet on the ground and her head was cocked to the right as the stranger walked towards her. He was tall with an average build. His hair was long, brown, and matched the facial hair that dominated his face. He was right-handed with a Colt-style rifle slung across the front of his body, the buttstock of the weapon at the top right shoulder of the man. It was tucked too high into his chest with a tight three-point sling that would make it difficult for him to aim down the sights. Tori knew this man was familiar with gear, but was not a veteran. The man boldly walked in close to her.

"Are you in need of assistance?" the man asked.

"Not at all. I'm trailing a group of friends that might have come through this way. Maybe you've seen them?"

Tori was confident that if Nathan had passed through here with a group of Marines, the man would most certainly know of it.

He didn't answer her question immediately. He strolled around Tori and checked out her gear. He noticed she was traveling light. There were saddlebags on either side of her seat, with a rifle holster and her Remington resting on the left side of the bike. When he had made a full circle, the man stopped with his back to the crowd that he had left behind.

"Yeah, we saw a group of military men coming through here, just today. They kept heading east."

The stranger pointed in an eastward direction, towards Marion.

"You're a brave woman to travel alone."

"I never said I was alone," Tori said. Her eyes locked on the stranger's eyes.

The man looked east and west, down both directions the road was heading.

"I don't see anybody, lady. You're all alone."

The man's arms were spread and his voice escalated as if to say *it's just me and me on this long empty road.*

"You forgot Bubba," Tori said with a calm quiet voice.

The man looked around again, but still could not see anybody.

"Who's Bubba?" he exclaimed, this time even louder and more obnoxious than before.

Tori wiggled the 1911 she had pointed at the stranger with her left hand. She wasn't left-handed, but at this range, it would matter very little.

The man looked down and was surprised that a female had the drop on him. His hands were no longer on his rifle, but were spread and locked in the position they were in when he came to the revelation that she had a 1911 pointed at his chest. He was afraid to move at this point and only uttered three words.

"Oh, that's Bubba."

"Keep your right hand in the air and slowly use your left

hand to detach the quick-release snap on that fancy little three-point sling you've got there. If you move suddenly, I'll blow a hole through your chest, I'll still take that rifle, and be long gone before your gangster friends get here."

"Easy, lady. I didn't mean any harm. I was just toying with you."

"You see, that's the problem, I'm not a toy. Quit stalling and drop that rifle."

"I've got a sniper on the roof."

"Then why hasn't he sniped me?"

The man finished detaching the sling, but it was still hanging around his neck. Tori slowly peeked behind him at the crowd and could see they were starting to figure out that something was wrong.

"Hurry now. You're almost there. Use your left hand to hand me the rifle and don't try anything funny."

Several hundred yards back, the sniper was resting his .30-06 on the bipod of his rifle. The man had originally placed the crosshairs of his rifle on Tori's forehead, but was distracted by an object he saw moving in the sky. The sniper turned his scope towards the hovering object and was so enthralled by the technology that he had forgotten what was happening below him on the street. Believing the man that he was providing overwatch for had the situation with the female stranger under control, he decided to take a shot at the strange hovering object.

Tori heard the sound of a loud rifle in the background and responded by shooting the man in the chest with her 1911. She caught the rifle as he was falling and latched the sling to her front right handlebar. She accelerated the Harley, but was being pulled to the right. She looked down where the rifle was dangling and noticed the man's arm was caught up in the sling and he was being dragged along the highway. She dragged him as long and as far as she could, using her right arm to push forward against the weight of the man dragging her to the right. She decided to pull over and cut the dying man free. She looked to the south and saw the crowd of people running in her direction, no doubt to catch her.

The sound of gunfire soon caught her attention. Tori couldn't find the knife she had placed in a saddle pouch, so she laid the bike on its side and attempted to untangle the man's arm from the sling. That proved fruitless and the crowd was getting closer. She found another quick-release snap and pressed the button. She placed the rifle on the ground and grabbed the handlebars of the Harley and lifted with all her might. By the time she had the bike standing again, the crowd was so close they were within range of their weapons. She saw the impact of bullets on the ground beneath her before she heard the cracks of the gunshots.

Tori straddled the bike and reached down to grab the rifle she had taken, but a bullet hit it and kicked debris into her eye. Frantic, she left the rifle and darted off to the east, with her right eye closed as she thought only of losing her eyesight.

December 6, 03:00 Hours, Tom Walker's Residence

Cade lay alone on the couch with his eyes wide open as he stared up at the ceiling. His head was neatly propped up against the arm of the couch and the pain had subsided. He had fresh gauze wrapped around his head with cotton plugged into the holes of his scalp. The bullet had gone in at an angle, somehow missing his brain and following the inner brim of his skull, finding its own exit. He was in very poor condition and certainly not well enough to travel.

His memories of his father were mostly what his mother had shared with him. She had raised Cade alone because Tom left very early in his life. Cade was about four years old when his father became dependent upon alcohol and started beating his mother. Sometimes, she would fight back, but she would only get hurt worse in the end. Many of the beatings were at night, after Cade had been put down to sleep. But the sounds of the abuse and the cries of his mother would stir him from his sleep and awaken him. If he cried, Tom would enter the room and beat him with his belt.

The information his mother gave him was true; although Cade remembered none of it, he had always harbored a dark desire for retribution. With his mother now deceased, he felt a compulsive urge to do what he had always dreamed of doing to his abusive father.

Cade gently sat up. Moving caused the pain to reenter his head, but that did not deter him. Cade was still filled with anger from his failure to kill Jessica. It never crossed his mind that he was acting irrational. His antisocial personality disorder had never been diagnosed, and it went unchecked in the Army. It was this disorder that voided out any appearance of social normality in his life. He felt very few emotions that a normal person might have, such as sorrow and joy. Instead, he was filled with a numbness and a sense of superiority. The more he thought of being bested by a girl, the more infuriated he became.

Cade sat on that couch in an upright position for about two minutes. There were others sleeping there, all of them on the floor. He quietly stepped over them and made his way to his backpack. He was looking for his knife, hoping it had been packed away. He quietly rustled through the bag for a couple minutes in search of the switchblade. Once he had found it, he made his way into his father's room.

A little bit of moonlight was streaming through the window, giving Cade the light he needed to look at his father and to say his goodbyes. He used his free hand to slowly open the blade and then he pressed through his father's nose and into his brain.

Cade hoped the sudden death hadn't startled anyone and that the blood would settle into the back of his skull. Gravity did its job and the blood did not pool forward out of his father's face. The only sign of respect Cade showed his father was giving him a quick and easy death and not lying in a pool of his own blood.

Cade snuck back into the front room and killed three more men before he grabbed his pack and his rifle and snuck off into the darkness.

CHAPTER 5

Benton, Illinois, about 160 miles south of Chicago

NATHAN STOOD OUTSIDE, at the head of his convoy, looking up Highway 37 on the southern edge of Benton, Illinois. Scratching his head, he couldn't help but ponder the complications it could entail going straight through the town. Interstate 57 would take them north, directly to their destination, Chicago. They had tried so hard to avoid interstate travel.

"Highway 37 runs north and south, along I-57 until Effingham," Nathan mumbled to himself.

Jessica, who was standing just feet away, heard him. "Are you rambling on again?"

"Yeah, this is a tough decision, Jess. Go through the seat of Franklin County, where only God knows what awaits us, or drive up I-57 and face certain conflict."

Ash, who had just shut the door of the HMMWV he was

rummaging through for a drink of water, came and stood next to Nathan, on the opposite side Jess was on.

"Do we even know what's in there?" Ash asked, pointing to Benton, then putting a black sock cap on his head.

"No, we don't, and that's the dilemma," Nathan answered.

Jessica put her arm around Nathan, showing him affection, and set her head against his shoulder, cuddling in next to him.

"Well, Nate, we know what awaits us if we go up I-57."

"Yeah, UN checkpoints. Lots of them, and absolutely no cover if things get bad."

"Look," Ash said. "We probably need to head into Benton anyway. We're short on supplies and haven't managed to recruit anybody since the early days of Marion. We need more water, too."

"Water makes you weak," Nathan said.

"What are you talking about?" Jess asked Nathan as she gave him a squeeze. "Is that more jarhead lingo?"

Nathan laughed. "It is," he said, "but it's true. Sure, you need it to live, but being trained to go without when you have to can help keep your head screwed on tight when you're running low."

"I can see that," Ash said.

"Okay, then," Nathan said, changing the topic back to Benton. "I say we go through. Rally everybody on me."

Ash and Jess stepped out away from Nathan and gave the *rally on me* hand signal.

HMMWV doors started opening and everybody in the group started to rally on Nathan.

Nathan felt the noise levels were a little high, so he shouted, "Listen up," and began his operational readiness speech.

"I know most of you know a thing or two about Benton. Let me just say that it's full of history and that makes it a popular location for Franklin County buggers. We have to go through to keep on a northward trek. I-57 poses more hazards than what we believe may be waiting for us in that town, but we won't truly know until we get in. Now, some of you have loved ones being held in the Chicago FEMA detention center; some of you don't have family anymore because the blue helmets took it upon themselves to execute judgment upon them for being American. Most of you want your country back, so you're here to execute a little justice of your own. Whatever the cause, we ride together, we fight together, and we die together!"

Nathan had no more finished his speech when the sound of a roaring freight train could be heard coming in from the south. Every person faced east and took notice of the railroad tracks headed alongside Highway 37 into Benton.

Everybody began scrambling back to their vehicles.

"You guys know the protocol! No noise, no movement, no shooting until you're being fired upon or given the go!"

All the vehicles began driving off the road and into a thin forest area on the west side of the street. Once all the vehicles were parked and facing the road, camouflage netting was pulled from the cargo areas of the HMMWVs and spread out over every vehicle that could fit. The others were hiding in the rear.

The heavy machine gunners were ready to enter their

turrets. Everybody had their weapons locked and loaded as they hunkered down and waited to see what would happen next.

Bicentennial Park, Northwest Indiana

Lieutenant Colonel Buchanan had been communicating with General John James for the past three days on a sophisticated radio frequency system using a SATCOM transceiver and ground relay station. Of many of the bits of information Buchanan had on the system, it included footprints, the rotation of the earth, the elevation of the satellites being used, their speed, etc. Buchanan felt it was all way over his head, but was all too happy to be using a radio that could reach across the state of Indiana.

He also felt that the idea of placing a Com Marine in his unit so that communications and radio-traffic security could be insured between the two groups was a genius idea, at the least.

Relations between the two groups were being solidified and Buchanan was ready to release the burden of command to his superior, Commandant John James. He had learned from James that the commandant still had an ace up his sleeve, but wasn't ready to reveal it to him just yet. He was hoping that sometime soon, perhaps after their official union, they would lay out all the cards, so to speak. Buchanan was eager to know what the general knew, and was very eager to share with him the intelligence that the oracle had brought.

Fort Wayne, Indiana

Michael shook the hands of John James and Belt McKanty one last time. He had made the decision to stay in Fort Wayne, where there was some semblance of liberty and the old ways.

"Thank you for all you've done, Michael. You have proven yourself to be a hard man. You would have been a good Marine, in different times."

"Thank you, sir. Coming from you, that means a lot."

Michael readjusted the strap on his rifle and snugged it up onto his shoulder, and headed out the gates, where he enjoyed patrolling the perimeter of the city.

John and Belt were packing up their belongings as well. They were loading their military vehicles with ammunition, MREs (meals ready-to-eat), and other essential gear for a long-term excursion outside the gates, where Operation Returning Liberty was going to officially kick off.

When John and Belt were finished packing, they shook hands and separated. The general had parted the convoy in two. The whole convoy would be under the general's command, but should there be an attack, they would be removed from one another in different parts of the convoy, assuring a commander would survive. John took the front portion, and Belt took the second portion.

Each of them entered their respective vehicles and they drove off in a westward direction, towards Bicentennial Park, Valparaiso, where they would finally meet Bravo One and his brave Marines.

The District

Executive Commander Abdul Muhaimin had waited patiently his entire military career to possess what he had now attained. His ambitions filled his head and overwhelmed his mind with new opportunities and avenues for advancement. He was not interested in the UN's version of what a global community should be. The UN's vision was summarized in their Agenda 21 policy and that conflicted heavily with his Muslim belief system.

Originally, Muhaimin was disgusted at the thought of entering the United States. After it had fallen, he felt it was by his hand. In the mind of General Muhaimin, it was by his command his troops came through the southern borders of America. It was his genius that the Mississippi River was used to float his machines of war and personnel into the Midwestern states. It was his word that brought soldiers to the East and West Coasts of America, and it would be by his command that America lived or perished.

When word came of Councilor Pao's opinion that America be exposed to a deadly viral pandemic in order to speed along the green-zoning process, it deeply offended Muhaimin. For Pao's act of attrition against the executive commander, Muhaimin sent a message to the would-be destroyer of his ambitions. In just a matter of a couple days, word would be reaching his ears that Pao had received his fair reward. But, for now, the executive commander was working on something else.

The upgrades for the Utah Data Center had arrived and Muhaimin was eager to test the ability of his new upgraded FLIES drones. In a couple minutes, the installation would be complete and the signal magnification would be expanded to unprecedented distances. Soon, every veteran who had ever served in the past fifteen years, having received an RFID chip, would be located, identified, and lit up on an E-Tech board, and they could be systematically rounded up or terminated.

Muhaimin sat in the Oval Office with his feet propped up on the Resolute Desk. He was anxiously waiting for the phone to ring with news from his Advanced Technological Weapons Systems czar that the upgrades were complete. After a half hour of waiting beyond the time he was promised, he stood up and straightened out his uniform.

"If you want something done on time, you have to supervise it yourself," he said. Nobody was in the office with the executive commander. He felt so vastly superior to others that he sometimes spoke to himself because he believed he was the only one sophisticated enough to speak to.

Muhaimin headed out of the Oval Office and proceeded to the White House Situation Room. There were two guards standing outside the room that bowed their heads when their executive commander approached. He waited for their heads to rise and then they opened the door for him. Muhaimin entered the room and first took notice of all the hologram technology that had been recently added to the room.

Payam Vahidi was the Iranian czar he had appointed over the Advanced Technological Weapons Systems. He was completely loyal to Muhaimin and would sacrifice his own life if asked to do so.

In his native Persian tongue, Muhaimin questioned his czar.

"What is the hold up, Mr. Vahidi?"

"Sir, I do apologize for the delay. The Utah Data Collection Center has informed me that we have successfully installed the software updates. However, the technology we have here in the District is outdated and required a software patch to complete the process."

"What kind of timetable are we looking at now?"

"Sir, the patch is downloading now and should be complete within an hour."

"Then we'll be live?"

"Sir, after the install, the system will have to be rebooted. All existing FLIES drones will need to be grounded before the system is finished rebooting. After that, the feed from the Utah Data Collection Center will be fed live to the District."

"Excellent work, Mr. Vahidi. The next time you experience a delay, do inform me."

"Yes, sir!"

Muhaimin walked out of the White House Situation Room and walked down the hall and around the corner. When he was alone, he stood in front of his window and pulled out his cell. After lighting up the screen with just a touch of a button, he hit one more button that called his contact in Beijing.

Outside the home of Councilor Pao, Beijing, China

Just a block south of Councilor Sung Pao's home was a luxury black 2032 LE BMW with tinted windows. Inside was an Iranian man, dressed in all white linen, watching the councilor's home. As he sat patiently, his phone vibrated.

Vvvv vvvv.

The man looked at the screen of his phone and then held it up to his ear, but did not say anything. There was a voice on the other end.

"Black Creek is on hold for at least another hour. Stand your post and await further instruction."

The man pulled the phone away from his ear and turned off his cell phone's screen.

The District

Muhaimin put his cell phone away and walked over to the nearest window. With both hands clasped behind his back, he peered out the window, the sunlight bathing his face. The executive commander felt confidently in charge.

Just south of West Frankfort, Illinois

Tori was parked on the side of the road, watching another freight train head north. The train was to the east of her with about seven hundred meters between them. She felt safe enough to watch from the distance with her left eye. She still had debris in her right eye from the struggle with the Carbondale bandit. She didn't have enough water to waste on a good rinse, so she tried her best to suffer through it. She counted about sixty train cars in all.

"I wonder where all these trains are headed?"

She started to move the bike's mirror so she could see the reflection of her eye. The mirror was stiff and offered a little resistance. As it began to give way, she saw the reflection of the road behind her as the mirror swept past her posterior view.

She saw several men walking up the road behind her. She saw their figures, but the mirror swept their reflection by too fast to get a number. She saw them walking in a strategic two-column formation. One column on either side of the road.

She remained calm and thought about starting the bike back up, but if it took more than one attempt, she risked being killed. She didn't know what the aggressiveness level of these men would be, so her thoughts of dying included going down shooting.

She hoped they still believed they had the jump on her, so she was careful not to make sudden movements that were out of place. She maintained the same posture and body language while she removed the rifle from the side of her bike and lifted her right leg up and over the seat. This move spun her around with the rifle at the ready and facing in the direction of the strangers.

The men stopped in their tracks.

Tori could see the men with her left eye but was in no condition to be in a gunfight. Even with two eyes.

With her one good eye, she could see twelve men wearing different patterns of camouflaged clothing.

"Easy, lady. We don't want any trouble."

The statement calmed her a bit, but she was too untrusting to let her guard down.

One of the men turned around towards the others and motioned with his left hand for them to lower their rifles.

They did.

Tori kept hers trained on the man that was now

approaching her. He had both of his arms in the air, but the rifle was still in his right hand. She watched as he slowly bent his knees, not breaking eye contact with her, and lowered himself to the point where he could place his rifle on the ground.

"Look, lady. If we intended you any harm, we would've shot you when your back was to us."

Tori believed the statement. It made perfect sense, but she was still untrusting.

"Take three more steps towards me and keep that rifle on the ground," she said.

The stranger could see she was struggling with her right eye. She couldn't keep it open and was turning her head frequently to maintain a wider peripheral with her good eye.

"Look, I can help. There's water in my butt pack," he said.

She remembered he was carrying the rifle in his right hand.

"Use your left hand to fetch it out. No sudden moves."

"Okay."

The man reached slowly into his butt pack and removed a canteen.

"Who are you?" Tori asked him.

"My name is Mike. I'm from Marion. Me and my guys were sent to track some murderers that headed in this direction."

"Mike, place the canteen on the ground and kick it towards me."

Mike did as she asked.

She lowered herself to pick it up and gave it a shake.

The canteen was about half full. She knew she wasn't going to be able to open it without compromising her hold on the rifle, but saw it as another test to try the man's integrity.

Tori gave up her advantage over the man to unscrew the cap on the canteen.

Mike saw an opportunity to lunge at the woman and take her by force, but he was a good man and his intentions to assist were pure.

When Tori saw Mike did not attack her, she walked back to her bike and place the rifle back into the straps that held it in place for travel.

She went to her mirror and canted her head to the side. This put her back to the stranger. She knew it was a risky move, but it would ease her trust level if he didn't take advantage of the situation.

She poured the water into her eye and flushed it with every drop that would pour out.

Standing back up and gently wiping her eye, she walked up to Mike and handed him the canteen.

"Thank you. My name's Tori."

"Mike. Mike Hammond," he said. "So what are you doing out here alone?"

"I'm tracking people, too."

"Killers?"

"No, just the opposite. I'm tracking a friend that did everything he could to save people before the Flip. I should've listened."

"Would you like to join us?"

"I'm afraid that wouldn't be feasible. You see, I have this

bike, and I don't see myself pushing it from here to your murderers."

"True, but you have a better survivability rate if you stay in a group."

"I can't argue with statistics. Grab your rifle. If you had plans to snuff me, you would have done it already."

Tori walked back to her bike and tried to pick it up.

"Would you mind helping me one last time?"

Mike walked over to assist her.

"I guess you're not staying with us?"

I'm sorry. You've been hospitable, but I need the company of people I know. Besides, I'm not giving up the Harley. Who knows, maybe I'll run into your murderers and do you a favor."

"I don't think we have the manpower to do it alone. They looked like a group of Marines and ragtag civilians. Our orders are to observe and report back, but we lost them. We don't want to go back empty handed, the boss has a bad temper."

It was Mike's comment *group of Marines* that caught Tori's attention.

"You know what? I think I'll try my luck with you guys. Help me hide the bike in those woods and I'll unpack my stuff and join your foot patrol."

"Cool."

Mike was eager to help her. He liked her spirit and there was something about the way his canteen water mixed with the dirt on her face that made her even more attractive.

Together, they pushed the bike into the woods, collected tree limbs and tall dead weeds, and covered the bike.

The first snowflakes of the year were beginning to fall.

The two of them stood in the woods and looked up into the sky. Tori could feel a cold flake as it landed on her cheek.

"I hate snow," she said.

"I love it. My mom used to collect snow and mix it with milk, sugar, and vanilla extract, and called it snow ice cream."

Tori, Mike, and eleven other strangers began their trek north, towards West Frankfort. The snow would eventually accumulate and be an alternate water source, but for now, it was just a nuisance to Tori and a pretty sight for Mike.

Hiding behind the trees several hundred yards away, Cade was lying in a prone position, looking through the scope of his rifle. He had his crosshairs on Tori from time to time, not out of ill will or a desire to shoot her, but he was using the magnifying zoom on the scope as he would a pair of binoculars, if he had them. He had heard Tori's motorcycle earlier and scurried off of the road to hide in the woods. Now that he had caught up to her, he saw that she was with a dozen or so men. He had lain quietly in the forest, watching, to see what he could figure out about the woman and the men. Strangely enough, the woman had lowered her guard to the men and they were now leaving together. He felt unsafe traveling alone and wanted to meet these people. If she could lower her guard for a dozen strange men, surely she would lower her guard to take in a single wounded man.

Cade took notice of where the woman had covered her motorcycle, and he passaged his way through the woods to the point where they had hidden it. By the time he reached the place where she met the strangers, they were still several yards ahead of him. He walked up to the motorcycle and uncovered it. There were saddlebags attached to it, but there was nothing to salvage from them. He covered it back up, not out of a sense of respect, but because he figured he might need to backtrack at some point and commandeer the bike. To do that meant he needed it to run, if and when he was to return to it.

Before Cade stepped out onto the road, he took a moment to develop a strategy. *Should I play the victim, or should I act normal?* he thought. Cade had a personality disorder that sometimes came between him and wise decision-making processes. He always assumed things would work out in his favor, no matter what that decision might be. In this case, Cade was fueled by revenge and that was coupled with the thought of his now deceased father, which was a move he regretted once he had time to rethink it.

I'm going to act normal, he thought. *If anybody sees how I'm wounded, they'll start asking questions.* Cade took the bandage off and ran his hand over the exit wound of the gunshot. The pain was excruciating to the touch. The hole was bigger than he had imagined, and he figured it would be better to keep it bandaged up. He carefully reapplied the gauze but couldn't get the tape to secure the end, so he tucked the end of the wrap under a previous pass, called it quits, and stepped out onto the road.

"Hello!" he called, but the pressure on his skull caused by the yell was painful and more than he could stomach. He barely got the word out, but they were too far ahead of him to hear his call anyway. To Cade, the mere fact that they couldn't hear him was as unbearable as the pain drumming through his skull. It wasn't long until one of the men turned to the rear to check their six.

"Hey, Mike," one of the men called out.

"Yeah?" Mike jumped out of formation, where he was preoccupied with Tori, and looked to the man in the rear patrol. "What's up?"

Mike saw him looking backward, to the north of the road they were patrolling, and saw a man waving a hand in the air.

"Check this out," Mike said, tapping Tori on the shoulder with the back of his hand.

Tori turned and stepped out of the two-column formation as everyone else stopped to check their six.

"Looks like a day for picking up stragglers," Tori said.

"Binos!" Mike exclaimed.

One of the men closer to him handed him a pair of binoculars. Mike held them up to his face and saw a ragged-looking man with a dirty bandage on his head.

"His lips are moving, but all I can read is *help*."

"May I?" Tori asked, reaching her hands out to accept the binoculars.

Mike handed her the binoculars and she looked through them. "He's looking a little rough. I don't think he'll survive these temperatures."

She aimed them a little higher over his head and saw two large birds flying in circles over his head, like vultures would do for carrion.

Cade could see that they had taken notice of him, but his condition had worsened since he had left. He was feeling severely drained and had the shivers. He struggled to maintain consciousness and continued to drag his feet to where the strangers were located. When he saw them moving towards him, he slowed his pace and eventually dropped to his knees.

I can't go on anymore, he thought. He dropped his pack and rested his back against it as he seated himself on the ground. Cade closed his eyes and his mind blackened.

As the group approached Cade, one of the men that was originally in the rear was now in the lead.

"Hey, Mike, it's that guy from the shooting by the train track."

Mike ran up to him.

"Hey, mister," Mike said as he gently shook Cade's shoulder, but he didn't respond.

"Hey, Kenny, do you still have that emergency heat wrap?"

"Yeah," Kenny said, taking the pack off of his back and opening the pouch that contained the heat wrap. He handed it to Mike and he took it and unfolded it, wrapping it around Cade's body.

Tori, using her motherly instincts, crouched down and felt his forehead. "He's burning up."

"Can you catch hypothermia with a fever?" another one of the men asked.

"I don't know," she responded. "I'm not a nurse, I'm a mother. Kinda the same thing, only different."

Mike heard the mother comment, but didn't reply.

She reached down and removed the bandage from his head.

"This is an exit wound, Mike," she said as she went around to the back side of Cade and found the entrance wound. "This man has been shot in the head."

"I know, I saw it happen. It's a miracle the man is even alive."

"What do you mean you saw it happen?"

"We belong to a group that controlled a few blocks in Marion. This man was walking the tracks with a lady that pulled a gun on him."

"Why do you suppose she shot him?"

"We never found that out, but it's the reason we're tracking the group now."

Tori looked into Mike's eyes, as if waiting for clarification.

"I don't know who shot first. Either she shot him, or we tried to save him by shooting at her; either way, he dropped and we soon found out they were not alone. A few Humvees with Marines and civilians came through, shooting back at us. They picked her up; we took cover and were later sent after them to gather information. Obviously, he hasn't fared so well. Now I need to know why he's here. Tom Walker would never allow him to leave in this condition."

Tori took the rifle from her shoulder, pointed it at his head, and aimed down her sights.

Tom hurriedly grabbed the muzzle of the rifle and pointed it in a safe direction. "What are you doing?" he exclaimed.

"He's going to die slowly if we don't put him down now."

"The world may have fallen victim to a hell we can't comprehend, but we're not animals, Tori. We don't kill each other, we protect each other. It's the American way of survival."

"He's just going to slow us down and be a burden to us."

"What's the big hurry? We should just head back now and tell Tom that we lost their scent."

"I'm not going backwards, and I'm going in that direction," Tori said, pointing to the north.

"Then you'll be alone again."

"That's fine by me. If you remember right, I was on my own just a little bit ago."

"What happened to your kids, Tori? Did you shoot them, too?"

When Mike said that to Tori, she lost all control and hit him with the buttstock of her rifle.

"My family was burned alive in our home by a band of brigands. I was rescued and cursed to live out my life regretting that I didn't die with them. The next time you insult my children's memory, I'll kill you, too."

Mike was holding his head where Tori had struck him. "I'm sorry, Tori. I didn't know."

"It doesn't matter now. Go be a white knight and save that guy. He's only got a couple hours if you don't get him hydrated and warm," Tori said as she readjusted her rifle sling onto her shoulder. She took off walking back to the south where she had laid her Harley in the forest. When she reached it, she noticed that the brush she used to conceal it had been disturbed.

The only person that could have disturbed my bike was that dying guy, she thought.

He must've been watching us.

"No matter now," she said out loud as she began removing the foliage she had used to cover it up. She touched the motor, for no other reason than to see if the engine was still warm, but it was cold. She was confident that the freezing temperatures would soon claim the wounded stranger's life.

By the time Tori had her bike out of the woods and onto the street, the group of men, led by Mike, had already constructed a makeshift field gurney to transport the wounded stranger back to Marion.

"They're stupid for this. It's more than ten miles back to Marion from here. He'll never make it."

She started the bike and looked northward at the men who were going out of their way to help a wounded man. She began to feel guilty for not lending them a helping hand.

What's becoming of me? Why am I allowing my compassion to erode? Is this who I am? A killer? Can I let a man die and not feel that I am somehow a part of his death?

She drove the motorcycle up to where the men were now taking turns carrying the wounded stranger, and pulled up in front of them.

"Latch it to the back of my bike. I'll take him back to Marion."

"You were going to finish him off a few minutes ago," one of the men said.

"I've had a change of heart. Do you want my help or not?"

Mike stepped forward and took out some 550 paracord and began to latch the handles of the gurney to the bike.

"You better use some of that stuff to secure him to the gurney so he doesn't slide off," Tori suggested.

The men wrapped him in all the paracord they had available, enabling Tori to pull him along without the worry of him sliding off.

"Eventually those sticks will erode away under the constant grind of the road," Mike said.

"I know, but I'm hoping the wet surface will help hold some of that at bay until I can get to some of those houses up the road that might have something I can use to lay under him, like a snow sled or something."

"Great idea. Just stay on this road until you come to some stationary train cars. Don't worry, they're broken down. Across from there, you'll see some shacks. One of our people will take you in and help you with whatever you need. We'll catch up to you later, I guess. Godspeed."

Tori nodded to them and took off towards Marion with the wounded gunshot victim in tow.

Just south of Benton, Illinois

The train was braking as it came near Benton. As it slowed to a crawl, it was apparent that this wasn't just another train, but mirrored the train cars seen in Marion and was eerily similar to the barges seen on the Mississippi river, just months prior. There was a Roman numeral five on every car, as far as they could see.

Jessica was near Nathan when they had taken their positions in the wood line.

"Nathan!" she exclaimed in a whispered voice. "It's the UN again."

"I know. I think they're using these larger towns as ports to pick up people for transport to the FEMA compounds."

"This one's obviously heading to Region Five."

"I would love to acquire the routes these guys are traveling, where they come from, etcetera."

The group watched as the lead car disappeared into Benton city limits and the train came to a stop. They couldn't see the lead or rear cars from their position, but it was an easy estimate to determine from the speed of the train and the distance into Benton city limits that the engine was well into, if not past, the town. The group stayed hunkered down in the woods for several minutes. Those minutes paid off when a convoy of UN-labeled HMMWVs came driving in from Benton along the road they were traveling. The convoy disappeared toward the rear end of the train until they had circled around and come back again. This time, they slowed to a stop and let several UN soldiers out of the vehicles. When they had unloaded their troops, they continued northward.

The group watched as the UN soldiers walked up to the train cars and began unfastening the securing mechanism on each individual car. Once the car was unfastened, they would slide the car door open and move on to the next one.

Nathan studied their procedure carefully, but there was nothing routine enough about what they were doing to develop a plan. He noticed the convoy was now gone and the soldiers were lingering in the area. Some of them jumped into the empty cars and sat down, others stayed on the ground, yet others were hanging out in groups of two or three and chitchatting.

The train cars didn't have any cargo, but the intention to fill it with cargo was there. Each car had a line of hand shackles running along the length of the back of the car. The group could see the hand shackles from their position, but do to their low profile, they couldn't see that there were also ankle shackles in the cars.

The train cars had been manufactured in the United States years prior. When the government began its work with the UN, the need to transport violent mobs of Americans became the problem of the day. When the president wanted plausible deniability, she assigned the decision making to the directors she appointed over FEMA and other disaster-related organizations, giving them each a budget. FEMA, together with the Department of Homeland Security, devised a way to *escort* the people to the *government-provided housing*. The trains were constructed and sat in an unused area on federal land until they were needed.

Ash was a few feet away from Nathan on the opposite side Jess was on.

"Hey," Ash whispered in Nathan's direction.

Nathan just looked his way with his finger covering his lips. "Shhhhh."

Nathan reminisced about the time he and Denny had coincided their shots to kill two UN soldiers, back in October. That's when they met Jessica. She was being held in a barge transport container similar to these train cars, except they were crammed into the barge containers and these cars were designed to have people shackled. Nathan could only imagine how they got people into them.

Jessica was having memories of her own. Lots had changed since Nathan's and Denny's daring rescue. Many friends had died and the small distance they had traveled seemed like a thousand miles and a hundred years ago. She took her eyes off of the train for a moment to look in Nathan's direction and saw Ash on the other side of him, with his head lying on the ground. His face was pale and his eyes were closed.

"Nathan," Jess said, catching his attention.

She received the same response he had given Ash, but Jess was adamantly pointing at Ash. "Corpsman," Nathan whispered, looking left and right.

"Corpsman," the members of the group began to whisper. There was no sign of Denny.

Nathan looked forward and saw that there was a UN soldier who might have heard the loud whispers. He was walking towards the woods, but never took his feet off of the graveled track. He was armed with an AK-47 and had it pointed into the woods, but at the low ready position.

Most of the group members were beginning to feel that their position had been compromised, so they remained quiet and watched, forgetting about Ash for the moment.

The soldier stood at the edge of the track until the train began to make loud, familiar clanking sounds that trains make when they're beginning to move. The soldier turned back around and rejoined the others, who were jumping up into the cars. They all loaded up and stood in them, hanging on to handles near the trim of the door.

The train began a slow crawl north. The soldier that may have heard the whispers was now out of the area, but there were more soldiers in the upcoming train cars.

Nathan took advantage of the noise the train was making to low crawl towards Ash. Once he reached Ash, he gave him a shake, but there was no response. He felt his face and it was clammy. About that time, Denny came quietly low crawling to the position where Ash and Nathan were lying.

"Sorry I'm late, boss. I lost you when we scurried into the woods."

"Ash is down."

"What happened?"

"I don't know. He called to me and I told him to be quiet. The next thing I know, he's out like a light."

"Is he diabetic?"

"I don't know. He never reported any such medical condition."

"I know this is a long shot, but I need orange juice or something with sugar in it that is rapidly soluble."

"This ain't good."

Nathan began looking around and came up with an idea crazy enough to work. He looked at Denny and said, "Pass this message along: Diabetic down. If you have any type of sugar product, pass it down."

Denny received the message and whispered it to the next guy. This continued on until a peppermint made its way back to Denny.

Nathan took one look at the peppermint candy and said, "What's the plan for getting a diabetic to swallow sugar?"

"You can't. If I force this into his mouth, he could choke and die."

Denny opened the candy and stuck it in his own mouth.

"What are you doing?"

Denny put his finger up to signal Nathan to wait a minute.

Nathan waited.

When Denny had produced enough sugary spit, he opened Ash's lips and spat the long stream of saliva onto his teeth and gums. He closed his mouth and waited.

"That was disgusting," Nathan said.

"Maybe so, boss, but we have to wait to see if it'll work."

"Have you ever done this before?"

"No, but he can't swallow and his gums and lips will rapidly absorb the sugar into the skin and ultimately into the tiny capillaries that will take it to his liver for processing."

The train came to a stop again and that introduced more UN soldiers that had been dropped off towards the rear of the train earlier.

Nathan sighed with a breath of frustration and said, "We can't stay like this, waiting on this train and having Ash in this condition."

"What do you recommend, boss?"

"Can you stay here with some guys while I take a team through the woods into town, to see what's going on there?"

"Not a problem."

Nathan low crawled back to Jess. "The next time the train progresses forward, we're going to get a team ready and head into town. We need sugar for Ash and to find out what's going on there."

"Okay."

It wasn't long before the train started moving again.

Nathan boldly took to his feet, walked in a crouched position, and started pointing at people.

"You, you, you," he said as he pointed. Taking with him about twenty men, old Posse members and Marines. They moved out the back way, with radios in tow, and headed north towards Benton city limits.

CHAPTER 6

The White House Situation Room, the District

Czar Payam Vahidi was standing before the giant hologram when the system had finally finished its rebooting protocol. It lit up brightly, with the location of all veterans who were in service after November 2018. The veterans that were serving at that time and all new recruits were required to receive an additional vaccination under the guise of the jihadist wars, which were escalating in the Middle Eastern countries. These *vaccinations* were actually tiny RFID chips that had advanced technology in them, consisting of data and GPS.

Mr. Vahidi ran to the phone and called Executive Commander Abdul Muhaimin, who was patiently waiting for notification of the new and enhanced FLIES drone system.

Muhaimin was having coffee with a UN military commander when he received the call.

The executive commander took one look at his cell phone and looked back at the UN commander. "Excuse me, Colonel, but I have business I must attend to."

Muhaimin walked away and pushed the answer option on his cell phone. Holding it up to his ear, he said in Persian, "Yes, Mr. Vahidi, please tell me you have good news."

"Sir, the drones have been reactivated and the signal strength has been broadened beyond our expectations."

"Excellent. I'm on my way."

He placed the phone back on his hip and went to the White House Situation Room.

Within minutes, Muhaimin had arrived. He walked into the room and took one look at the hologram map of the United States.

"Mr. Vahidi, why is the map red?"

"Sir, you wanted to locate the veterans of America's armed services. The red indicates their locations."

Muhaimin was shocked at the multitude of veterans that had been located and he suddenly felt incapable of the task before him.

"Impossible," Muhaimin said under his breath.

"Sir?"

Not willing to let his subordinates hear the word uttered from his lips, he said, "Nothing, Mr. Vahidi. Can the screen zoom in?"

"Yes, sir."

Vahidi zoomed the screen in on their location, but it hazed out the more zoomed in it became.

"It must be an anti-spy program that the United States had installed before your rise, sir."

"Zoom in somewhere else," he commanded.

Vahidi zoomed in on a random town in the Midwest.

The closer the satellite zoomed in to the area, the more veterans it located. The satellite had placed a red square around each and every RFID-chipped veteran. No matter where the veteran moved, the red square was on them.

"How does this work, Mr. Vahidi?"

"Sir, the technology appears to use a system of triangulation to locate the veterans."

"Explain."

"The FLIES drones that are active have a signal magnification program downloaded into their chipset. These GPS devices are not only communicating with each other, but are also relaying information back to the satellite and then relaying it to the Utah Data Collection Center, where the live feed is being streamed to us, in the District."

"This is excellent news, Mr. Vahidi. Is there any further use for our friends in North China?"

"No, sir. I believe we have a workable program that can be used for the purpose you requested."

Muhaimin walked out of the White House Situation Room and pulled his cell phone out.

Outside the home of Councilor Pao, Beijing, China

The stranger sitting in the black luxury 2032 LE BMW received a vibration from his cell phone. He picked it up, held it to his ear, and heard the words "Operation Black Creek is a go."

The stranger looked at his phone and scrolled through the settings until he came to an option to restore manufacturer settings. He selected it and then placed the phone in a pouch that was strapped to his body beneath the white linen. The man had explosives attached to his body and they were not visible because of the white linen garment he was wearing. The man grabbed a device that was located inside the center console of the car, between the two seats, and exited the BMW.

Councilor Pao walked outside of his home to greet the mailman that had just walked up to his mailbox. With a respectful greeting, the mailman handed Councilor Pao his mail and then walked off. When the mailman was walking away, Pao looked up to see a man dressed in fine white linens walking towards him from a luxury BMW. Pao attempted to greet the stranger. By the time he saw the detonator in the stranger's hand, it was too late. The stranger pressed the button, igniting both himself and the car in a tremendous explosion that instantly killed both men, the mail carrier, and rocked the neighboring homes.

Bicentennial Park, Valparaiso, Indiana

Lieutenant Colonel Buchanan, Captain Riley, Sergeant First Class Reynolds, and Gunnery Sergeant Franks, along with their soldiers, Marines, and militiamen, had just received word that the commandant of the Marine Corps and admiral of the Navy were just minutes away from their location. Using the latest in high-tech satellite communications and a vast array of encrypted SATCOM frequencies, the two groups had maintained a tight long-distance relationship. By now, Buchanan could see that the CMC, whom he had never met, ran a tight ship. He was eager to hear his story of survival and how he and the admiral escaped the District and were able to get out undetected.

Buchanan had selected the nicest pavilions for their meeting, and had set up the tightest possible security, with an extended perimeter as a precaution. The formalities of having a freshly pressed uniform and locker inspections were long gone. This new America called for fewer formalities and more practicality. Prior to the Flip, Buchanan had monthly JOB (Junk on the Bunk) inspections. These inspections meant that every Marine would have to make sure that his appearance was the absolute best. Loose strings, or Irish Pendants, as the Marines called them, were not allowed. Every piece of clothing and uniform assigned to the inspection had a specific measurement that had to be exact. Every piece of gear had your name stamped onto it in a precise location. Weapons received extra attention to detail. Buchanan would wear a white glove and pass through the ranks for an inspection arms drill. He would randomly select a Marine's rifle and snatch it from their grasp, inspect it for cleanliness, break it down, and run the finger of his glove through the normally carbon-caked parts of the bolt and chamber. Nothing went unnoticed. Now, Buchanan found himself applying that same attention to detail to the place of the meeting. It was hard for him to let go of a mindset geared towards perfection. All that training served its purpose. He taught his Marines that details are important; forgetting one could be life threatening.

After several minutes had passed, Buchanan and the others could hear the faint sounds of a convoy of HMMWVs ripping through the hills. The layout of the land muffled the noise and gave the sound of the vehicles an effect similar to a ventriloquist throwing his voice. Nobody knew where the convoy was coming in from, and secretly everybody hoped it wasn't a different convoy, perhaps an enemy troop, that was driving in. Just before Buchanan's nerves had the best of him, the Hummers came into view. Some of them were Army class and some were Marine class Hummers. It was a welcomed sight, regardless.

Buchanan turned towards all of his men and said, "Fall in! Active duty there and militiamen there." The men and women ran to their respective positions. The veterans and active-duty Marines, soldiers, and seamen jumped right into formation, while the civilians scrambled to find a way to look as neat and orderly as the experienced ones. When they caught on to what they were doing, they fell into columns and formed platoon-sized groups. The civilians weren't standing as uniformly as the military veterans, but they were capable of producing the appearance of uniformity.

Gunnery Sergeant Franks was a battle-hardened Marine. The fatigue of life after the Flip had the same effect on him that it did on his commander, Colonel Buchanan. When Buchanan was calm, it had a reassuring effect on him. Franks looked at Buchanan and could see the nervousness, and that brought on a sense of battle readiness that he wasn't prepared for. When he saw the HMMWVs for the first time, he took a deep breath and exhaled it slowly; calming his heart rate eased his tension.

General John James was a bit nervous as well. Life after the Flip had taken a toll on the lives of every American. Narrowly escaping death on multiple occasions had made John weary. A heightened sense of self-awareness coupled with a heightened state of environmental awareness was extremely exhausting. His body wasn't tired, but his mind was, and that sometimes brought on a little paranoia, which wasn't necessarily a bad thing in the America he now found himself. He reached looked to the rear of his HMMWV and asked for the mic.

"Romeo Lima Two from Romeo Lima One. Over."

When Belt received the transmission from John, he knew that was his cue that they were arriving at their destination.

"This is Romeo Lima Two. Go."

"Romeo Lima Two, we are on site. Hold your convoy back until I can make an assessment. Will notify. Over."

"Copy," Belt said back on the radio.

Belt turned his attention toward his driver and said, "Pull over here and wait for clearance. They've arrived at their LZ."

The second half of the convoy pulled over and waited on John to assess the situation.

John's convoy was now pulling into the area where they had agreed to meet. He was impressed by the low-key, yet detailed appearance of the pavilion that Bravo One had set up. John still did not know the real name of the brave southern Illinois Marine. Buchanan had kept certain details secret, including his name, the size of his force, and his speechless friend, known only as the oracle, who had intel on the FEMA compound layout in Chicago. John was about to receive the answers to all of the questions that had been plaguing his mind.

Besides the pavilion that had been brightened up, the first thing he saw were the ranks of men and women standing in formation. He could instantly tell the civilians apart from the others.

The platoons of veterans and other active-duty military branches were mix-matched in their respective platoons. Marines were in battle fatigues, standing next to seamen, who were standing next to soldiers in their battle fatigues, and so on. John was one for more order, but also had a deep understanding of the different era they now found themselves.

His convoy came to a stop. A group of military men filed out and secured the area. Buchanan noticed that his force was much smaller than his. Not that he had envisioned a larger group, but seeing the commandant of the Marine Corps with only a couple platoons didn't seem right.

Once all the men were in place and John saw that there was no threat, he exited the HMMWV and walked into the pavilion. Buchanan was already standing in the center of it and only had to take a couple steps to meet John.

John saw Gunnery Sergeant Franks and Sergeant First Class Reynolds standing next to him. When he extended his hand to Buchanan, Buchanan gladly extended his in return.

"It's nice to see some more brass again. I'm General John James."

"Charles S. Buchanan. It's a pleasure to meet you, sir."

"The pleasure is mine. I'm very excited to see some

rockers, too," John said, referring to the ranks of both Reynolds and Franks.

John extended his hand to Franks first.

"Gunny."

"Sir, it's a pleasure."

"Sergeant First Class," John said, acknowledging Reynolds.

"Sir, thank you for meeting us here."

John returned his attention to Buchanan. "Colonel, may I call you Charles?"

"Sir?"

"We're living in a different world now, Colonel. The Corps is not the same, America's not the same." John pointed back to the platoons of mix-matched military men. "This is what we have now, Colonel. A band of patriots, some more experienced than others," he said, pointing back to the civilians. "You're not a colonel to them. You're a leader and a man with knowledge, grit, and experience. They look to you for strength. The point I'm trying to make is this, we can't let down on an ounce of discipline, but we can sacrifice formalities, and do it without compromising strength."

"In that case, John, you may call me Charles."

"Excellent. How far out did you secure our perimeter?"

"Maybe a half mile."

"That's good. Let's take a walk and chat a bit."

Charles and John launched out into the park and began a long walk through the twisting trails.

"Charles, I understand you have come a long way to get to where you are today, both professionally and geographically. We have a long fight ahead of us and we can't do it without numbers."

"I agree, sir."

"Please, it's just you and I out here. Call me John."

"John, I've been accruing numbers since the Flip. Most Americans are decent at heart and only turn to violence when their lives are at stake."

"That's the problem, Charles. People are going to become whatever is in their heart. I partially agree with you, but I think in times of tribulation, man is ebbed down to the basest of humanity. If their heart is truly good, they probably won't survive out here."

John stopped walking and turned to face Charles. Charles followed John's lead, stopped, and listened to what John was about to say.

"Freedom, Charles. Freedom is why we joined the military. It's why we fight and struggle to bring back balance, to both the people and its government."

"I think the people are done with government. Twice now, it has betrayed them and twice it has forced a revolution."

"That's where we find ourselves now, Charles. At the cusp of a second American Revolution. There's no way around it. So, what is the answer? If the people are through with the government, what are we to do? Anarchy is what we have now. Limited government works, but it always grows beyond its boundaries and it overreaches into the lives of the people."

"I was thinking of reinstituting the Constitution. Perhaps

restoring it and amending it. In that regard, we can fix the holes that led us to this day. America changed."

"No! That's the thinking that got us to where we are. The people stopped respecting the Constitution and its elected officials disregarded it. But the people continued to enjoy their freedom at the expense of the wealthy. The wealthy became slave to the government and it cost us liberty. That's not the American way!"

"You're talking about life, liberty, and the pursuit of happiness."

"Correct. The Declaration of Independence set the stage for individual liberty."

"But individual liberty was swallowed by democracy."

"Correct again. We have to get America back on track. What type of republic is the question."

"We are to be a constitutional republic."

"I see now why you command so many men, Charles. When you strip away the Constitution, what do you see?"

"Absolute tyranny."

"Absolute tyranny is correct. When the people are governed by a Constitution that protects individual liberty, it allows them to be free of tyranny, only because one person's rights cannot trump another person's rights. Without a constitutional republic, the people sink into a state of degradation that allows them to herd into larger bodies of people. When that happens, the majority gain control of the rights of the minority. In absolute tyranny, this happens on a smaller level. It happens individually."

"One man's desire will become the rule over another."

"Democracy and tyranny are not distant relatives. They're bedfellows."

"Where are you going with this, John?"

"I have a Marine Corps regiment in South Dakota. We must reach them if we are to have any chance of salvaging America."

Charles was shocked at the idea of a fully functioning Marine Corps regiment. The possibilities would be endless and would certainly turn the tide and set the course for a successful second American revolution.

"That's the best news you could have given. But I fail to follow your point with the tyranny line of questioning."

"Charles, I had to do some brutal things to get here. I'm not proud of what I've done, but I did it without commanding a single person to follow me. When I was given men, I made them strong and they learned to stand on their own. I'm not going to command you or your men to go with me to South Dakota. That would be tyrannical of me. I'm not going to call for a majority vote, because that would be tyrannical, too. I'm going to ask for volunteers and hope that I have enough support to safely make the journey."

"And if you don't?"

"Then I continue on, as I have."

"Well, since you're sharing secrets, I have one of my own."

John's curiousness was noticed by Charles in the way he raised his eyebrow.

"John, we have been working our way toward Chicago, where we have intelligence on a FEMA camp. The camp is located on Goose Island and is heavily fortified with walls, towers, and rivers surrounding it."

John felt a little let down.

"That's not a secret. Not to me, anyway. Being a Joint Chiefs member, I had access to all kinds of black documents. There's twelve FEMA headquarters and far more FEMA camps. Before the Flip went down, there was a meeting with President Baker on the transitioning of federal prisons into FEMA detention centers. Virtually every prison and many state prisons were being looked into for modification."

"I also have a man that escaped from one of them. The guys call him *the oracle* because he knows so much about the Chicago FEMA camp."

"Then I suggest you use him. But he's a bag fry. There's many more needing saving and we need the numbers to make it happen."

"I'll have a meeting with my top NCOs and let them in on everything."

"I look forward to moving forward with you, Charles. I just hope it's in a westward direction."

Both men smiled and shared a short chuckle before John said one more thing.

"We better head back, I almost forgot the admiral."

"The admiral?"

"Yes, I brought a squid along. He's an alright guy. I've known him for years. The two of us saw this coming for years and had developed a contingency plan just in case. It all worked out. His name is Belt McKanty."

"Belt?"

"I don't know," John said confusingly. "That's what his mammy and pappy called him at birth."

"Popeye! Good one!"

General John James and Colonel Charles Buchanan made their way back to the pavilion and spent the rest of the day getting to know each other.

CHAPTER 7

Just outside the residential area of Benton, Illinois

NATHAN HAD SELECTED Jess and a few others to sneak into Benton city limits, along with them was a small group of reconnaissance Marines that they had met months earlier at their old homestead in Gorham.

As they approached the outskirts of the residential areas, Nathan was taking in any type of movement or sounds he could pick up. Jess was doing the same, but facing in a separate direction. Nathan maintained a low profile as he moved from point to point, walked up to one of the Marines and said, "Can you take your team northeast into town and head toward the square?"

"Yeah, not a problem," Sergeant Banks replied.

"Great, you'll be looking for a federal building in the center. I suspect there'll be some activity of sorts."

The Marines checked their equipment again, for operational readiness, and stepped off.

"Jess, it's great having my Marine Corps brothers along, but it's more like home when it's just us."

"Are you suffering from low blood sugar, too?"

"No, why do you ask?"

"Because you're getting mushy on me. Stay on target, Marine."

"That's too funny. I'm glad you find humor in despair."

"Just making the best of things. So, what's the plan?"

"Plan? No plan. We just head northwest and towards the square. See what we can see and head back. Simple."

Nathan looked back at the group. He had about ten with him, including Morgan and Blake, two members of the original Posse, and others he didn't know real well, but knew how to handle their firearms. From that he had gathered they were experienced to some degree.

"I'm not sure what we'll run into, but if we find a SNAFU, everybody is to meet back here! Copy?"

"Forgive my ignorance," Jess said, "but what is a SNAFU?"

"Situation Normal: All Fouled Up," Morgan answered before Nathan could open his mouth.

"He's right. If things get foul, or go south, meet back here. Then we'll head back and rejoin the rest as a group."

Nathan led them into a house with an open back door. The smells were horrendous. Nathan was hit first by the pungent odors of old human waste. He looked back at Jess and saw that she was tying a handkerchief around her face, the way the old American West bandits used to do. Her eyes were visible, and he couldn't help but wonder why she would think the handkerchief would filter the smell. He just smiled at her as they made their way through the house. In doing so, they walked by the bathroom and saw that the toilet and sink were full of human excrement.

"There's the source for the perfumes of tomorrow," Nathan joked as he whispered with a smile.

"You're disgusting!" Jess said, striking Nathan in the shoulder. Her shoulder had healed up nicely since she was shot, but every once in a while, she would feel a tight pinching sensation when she exerted a little force on it. This was one of those moments. She struck Nathan and that made her wince.

Seeing her wince caught Nathan's attention. "Is your shoulder still bothering you?"

"Yeah. It only happens once in a while."

As the group made their way to the front door, Nathan stopped them and peeked out of the curtains.

"We're going to have to travel from house to house like this until we reach the square."

"That's going to take us hours," Morgan said.

"Do you have a better plan?"

Blake interrupted and said, "Why don't we send one guy a block ahead and he signals us to move forward?"

"Okay," Nathan said. "Who's going to volunteer for that detail?"

Morgan looked back to Blake and saw that Blake was looking at him.

"Don't look at me; it was your idea."

"Rock, paper, scissors?"

"No way!"

"Fine, I'll do it," Blake said. "Me and my big mouth."

Nathan stopped him at the door. "You don't have to do this. We can continue on as we started and use the houses as cover and concealment."

"If I can get us there quicker, I'll gladly donate myself for the detail."

"Okay, then. Be careful, check yourself for danglies, and make sure you're as silent as a ninja."

"Danglies?"

"Things that hang from your gear and cause sounds."

Nathan helped him search for any noise makers and secured a couple straps with electrical tape.

"Good luck," Nathan said, patting Blake on the back.

Blake stuck his head out the door and looked both ways. When he felt it was safe to move, he inhaled deeply and stepped out. Nathan caught the screen door and watched closely from the window.

As soon as Blake reached the next street, he looked back at the group and motioned them to proceed forward. This tactic lasted several blocks before they saw their first sign of life.

The group was now entering what used to be the business district. Blake saw a child run from the outside of one of the buildings into the back door, where he vanished from sight.

Nathan was waiting a block back and saw Blake enter the building.

"What's he doing?"

"What do you see?" Jess asked.

"Blake just ran into the back door of an old two-story storefront."

"Wonderful," Jess said sarcastically.

"That's something Ash would have done," Nathan blurted out. The comment made him remember their mission. "Has anybody seen any sugar products that they can take back to Ash?"

"We're out of the residential living area now, Nathan," one of the guys said. "If we're going to find anything, it would be from some of the homes we passed, instead of going through."

Nathan looked back at Morgan and said, "Would you mind heading back the way we came, checking the cabinets of the homes for any sugar products you can salvage?"

"Sure, can I have a couple guys?"

"Of course. Anybody want to head back with Morg?"

Two men raised their hands and the three of them headed back.

Nathan was down to six members. He looked at each of them and said, "You guys okay with going into that building?"

They all looked at each other and everyone volunteered to tag along. They stepped off and traveled a block ahead. When they reached the back of the building, Nathan quietly opened the back door and peeked in. Inside the door, he saw a blackened-out staircase that went upwards at a steep pitch. Stepping in, he pointed his rifle straight upwards towards the overlook that he could barely see from his position. He whispered to Jess, who was right behind him, "Prop the storm door open so we can see the stairwell."

Jess passed the word down to the sixth person in line and

he locked it open with the locking mechanism on the storm door closer.

Nathan was now in a position where he had to awkwardly step up the stairs in a side-strafing pattern so that he could keep an eye on the stairwell overlook. When the group reached the top, there was another door that was slightly cracked open. Nathan signaled for Jess to walk up next to him for a possible breach entry. He could hear voices coming from the room but had no idea how many people were there, only that the voices weren't Blake's. Nathan stepped to the left side of the door to make room for Jess to take the right side. The others staggered behind Jess and waited for the word.

North Marion, Illinois

Tori was now entering the northernmost parts of Marion. She hadn't taken this exact route earlier, so the location was all new to her. She had stopped along the way and rummaged through an abandoned house; finding a pair of tennis shoes, she latched them onto the ends of the gurney to prevent them from grinding away against the surface of the road.

She had finally reached the destination as it was explained to her by Mike. Her motorcycle came to a slow and steady stop. Her legs now firmly planted on the earth, she turned the bike off to listen for sounds of life. She could clearly see the signs of a battle on the sides of the train. They told a story as she read the clues. According to Mike, a group of military men and a ragtag group of civilians came through here. She could clearly see that bullets had left their sting as the Marines were missed and returned fire back towards the homes, where a trail of machine-gun fire was visible across the siding.

When she had completed her initial examination of the evidence, she removed her rifle from the latch on the saddle-bags. She put her kickstand down and leaned the bike against it. Maintaining a constant eye on her environment, she became concerned that perhaps she was being watched, and that feeling irritated her and made her feel vulnerable; a feeling she had promised herself that she would never succumb to again.

"Hello?" she called, in an attempt to discover the men. "Mike sent me. I have a man that was wounded here. Mike asked me to bring him back."

She stopped talking for a moment to wait on a reply. As she waited, she looked back at the wounded stranger and saw that his bandages were in need of replacing.

"This man is wounded. He has a fever and needs new bandages," she called.

Inside the shacks were several men taking cover in the shadows. The day had been long, and the evening sun was casting a long shadow to Tori's benefit. The men were not moving because they had the sun in their eyes, but soon it would be below the train. Tori knew that soon she would be caught in the dark, so she had to make a rash decision.

"Sorry, dude," she said to the wounded stranger, "but this is where we part ways."

She walked to the back of the bike, and keeping her rifle pointed towards the shacks, she unfastened the gurney from her bike and left Cade near the ditch.

When the lady on the bike was gone, the men came from the shacks and had several rifles pointed in all directions.

"Be careful, boys," one of the men said. "I smell a trap."

When they had walked up to the man on the gurney, they could see it was Cade.

"It's Cade, Tom's boy," another man said.

"Let's get him inside. It's freezing out here," he said as he knelt down to touch his forehead. "He's on fire."

"Is he going to make it?"

"How would I know? I'm not a doctor."

"Well, if he's half the man his father was, he'll pull through."

Another man stepped forward and said, "Wait a minute, guys. Let's not forget that Cade came up missing the night Tom, Ralph, Ted, and Steve were killed in their sleep."

"You don't think Cade killed his own father, do you?"

"I would certainly hope not, but I feel more comfortable keeping him secure until we get answers."

"Then move him inside. Be quick about it. If he's caught the fever, he'll be dead in this weather."

The men moved Cade inside one of the shacks where they had a wood-burning stove. Several logs were already in the fire. They moved Cade close to the fire, but had taken off a couple layers of his clothing to help break the fever. Clean bandages were long gone, so one of the men used a sheet to cut strips for wrapping his head.

"That's about all we can do for him right now."

"Hey, Donnie," one of the men said to another.

"Yeah?"

"That girl on the bike, was that the same chick that tried to blow his head off?"

"I don't think so. The girl that shot Cade had long brown hair. This girl had short black hair."

"I don't think so," another man said. "That was the girl. That's the only reason I didn't take her out. I figured they had come back to finish us off."

There was a great disagreement in the room about the appearance of the girl that shot Cade. While they were arguing, Cade had awakened from his sleep and was eavesdropping on their conversation. At first, he was unaware of his whereabouts, but soon recognized some of the faces and realized that he had been compromised by being brought back to Marion. He could tell by their discussion that they didn't know he was responsible for killing their friends.

In a low mumbled voice, Cade picked up the conversation. "It was her."

The men heard Cade speak and moved to his side.

"Take it easy, brother. You're in bad shape and need more rest."

"The girl," Cade continued. "She's the one that shot me in the head. She came back for me while we slept. She took me at gunpoint and threatened to finish me off if I didn't cooperate. I think she hurt my dad."

The men looked at each other and were saddened to have to be the bearers of bad news.

"Cade, she killed your father," Donnie said.

"No! I don't believe you," he cried out. His act of anguish fooled all of them. "Take me to him."

"We buried him out back, Cade. We had a really nice memorial for him."

Cade closed his eyes and feigned sleep.

"The poor guy has been through so much," one of the men said.

"We've got to come up with a plan to stop them. This can't continue. They're just toying with us."

"We need some wheels if we are to have any hope of catching up to them."

"Stop and think about what you guys are saying! This is a suicide mission!" Donnie barked.

"It's one girl!"

"She's just the decoy. It was just her before and then the storm came."

"Old man Sutton still has a running car," yet another man blurted out.

"If you guys go after them, I'm out. It's a sure death," Donnie said.

"Go ask Sutton if he'll trade the car for a hunting rifle with ammunition."

It was as if the other men weren't listening to the words that Donnie was saying. He was sure that this was a different girl than the one that shot Cade, but the others weren't hearing it. They had made up their minds that she was the guilty one and they were going to catch her and stop her murderous rampage. Cade heard everything and was keeping mental notes. He lay there quietly, biding his time, as the sun was coming down on Marion.

Benton, Illinois

Jess watched Nathan carefully for the signal to breach the door to the apartment. The faint muffled sounds of human voices were in the air as Nathan held out his fingers and counted down from three. When he reached zero, he kicked the door the rest of the way open and the group filed into the apartment room with guns aiming center mass on several dozen men, women, and children, both standing and lying on the floor, and furniture. They were coughing into the air as they were both startled and scared at the strangers' unwelcomed entrance.

Nathan saw Blake helping a man lying in the corner.

"He's dead," Blake said.

"What have you done?" Nathan said.

"I'm helping these people. They're sick."

"You've put us all in danger. Outside, now!" Nathan commanded.

"These people aren't violent. Look at them!"

"Yeah, look at 'em! They're sick and now you've exposed not only yourself but us to an unknown sickness."

"Blake," Jess said, "he's right. We don't have hospitals or vaccines or pharmacies. If we get sick, that's it."

Blake stood up and walked over to the doorway. Nathan provided cover to the rear of the room and looked upon the sick people. He knew their fate was sealed, but was more scared that the group might now be exposed to the same sickness. Blake had been touching them and there was no running water or soap to wash his hands. It was a truly frightening scenario for Nathan, who had tried so hard to protect the Posse.

Blake was now leading the way down the stairs and out of

the apartment. His rifle, which was slung over his shoulder when he was trying to help the sick people, was now at the ready as he prepared to exit the storm door. Jess was directly behind Blake, just two steps up, when he took his final step. A high-caliber shot was fired from outside the building, and the round penetrated Blake's chest, exiting just inches away from Jess's legs. Blake fell straight down, as if his legs had been taken from him. In a quick reaction, Jess lunged forward to catch Blake. That's when she saw a squad of UN Biocontrol troops armed with AK-47s. They were garbed in white, head-to-toe hazmat suits and had breathing apparatuses on their faces and heads.

Realizing what had happened, she turned and shouted, "Back up the stairs, now."

Everybody ran backwards up the stairs. Jess was the last one in the apartment. She kicked the door closed and was thoughtful enough to not touch anything with her hands.

"What happened, Jess?" Nathan shouted.

"UN troops, outside, in biogear."

"Blake!" Nathan called out.

"He's done, Nathan," Jess said. "They hit his spine and dropped him. He's dead weight now."

Nathan's mind was racing as he looked at the sick people and realized he was stuck in the worse possible scenario.

Nathan looked at Jess and saw that she still had a handkerchief over her face.

"Cover your faces," he told the group.

Looking at the sickened people, Nathan found the boy that was walking around and appeared healthy.

"Where's the front door?" he asked the boy.

The kid pointed to the right, down a hallway. The group started in that direction, stepping over people that were lying on the floor as they went. The group cleared two rooms and found another staircase leading down. Nathan kicked the door open and the group ran outside with their rifles aimed in either direction up the street. As they ran in a northward direction, Nathan kept in mind that he needed to head back south, but the UN troops were most likely waiting for them on the other side. When they had cleared the street, the men that shot Blake came awkwardly running around to the other side of the building, where they now had visual on Nathan, Jess, and the others as they were heading deeper into town.

As they maneuvered from block to block, avoiding armed UN troops in white hazmat suits, they began seeing more signs that had apparently been set up by Civil Obedience and Biocontrol units. The signs ranged from UN-Controlled Zone to Biohazard Zone to Martial Law. Blocking the rim of every city block within eyesight was concertina wire. The sight reminded Nathan of some of the postapocalyptic novels he once had sitting upon his bookshelf. Not only did he enjoy reading them, but it had an allure that satisfied his curiosity about how the end would come. He tried reading zombie and nuclear biohazard novels, but could never find a niche in such a possibility. The real-world novels, like EMP attacks, martial law, and cataclysmic natural events, interested him most. He gleaned whatever he could from the authors that had studied such things, but nothing could have prepared him for what life after liberty would offer.

Gunfire picked back up, causing Nathan, Jess, and the others to tuck their heads as they ran along the concertina wire and into another building that was across the street west of the concertina wire.

"This is not ideal," Nathan shouted. "This is not how the story ends."

This building was all lower level and had boarded-up windows. It was impossible for the group to see what was waiting for them, if anything at all, on the back side of the door.

There was limited light in the building, making it difficult to see what was in the room.

Jess, like the others, had broken from the group once they were in the building, and began searching for other exits.

"Over here!" she shouted, having found a doorway that led to yet another room with an exit sign above the exterior door.

The group ran towards her while she peeked her head outside to see if it was clear to exit. Hearing only voices, she said, "Move, now!"

The group moved as a unit back out onto the street. Jess attempted to lead them south, back to the rally point, but they were hearing lots of gunfire in that direction.

Nathan looked over his shoulder and saw several Biocontrol troops chasing after them. Nathan, thinking quickly, grabbed Jess by the wrist and said, "This way."

The group turned towards Nathan and Jess and ran down an alleyway, around the corner, and into another building.

"Upstairs," Nathan shouted.

The group ran up the stairs and into an apartment building, above an old storefront, that had been abandoned for years.

"Seems like nothing's locked up these days," Jess said.

"Is everybody okay?" Nathan asked the group, looking around at each of them, then turning to the window curtain for a vantage point. "It's no use. It's getting too dark to see anything."

"We're going to have to stay here until we can see where we're going," one of the men said.

"I'm going to have to agree with that. Jess, do you have any chemlights left?"

"Let me check."

The old Posse members had been told to keep their equipment wherever they wanted, but consistently keep it there. Then, in the event of an emergency, you would know where to look.

Jess took her pack off and went right to the position of the chemlights and took them out.

"I have two," she said.

"Don't break them yet," Nathan instructed. "Does anybody else have any?"

The other members of the small group took their packs off and located only two more.

"That's four. Save them until we absolutely need them."

"It's freezing in here," Jess said.

"I know."

Nathan looked around the room and at the window.

"What's running through your head?" Jess asked.

"Did you see that old stove in the kitchen?"

"Yeah."

"It's got a vent. Maybe we can heat the kitchen with a small fire over the stove and not have to worry about the light being seen from that window."

"What about the smoke?"

"I don't think there'll be enough smoke to make a stink. Besides, it might be concealed under the cover of darkness."

"I have a roll of duct tape," one of the men said.

"Perfect," Nathan said, taking the duct tape from the man. "Thanks, Bill."

Bill was a quiet man and always willing to help. He'd joined the group in Marion and had since proven himself an asset to the team.

Nathan started placing tape on the window in strips that ran vertically, until the entire window was lightproof.

"Wood?" Jess asked.

"There's furniture right there. Chemlights, please," Nathan asked as he pulled his Ka-Bar out of its sheath.

Others joined Nathan as he began dismantling a couch.

"Too bad for the couch. I was hoping you men would let the lady sleep on it tonight."

"What lady?" Nathan asked.

Jess slapped his arm and looked over to one of the men leaning back on the door that they had come in. She was thankful to have a good team and individuals with clear heads enough to think about the important details, like guarding a door.

It's going to be a long night, she thought.

Pyongyang, North Korea

Kil Jong Ho was a ruthless North Korean dictator. He had inherited his rule from his ancestors who had ruled before him. The iron-fisted approach to control had been the norm for several decades. For years, his regime and the regimes of his forefathers were kept under the thumbs of the Chinese dynasty. Years of appeasements by the United States led only to a more emboldened North Korea. Sanctions placed against the evil regime barely had an impact. The people of North Korea starved while the ruler lived in luxury. Secret financial aid from China always seemed to find its way into his mansion. The Chinese knew they were paying for a friend, but the people of North Korea only saw empty tables. Kil Jong Ho blamed it on US sanctions, causing hate to brew in the minds and hearts of the ignorant. As far as Kil Jong was concerned, Councilor Pao was a friend, loyal to the communist cause of North Korea. When Pao was murdered, he blamed the Americans and forged a campaign to further his anti-American rhetoric.

Kil Jong had no patience for the Russians, the French, or the Iranians, so when the time came to launch an attack on America, he did not hesitate.

For years Kil Jong had been gloating about his missile capabilities and saw no reason why he shouldn't demonstrate North Korea's might.

Several years earlier, North Korea announced its sovereignty and defied the global community by revealing its uranium-enrichment programs and testing them over international waters. North Korea, now fully nuclear, often touted its sovereignty.

The fact that America was now being controlled by a

global movement, or so they thought, did not deter Kil Jong, who, although ambitious, was way too clever to launch a nuclear assault on the US. Instead, he chose to dismantle what technological edge America still held. His goal was to detonate a massive electromagnetic weapon above American soil. After such a technological weapon had been deployed, his technology could be brought onto American soil, where his army would have sole discretionary use of it and have the edge over the patriot resistance and any international force that may be operating within the former US. Such a monopoly hadn't been employed yet. To Kil Jong, it was bold and demanded respect; for who could bring America to its knees? Nobody but Kil Jong Ho.

Nuclear electromagnetic weapons were outdated in 2032. Newer technology had been in the development stages for years. The UN, pretending to send inspectors into sanctioned countries, only emboldened the rogue nations to continue their development.

Direct energy weapons, or *dewies*, as they were called, were at the top of North Korea's advanced weapons lists. After that, harnessing the power of electromagnetic energy that only permanently disabled electronics was the focus. Kil Jong Ho's ambitions were riding higher than ever and he was feeling the need for recognition. The death of Councilor Pao was only the excuse.

Kil Jong knew that the American power grid was down, all except those controlled by the existing government. His desire was to reach the West Coast with an electromagnetic attack, wiping out key electrical infrastructure. His ability to make a surface-to-surface attack was not possible, and may not be an available option for at least another year of development. After having a sit-down discussion with his generals, he had learned that they could improvise a device that may not be able to reach American soil, but could be detonated off the American West Coast with an effective range up to 1,300 miles, reaching the states of Montana, Wyoming, and Colorado, providing they could at least reach a few hundred miles from the western coast of Oregon.

The option sufficed for Kil Jong Ho and he gave the go-ahead to make the preparations and to have the missile on standby, waiting for his word.

CHAPTER 8

Bicentennial Park, Valparaiso, Indiana

DAWN CAME EXTRA EARLY for the men of Weapons Company 2nd Battalion, 24th Marines, Company C, 6th Engineer Support Battalion, and Company E, 4th Recon Battalion. Buchanan had sustained losses along their trek from Peoria to southern Illinois, and north to northern Indiana. What Buchanan thought was a small supply of treasure John James was bringing turned out to be a heavy supply of much-needed infantry Marines. 3rd Battalion, 25th Marines was made up of four companies of Marine Reserves, from Tennessee, Ohio, and Pennsylvania. They were the companies of India, Kilo, Lima, and Weapons. The 3/25 designator Buchanan had heard on the radio was lost in the excitement of meeting the commandant of the Marine Corps.

Charles was lacing his boots when he was approached by John.

Charles was just remembering the conversations they'd

had the night before. He learned of the commandant's secret Marine Corps regiment located in an undisclosed location in South Dakota. John was unwilling to provide him with the location, stating that it was of utmost confidential and classified information.

"Good morning, Charles."

"Good morning, John."

Belt came walking up to the commander's table.

"Good morning, gentlemen."

"Good morning, Belt.

"John, I was thinking," Charles began. "I know you're trying to accomplish a very important mission objective by keeping the secret Marines name and location to yourself. But if something were to happen to you and Belt, that mission would go belly up. Don't you think it's wise to share this information with as many confidants as you can, to ensure mission accomplishment?"

"I agree with your comment, Charles, but the more people I tell, the more likely the chances to activate them get leaked. They are waiting for me, and me alone. The structure is complicated, and I would love to tell you details, but I must have your absolute and sole discretionary silence on the intelligence."

"You have it."

"Let's take a walk," John said to Charles. "Belt, you're welcome to come along."

Charles finished lacing his boots and stood up with John. He, John, and Belt went for a morning walk along the winding trails of the park.

When the men were a good enough distance from prying

ears, John said, "Charles, Belt and myself have been in service to this country for decades. We have served faithfully and honorably every bit of that time. Along the way, there was a metamorphosis of the nation. It began to spiral out of control as the people became sheep, and the sheep became herds. They were no longer thinking as individuals, but were lost in the pack mentality. When I saw our country's leaders exploiting them, I knew it was the beginning of the end. I met with Belt and we had a private meeting to discuss possible eventualities. We developed a plan B that included our own evacuation from the District. A day after our initial meeting, I couldn't sleep. I lay awake at night, staring at the ceiling and pondering how we could rise above the ashes.

"Well, being a Joint Chief and commandant of the Marine Corps are not without their perks. I began cooking the books, so to speak. At the end of the week, I had secretly reactivated an inactive Marine regiment and funneled finances and equipment to them under the guise of the Federal Emergency Management Act. The government had so much funding going out, it wasn't being watched and nobody was being held accountable. When the spending came up for FEMA, it was approved for the budget. This went on for years. To make a long story short, the 21st Marine Corps Regiment was reactivated and is now fully operations capable. Their commanding officer, Colonel Edward B. Hensworth, a loyal patriot and Marine, was in full agreement when I appointed him. He now waits for further instruction, from deep within the secret South Dakota interior."

Charles was both amazed and impressed at John's perseverance through those times. He embodied the spirit of the Marine Corps.

"Well then, we had better head back and start gearing up for the trip to South Dakota."

Black Hills Ordnance Depot, Edgemont, South Dakota

Colonel Edward B. Hensworth, or Hensy, as his friends called him, was handpicked by the commandant of the Marine Corps with a detailed and classified mission, to maintain a Marine Corps regiment in the southern pine-clad mountains of the Black Hills Great Plains region just west of Edgemont, South Dakota. The commandant, General John James, had spent days scouring through military files in search of the perfect candidate to help him reestablish the Constitution. When he found Hensworth's file and saw that it was red-taped, he knew he was on to something.

Red-taping was a term the government began using in the mid-2020s. It involved placing a red piece of translucent tape on the file of military personnel. It was a way of quickly coinciding the personnel file with the names the government maintained in the red list. The *red list* was a list of personnel the government believed would be problematic in the event of a national crisis, where civil obedience would be enforced. To be on the red list, one would have to be a veteran or a currently employed member of the armed military; have outspoken views that are inconsistent with the government views; be a conservative; have at least once in their lifetime purchased a firearm; be the child of a person who has purchased a firearm; and also included all previous law enforcement personnel, including retired members of the FBI, CIA, NSA, DHS, etc. The government wanted to keep a close eye on individuals that had the training and capacity to resist.

In Hensworth's case, he was red-taped because he was a very outspoken conservative and often discriminated against gays serving in the military and had made comments about homosexuals serving in his "beloved Corps." These comments often reached the desks of his superiors and on at least one occasion led to a demotion in rank. Such a demotion usually ends the career of an officer, but Hensworth knew how to play the cards. Before he had reached the rank of lieutenant colonel, Hensworth was already on his way to being a popular voice in the Marines. When his demotion came, those under his command loved him even more. He once told them that he would eventually reach the rank of colonel, but they laughed him off. He didn't take the laugh as a sign of disrespect, rather he took it as a challenge. Then Captain Edward B. Hensworth went before the promotions board and declared the reason why he was making anti-gay and inflammatory remarks about homosexuals was because he was also gay and was attempting to conceal what were otherwise considered unnatural urges from those under his command. Of course, the lie worked, and Hensworth was reinstated as Major Edward B. Hensworth. Integrity is at the core of everything taught in the Marines, but he understood the significance of serving in the military and that the use of integrity was fluid. He lied, not because he was lacking in integrity, but because he saw what his country was becoming and he wanted to be poised in the right place at the right time when his government turned against its people. That was integrity in his mind: doing his part for America, seeing the gray colors and not just the black and white by-the-book mentality.

The Black Hills Ordnance Depot was once a munitions storage and maintenance facility run by the US Army. It was active decades prior but eventually fell off the books of record keepers. John James never forgot about the depot, but kept it quiet for such an eventuality. The bunker, now loaded for bear with munitions and Marines, was ready and waiting for Buchanan's command.

"Where's my lieutenant colonels?" Hensworth shouted from his bunker headquarters.

Five lieutenant colonels came walking into the bunker. He was wearing a radio on his back, as was customary for him. The colonel was never seen without it, and nobody knew why.

The winter snows had already come to South Dakota. So when the lieutenant colonels came walking in, they tracked in snow mingled with dirt onto Hensworth's deck.

"Each of you are going to be supplying a working party to clean up your nasty animal tracks. Come on, you're supposed to be officers of the Marine Corps, act like you have a little courtesy."

The men followed Hensworth deep into the bunker, where he walked up to his desk and pulled out a chair and sat in it.

The men stood in the same formation once a week. The only difference this week was that they were called in a few minutes earlier than usual. This caught them off guard because they were used to a very stringent and ritualistic schedule when it came to their commander. Each of them were left wondering why the sudden break in routine.

The colonel had the 21st Marine Corps regiment divided into five battalions, each consisting of five companies. In the old world, an infantry battalion would consist of three primary infantry companies, or grunts, as they were called, a weapons company, and a headquarters company. The need for a headquarters company seemed like a waste to the colonel, so he set up a rotation system that required the use of just one platoon to maintain the munitions and the distribution of supplies and rations. The rest of that company could retain its combat readiness as an infantry unit. It was a heavy duty for just one platoon to support themselves and twenty-four other platoons, but it insured a readiness protocol, with effective numbers ready to fight should the rubber meet the road.

The commandant had also reallocated tanks, helicopters, artillery, and the instructors necessary to make grunts into heavy-armor support, cross-training them to be dual-purposed infantry units.

The lieutenant colonels now stood in front of the colonel's desk. From left to right, as the colonel was looking at them, was Cody Barker, Zachary Barnes, Jack Wright, Bobby Cox, and David Howard. Each of them capable Marine Corps commanders, but lacking Hensworth's resolve. They were slowly growing bored; having joined the Marines to serve an oath to country, it was now seeming futile. None of them were married, nor had children, and had no one outside Black Hills Depot to run home to. The colonel had taken the same tedious approach to locating these men that the colonel had used to locate him. They were ready to fight and to lead in the good fight, but were growing weary of the lack of action and purpose.

"Gentlemen, when I was given this assignment, I was entrusted with a very detailed set of ears-only classified instructions. I am happy to say that I am now at liberty to begin sharing some of the details of the operation with you."

All of the officers began looking at each other with half grins. They were ecstatic to finally get some news.

"One of the details of the operation was that I would tune the frequency of this radio to a very specific number and leave it there. Under no conditions whatsoever was I allowed to change the setting once it had been established."

Hensworth was pointing at the radio that was now feet from his desk, sitting upright in the corner behind him.

"Since the day I received this radio until now, we have been under strict and absolute radio silence. But today we have received word from General John James that our wait is over."

Hearing the news caused the men that would normally have full military composure to break down into cheers and handshakes.

"That's right! The commandant is coming here, to our location, and is suspected to be on our threshold within a couple days, providing resistance is minimal. He is burdened with purpose and a refreshed zeal for our beloved Corps. He is not coming alone, but is bringing more Marines, soldiers, and even some of our sisters from the Navy. I have been instructed to continue radio silence until

I hear otherwise. For now, this is ears only, so I want you to prepare your men and set up LZ security. I also want drills every ten to twelve hours until the CMC arrives so that we stay sharp on our security perimeter. Do you have any questions?"

The men all said no as they continued to smile at one another.

"Then dismiss yourselves, and remember, ears only!"

The District

Executive Commander Abdul Muhaimin received a phone call from the White House Situation Room, where veterans and active-duty military personnel were being enumerated. Muhaimin was hoping to hear some good news from his Advanced Technological Weapons Systems czar.

When the executive commander arrived, the czar stood and saluted him.

"At ease, Mr. Vahidi. What is it you have found?" he asked him in his native Persian language.

"Sir, I'm afraid the number of active-duty American military men and veterans reach numbers upwards of four million. That's figuring the three million that are RFID chipped and guessing another one million for those veterans who are not."

"That's a very high number, Mr. Vahidi. Have you double-checked your work?"

"Triple-checked, sir. The numbers are accurate—three million chipped. There could be more than a million non-chipped veterans still existing, sir."

"We'll have to focus on group numbers," Muhaimin said, pointing at the hologram of America.

"The map is almost completely red, sir. They are everywhere and it's difficult to see from this altitude, but when you zoom in," Vahidi said as he zoomed in on South Dakota, "you can see in great detail who's amassing where."

Muhaimin looked at the screen and saw that the Black Hills Depot had thousands of RFID-chipped men walking about the area.

"What is this? What am I seeing? There must be thousands."

"Two thousand five hundred, give or take. They are not with us, sir. You can see that they are alone. There are only RFID-chipped American soldiers. If they were ours, they would be working alongside UN soldiers, who are not RFID chipped. They would appear next to them as people walking, not having a red square assigned to their location."

"How can we find out who they are and what they're doing?"

"I'm afraid what they're doing cannot be discovered, but they are living in underground bunkers, because we lose their signal when they go twenty feet below the surface of the earth. But, we do know who they are," he said as he walked over to another system and tapped a few buttons on the keyboard.

Muhaimin looked back up at the hologram while Vahidi highlighted a person with the tab key.

"Now we can know who they are by sorting through them like this," Vahidi said, tapping the tab button on the keyboard.

As Muhaimin watched, an information block sorted through each individual on the grid. The information block contained the name, rank, branch of service, years served, living family members, and more.

"Sir, these are active-duty Marines. A regiment-sized unit and each member comes from a different unit. It's like they amassed to this point out of the blue."

Vahidi pressed the tab key and selected a Marine.

"This Marine is supposed to be assigned to 2nd Battalion 4th Marines located in Camp Pendleton, California. This Marine," he said, selecting another member on the hologram, "is supposed to be assigned to 1st Battalion 2nd Marines, Camp Lejeune, North Carolina. As I search through the personnel files," he said, walking over to yet another system, "I find that they were reassigned to a classified unit and location, a complete black op, with no further history of their location until now."

As Muhaimin was watching in bewilderment, he saw five members filing out of a bunker.

"And who are they?" he asked, pointing to the screen.

Vahidi tabbed to the members and highlighted them, showing a service record of active-duty Marine Corps lieutenant colonels.

"Mr. Vahidi, watch that bunker and report to me immediately if you see a high-ranking Marine come walking out. I want answers and I want them now. Keep the drone out of sight until you can tell me more."

"Yes, sir. It shall be done."

Pyongyang, North Korea

Kil Jong Ho came riding up to the launch site and exited his car. The entourage of security and military commanders were on site to greet him. The dictator walked up to his chief scientist and military commander.

"Is it ready, then?"

"Yes, Your Highness, we have done as you commanded and we now await your word."

"First tell me what you have done."

"Yes, Your Highness, we have retrofitted a surface-to-surface intercontinental inertial-guided ballistic missile with a timed air-burst electromagnetic detonator. With the technology we have available to us right now, we have improvised this missile so that it will explode four hundred miles off the western coast of Oregon. It will be an air detonation over the Pacific Ocean, causing all electricity and technology within the effective range to be destroyed."

"And what is the effective radius?"

"Your Highness, the best we could do is an estimated thirteen-hundred-mile maximum effective radius. We are unable, given our technology, to produce both the required distance and the altitude to affect the entire surface area of America."

"How much of America will suffer?"

"Your Highness, we estimate that the states of Oregon, Washington, California, Nevada, Utah, and Idaho will receive total exposure. Arizona, Colorado, Wyoming, and New Mexico will experience only partial exposure."

"And these states will no longer be able to use their technology again?"

"Your Highness, all exposed electronics will cease to have any usefulness at all, irrevocably."

"Loss of life?"

"Your Highness, there will be no loss of life caused by the missile itself. What electronics currently exist will cease to function. If any of those items are being used for life sustainability, they will cease to function, and those on life support will cease to exist."

"How long will it take the Americans to restore their electrical grid?"

"Your Highness, it will take months, if not years, to restore the grid."

Kil Jong Ho looked at his military commander and said, "Make the launch."

His military commander saluted him and walked off in a hurried shuffle to the launch room, with the scientist in tow.

Kil Jong went back to his car and lowered his window. He looked at his driver and said, "Stay here. I want to watch this."

Within minutes, the missile's cryogenic propellants were ignited and it was lifting into the air. Kil Jong watched as it vanished out of eyesight at an unbelievable speed.

"Now America will know the legitimacy of Kil Jong Ho."

Benton, Illinois

Bill had the last firewatch of the night. His rifle was slung forward across his chest and he had a tiny piece of duct tape removed from the window so that he could see the early morning activities outside. The others were still asleep in the room that seemed as midnight from the darkness. For Bill, the bright light coming through the tiny opening in the tape was piercing.

On the ground level just across the street and at the end of the block, Bill had seen the UN vehicles pulling up. They seemed out of place for a Biocontrol zone. Bill's left cheek was pressed against the glass as he looked at the tight right angle to see what was happening. Two OD green-colored military vehicles that read *UN Mobile Command* on the side, in bold white letters, had pulled up. One of them had a mechanized-looking trailer that began opening along the center length of the trailer. It split in two and widened horizontally until the two parts could not separate any further. Then a rounded dish began rising up from the center of what used to look like a trailer. It was some kind of satellite dish that was rotating in a circular motion. After a couple minutes of watching this, several men dressed in white Biocontrol uniforms came piling out of the rear trailer. They were all armed and pointing in his direction. Alarmed, Bill backed away from the window and found himself closest to Jess. Not wanting her to inadvertently yell out, he placed his hand over her mouth, at the same time giving her a shake to wake her.

Startled and defensive, and weary from the long road of heightened awareness, Jess reacted, shooting Bill in the chest and throwing him off of her. The gunshot awakened everybody in the room. They jumped to their feet with guns drawn and pointing at the shadows on the floor.

Nathan ran to the window and began shredding duct tape from the window, hoping to let some sunlight in so they could see what had just transpired. Those in the room that were standing around Bill and Jess saw that he had been shot by her, and she still had her pistol in hand. Nathan, also concerned and curious about what had happened, had no time to ask. He immediately saw the men outside and that they were taking cover on the opposite side of several armored vehicles that were pulling up. He saw the satellite and the trailer labeled *UN Mobile Command*, but what alarmed him the most was another vehicle towing a large tubular device with two other smaller tubes attached to computerized gadgets, all self-contained with an armored anterior design.

The entire device was a technological breakthrough in electronic weaponry. For the past decade, North Korea had been leading the way in the development of direct energy weapons. The Chinese had hacked their networks and stolen the blueprints and beta designs for the weapon systems. What North Korea lacked financially to continue with development, China made up for. With development finished, it was time to put these new weapons to the test.

———

DOWN THE ROAD FROM THE POSSE, THE MOBILE command unit was being supervised by Captain Rashoutan Siroosi, an Iranian commander of Advanced Weapons Technology. His name and rank, sewed on his Biocontrol uniform, gave his identity away to others. He was not normally assigned to the areas under quarantine, but the new upgrades to the FLIES drones system had alerted him to the location of high-value targets within the quarantine zone. The mobile command unit was well equipped with computerized GPS and location services being streamed from the Utah Data Collection Center. In addition to the stream, they were receiving real-time information from personnel assigned to the Advanced Weapons Technology Department in the District.

"Where are they now, Sergeant?" Captain Siroosi asked one of the operators of the direct energy weapon.

"Right over there, sir. On the back side of that building, in the alley."

"You're absolutely positive that they are Recon Marines not assigned to us?"

"Yes, sir."

DENNY, MORGAN, AND THE RECON MARINES HAD reassembled back at the rally point the night before. Morgan, having found some honey, was able to save Ash. Working with the Recons, Denny put together a search and rescue mission to find Nathan, Jess, and the rest of the missing members. So far they had tracked them to the correct building, but were one floor away from making contact.

Denny heard the shot that Jess had made, and that brought them to their present location.

"WE'VE GOT TO GET OUT OF HERE, NOW," NATHAN SAID.

"I've shot Bill," Jess said in a panic.

Running over to Bill, Nathan looked at the wound. "He's not going to make it, Jess."

"What do you mean I'm not going to make it?" Bill gargled.

"You've been shot through the lungs, my friend. You're going to die."

"I don't want to die this way. Not by friendly fire."

Jess was starting to cry. "I'm sorry, Bill. I didn't mean—"

Bill interrupted Jess, "I forgive you, brown eyes. Revenge me. Kill some blue helmets."

"We've got to go, now," Nathan said, looking out the window again.

Jess wasn't willing to leave Bill behind, but when he started gasping for air, she couldn't stand to watch the life leave his eyes, so she kissed him on the cheek and headed out the door.

The remaining members ran out the door and down the stairs into the abandoned storefront.

Denny, Morgan, and the Recon Marines were already in the storefront when they came running through the door.

"'Bout time," Nathan said, hugging Denny. "What took you so long?"

"Well, you know, the apocalypse slowed me down."

Nathan saw that the Recons were looking through one of the boarded windows at the UN movement.

"They have dewies!" one of them exclaimed.

"What's a dewie?" Nathan asked.

"Direct energy weapon. We can't stay here," the Marine shouted before he left the window. "Take cover, now!" he yelled, and jumped down behind the old counter.

The others didn't have the same amount of time to take cover, or their reflexes were slower than the Marine's. The wall blew inward as if hit by a six-foot-diameter torpedo. Shards of wood, glass, and brick went flying from the wall to the interior of the store.

Everybody inside the room fell victim to the blast. There was no person left standing when the dust settled. Nathan was disoriented and his ears were ringing. The room was spinning and he had no concept of direction. His face was numb, as if it was hit with a two-by-four at a hundred miles per hour. Next to him, he saw Jess. She was unconscious from the shock wave that rattled her brain. With the room still spinning, he saw two Marines still standing and walking towards him, throwing debris out of the way. He was able to sit up and turn his head, but for the most part, he was lacking the fine and gross motor skills necessary to stand himself up and move about.

A shout pierced its way through the ringing in his head, but he couldn't make it out.

"Let's go! Up and at 'em, Marine!" one of the Recons shouted to him as they grabbed his arm and attempted to pull him up.

The shout was now making sense, and the ringing in his head was subsiding. Nathan found himself on his feet, with the aid of the two Marines that were helping.

Gunfire began erupting from the Biocontrol troops that were stationed outside. Nathan grabbed Jess and clumsily threw her over his shoulder into a fireman's carry position.

"Let's go," the Marine shouted. "We can't save everyone."

Nathan looked about the room one more time in search of

Denny, but could not see him. The UN troops were closing in on their position quickly, so Nathan had to make one of the most difficult decisions of his life: leaving behind his most loyal and best friend, Denny Ackers.

Nathan made a one hundred and eighty degree turn back towards the door and left with Jess over his shoulder. When he exited the building, he saw a few more Marines laying down some support and cover fire so the wounded could be evacuated from the building. Once Nathan and Jess were moving in a safe direction away from the gunfire, the Marines pulled out of their shooting positions and provided rear cover for the now fleeing Posse leaders as they sought a new cover in the suburban combat zone.

West Frankfort, Illinois

On her way back from dropping off Cade Walker, Tori had found the backpacks of Mike and his men, emptied and strewn out upon the snowy roadway. The tracks were faint, but she could see that several men had come from the train that was stopped here the day before and took them away. There was no sign of struggle, just several tracks walking up to where they had been hiking and leaving with the men back to the train. The one exception was a solo pair of tracks that appeared to have run away from the site, away from the train.

Since then, Tori had found an abandoned home to rest her eyes and catch some well-deserved Zs. The strange disappearance of Mike and the men were on her mind when she went to sleep, and it was the first thing she thought of when she awakened.

The house was cold, but she was well bundled, with several layers of clothing she wore for these kind of nights. She had also taking some drapes down off the windows and used them to shield herself from the cold. Every bit of insulation she could find helped sustain her warmth for the night.

Stretching out and listening to the early morning songs of a cardinal was refreshing and reminded her of better days. The birdsong brought to memory a time she and her daughters, Charity and Amelia, worked together to paint birdhouses that her husband, Richard, had built from spare lumber. They sat out in the garage, as a family, and smiled as they talked about giving homes to the homeless birds.

It was barely a thought, but it was enough of a happy memory to bring a tear to Tori's eye. She was lonely and missed her children, husband, and friends. She had to keep her mind occupied or she would go mad with survivor's guilt.

I can't continue to let these things cloud my mind. I have to stay sharp, she thought.

Tori stood up and took off her heavy outer layers of clothes. Packing them tightly into her bag, she made sure she had everything and then grabbed her rifle and headed to the kitchen area, where she had the motorcycle. She found herself studying the exit strategy for backing her bike out of the door of the kitchen. Pushing it in was easy, but pushing a motorcycle backwards out of a doorway was going to prove difficult.

Once she had the handlebars of the bike beyond the threshold of the door, she felt easier about getting it out, but the rear tire landed hard when it dropped off the six-inch back patio. That caused her to lose control of the bike and it fell off to the side, landing on a barbeque grill and causing a great deal of noise. Tori quickly took her rifle off of her shoulder and spun it forward, backing herself inside the shadow of the kitchen, where she sat still and waited for somebody to reply to the sound. After several minutes of no response, she began to move back to the bike. She proceeded out of the door with great caution, but inevitably had to shoulder her rifle to lift the bike back up.

Lifting motorcycles was no easy task for Tori. She was an average-sized female trying to muscle a three-hundred-fifty-pound bike. She had found the best way was using leverage. She started her lift by using her legs, and then walked in closer to it. The tighter she was to the bike, and the higher the lift became, the less it seemed to weigh.

As soon as she had the bike upright, she was grabbed from behind. Knowing only that a man had snuck up on her, had covered her mouth, and that she was being dragged backwards into the kitchen, she grabbed her shiny 1911 from her waist and bit the man's hand, causing him to release her. She spun around and pointed her pistol at the man.

No sooner than she had said, "Meet Bubba," she recognized the man as one of Mike's patrol team.

He was already shot and bleeding.

Tori put the 1911 back in her waistband and pushed the man in the chest. "What are you doing? I almost shot you."

"I didn't want you to scream."

"Why would I scream? Because I'm a girl? I'm so sick of effeminate clichés."

"I've been shot through."

"What am I supposed to do? Kiss it and make it feel better?"

"Look, I'm sorry. I misjudged you."

"Let's take a look at you," she said as she began lifting his shirt.

The man was shot in the back and it went through the soft tissue and penetrated his kidneys, exiting his front side.

Tori sighed. "Well, do you want the good news or the bad news?"

The man was looking green and could barely stand. "Just give it to me."

"The bad news is, you're done. You have a serious infection in that wound and you're toxic from having a ruptured kidney."

The man slid down the wall into a seated position with one leg crossed. He took out his pistol, pointed it at his head, and pulled the trigger. The man died instantly.

Tori didn't miss a beat before saying, "The good news is, you don't have to live in this hell any longer."

Tori grabbed the dead man's gun and placed it in her pack, but not without checking it for ammo. It was a Sig Sauer 9mm P226 with a twenty-round super-capacity magazine. She looked around for the man's backpack, but remembered the count of backpacks that were on the road.

He must have given up his pack before he ran for it, she thought as she went back to her second attempt at lifting the bike.

Benton, Illinois

When Denny finally came to, he found himself in a dimly lit room with Morgan sitting in the opposing corner. He had a severe migraine and his nose had been bleeding. His face was numb around the area of his lips and the bridge of his nose.

"Where's Nathan?" Denny asked his friend.

"I don't know, man. That dewie thing knocked a hole in the wall the size of a wrecking ball and left no sign of shrapnel. Everybody scattered or vanished or was taken, I don't know, man."

Denny felt his nose and knew that it was broken. "Where are we?"

"You're a heavy cat for your size, bro. I carried you two blocks before stopping here. Wherever *here* is."

"I need a pen or a pencil. Something long, narrow, and about the same diameter."

"Why? You gonna write a love letter to Nathan?"

"What's up with the attitude?"

"I'm sorry. It's just that this is wearing me down. I'm getting grouchy," he said as he took off his pack and tossed him a china marker.

Denny caught it and stuck it up his nose.

"Whoa, whoa, whoa, man! What are you doing with my grease pen?"

Denny lined the china marker up with his nasal cavity and snapped the cartilage in his nose back into position and then tossed the marker back to Morgan.

Morgan didn't catch it; instead he dodged it and let it hit the wall. "Really? I woulda let you keep it."

"Nah, I've got one."

"What?"

"You didn't think I was going to stick my own china marker up my nose, did you?"

"Whatever, man. What do you think they shot at us? That jarhead called it a dewie, and said something about energy, or whatever."

"I'm not sure, Morg. That's all way over my head. I use this," Denny said, pulling out his Karambit. "And this," he continued, grabbing for a rifle that he couldn't find. "Oh no," Denny exclaimed.

"What is it?"

"Where's my rifle?"

"It must've got lost in that energy blast."

"I don't travel without my rifle. That's the same as suicide."

"We can't go back there, man. They'll catch us for sure."

"I'm going back. I never mentioned *we*."

"If you go back now, you'll be killed. They're looking for us."

"Again, you're putting words in my mouth. I never said I was going back *now*."

"Then when?"

"I'll probably head in when darkness falls. I've noticed those goons don't go room clearing at night. It's bad for their health."

"Yeah, well, we've got the home-field advantage, too."

"You know what would be cool?"

"What's that?"

"If all these foreign invaders caught an illness that would

kill them off. Something that we Americans already have an immunity too."

"Man, you're talking some Orson Welles craziness."

"Maybe so, just saying it would be cool. So, you never saw what happened to Nathan?"

Denny could see that Morgan was trying hard to remember the facts surrounding the direct energy weapon attack.

"No, I think I blacked out, too. I popped up and saw people scrambling, just shapes, really. I saw you were still breathing, so I grabbed you and hightailed it out of there."

Denny was more concerned about Nathan than anything else. He found himself in his current situation because he ran into town towards the sounds of gunfire. He knew Nathan had headed in that direction and that he probably needed their assistance. He didn't believe for a second that Nathan would have left him behind. He was fairly positive that Nathan was either killed or rendered unconscious.

"I can't stay here. I'm getting the itches thinking that Nathan might need my help."

"If you go out that door, they're likely to see you."

Denny stood up and started collecting himself. "Whatever. I'm going to see what I can find out. I'll be careful."

Morgan stood up. "Fine, I'm coming with you."

When Denny had smiled at Morgan and turned his back to lead the way out of the room, Morgan struck him in the back of the head with the buttstock of his rifle.

Denny went limp and fell unconscious again.

"I hate to have to do that, man, but if you woulda walked

out that door, you woulda jeopardized us both, and I can't be havin' that."

Morgan took Denny and pulled him back to the corner and propped him back against the corner wall where he had him before. He situated Denny's backpack behind him so that Denny was leaning upright.

Morgan opened an MRE and began eating the spaghetti and meatballs.

"I'll never get used to this stuff. I can't see how you veterans ate this stuff all the time."

Morgan's plan was simple. Watch over Denny, and wake him up when it gets dark. That was the only acceptable plan of attack that he was willing to work with.

FEMA Compound, Sheridan, Western Oregon

What used to be a 1980s-designed federal penitentiary was now serving as a FEMA compound. Virtually all federal and state prisons were converted to FEMA compounds when the Flip occurred. Even before that, preparations were being made, early in Adalyn Baker's presidency, to turn all high-security facilities into emergency government housing to provide for civil disobedience, which was the buzz word for Americans who failed to comply with martial law.

This day started out like every other day since the Flip. Busses were actively bringing in loads of *fresh meat*, which is what the federal employees called new admissions. The busses pulled up on a scheduled basis, the gates opened, and the people piled out at gunpoint. On this day, the gates opened, and then the busses stalled out, the generators stopped humming, and the guards were left wondering what was going on.

"Control from SE Gate. Over," one of the guards said into his radio, but received no reply.

Looking closer at the radio, he found that it had stopped working. He removed the battery and put it back in, but it still did not function.

Looking at his digital watch to get the time, he saw that the screen was black and not functioning.

The guard walked up to the bus driver, who opened the door and told the guard, "My bus stalled out. Everything analogue that's running directly off the battery is fine, like the wipers, but nothing digital or electronic."

The guard walked back over to the control for the gates and pressed the button multiple times in a futile attempt to secure them.

Once again, he called on his radio, "Control from SE Gate. Over."

There was no reply.

The gate guard looked up to Tower One and saw the tower guard standing outside his post, on the catwalk.

"Hey," the gate guard yelled up to the catwalk. "We don't have any power."

"Me either," he yelled back down. "The magnetic locks just stopped working. Everything is down. I think the generators went out, too."

"Nothing's working! Not even the RFID scanners."

"I'm going to fetch a chain and padlock. We're going to have to manually secure them until we find out what's going on."

"Sounds good."

The man left the catwalk and returned to his post. When he walked in and pulled the magnetic door closed, it just swung back open.

Meanwhile, at Tower Three, the tower guard was bundling up because his electric heater was not warming his post. Before he could finish putting his heavy coat on, medical assistants came running out of the Bioengineering and Research Building. The guard was trying to hear their conversation, but the distance from the Bioengineering and Research Building to his post was too far. He pulled out his binoculars and tried reading their lips. Their conversation was reaching his ears after the fact. He was only able to make out a few words: *"unstable in cooler temperatures"* and *"no power to sustain."*

It was enough to frighten the tower guard, who immediately abandoned his post and walked out Gate Two, leading the way for the medical assistants, nurses, doctors, and scientists to follow. Everybody that came out of the Bioengineering and Research Building stripped their biohazard suits and fled on foot.

One guard that was working inside the building, and had the sole responsibility of insuring everybody left decontaminated, came out last. He was distraught, walking backwards from the building and holding his head with both hands. When he was well outside, he looked around and saw that he was alone. He fled out the gate.

Camp Parks Army Reserve Forces, Dublin, California

Soldiers of the Army Reserves Forces, Camp Parks, had just secured the Dublin federal penitentiary when the lights went out. They rescued several hundred men and women from the FEMA compound and managed to secure the radios, transponders, frequencies, and virtually every manner of electronic communication that was available.

"Sergeant Briggs, the radios stopped working the exact same time the power went out," Corporal Tina Wheeler said.

Sergeant Briggs was a five-year serviceman and sergeant from Asco, California. His father was a lifetime soldier and raised him on the Army base. There was no soldier more dedicated to the virtues of the Constitution than Sergeant James Briggs.

"Can't be a coincidence. The District probably found out about our little raid and thought it would be easier to EMP us than to suffer more casualties. We saved them, that's what matters most, Corporal. Let's gather up whatever intel we can find and get out of Dodge before they send something worse."

The District, White House Situation Room, 14:36 Hours

Payam Vahidi was working frantically to bring life back to the computers that had mysteriously shut down at the Utah Data Center. None of the FEMA employees or UN commanders assigned to that area were answering their phones. The live feeds had stopped coming into the White

House Situation Room and there was no explanation why or what was happening.

Vahidi was understandably afraid of bearing bad news to the executive commander. It wasn't until he had exhausted all possible efforts that he finally dialed Muhaimin's number.

The District, White House Oval Office

. Muhaimin was meeting with his top commanders and going over final preparations for the assault on the RFID-chipped veterans and active-duty personnel, primarily the group located in South Dakota, when his cell phone rang. Muhaimin reached into his coat and pulled out his cell phone.

Looking at the call, he said, "Excuse me, gentlemen, I have an urgent phone call that I must attend to."

"Mr. Vahidi, this had better be good news. I was not expecting a phone call."

The commanders were overhearing his end of the conversation.

"I see. Thank you for the update, Mr. Vahidi."

Muhaimin pressed the button that disconnected his call from Vahidi, and looked at the commanders.

"Gentlemen, I'm afraid there's been a stall in our plan of action. I will be in touch with further updates. Continue to stand down until you hear from me."

The commanders saluted him and he walked away without returning the salute.

A few moments later, he joined Vahidi in the White House Situation Room.

"Tell me again how you failed me."

"Sir, I have been unable to make any connection to our contacts on the West Coast. Our systems are still running, but it's like their systems crashed. We are no longer receiving feeds from the FLIES drones or the RFID program. Nobody west of South Dakota has contacted us. It's like they vanished."

Muhaimin looked around the room and saw several operators answering phone calls.

"Who's calling them?"

"They are receiving phone calls from our units east of Wyoming. They are technical support employees, but all of our forces on the ground have no further access to the RFID-location protocols that we have recently upgraded."

"This is obviously a retaliatory attack from the Chinese."

"Sir?"

"Mr. Vahidi, you've outstayed your welcome. It's time to move on."

Muhaimin pulled his pistol from the holster and pointed it at Vahidi.

Vahidi said, "Sir," but was shot in the chest three times before he could beg for his life.

"You were a good friend, Mr. Vahidi, but I can no longer tolerate the embarrassment you've given me."

Muhaimin turned and walked out while Vahidi fell to the floor and slowly died, unassisted.

Benton, Illinois

Captain Siroosi was pursuing the Recon Marines,

utilizing the RFID protocol, when the signal dropped at 16:23 hours. He sent several work orders to the UDC and to the District, but never received anything but a dead tone from the UDC, and the requests to the District went unanswered. Having been stricken with the sudden lack of actionable intelligence, Siroosi stopped firing off the TITAN 1, which was the official name for the direct energy weapon. Frustrated, he selected twelve UN ground troops and geared them up in Biocontrol uniforms, charging them specifically with killing any American that looked active military or capable of effective resistance.

To the UN soldiers, this was like a blank check. Each of them were feeling power hungry from watching the TITAN 1 being shot towards the Americans. From where they were standing, behind the TITAN 1, their chests were vibrating vigorously each time the TITAN 1 would charge for the next shot. It filled them with adrenaline and psyched them up for a fight, like school kids listening to their favorite speed metal song before they ran off to do something juvenile and brazen.

The twelve soldiers were being led by Sergeant Feliks Paparov (or Papa as his men called him), a bloodthirsty Russian combat veteran. He was smart and adapted well to any combat environment, whether it be desert, urban, jungle, or woodland.

Papa saluted the captain he was detailed to work with, and rounded up his men for a duty gear check. In his Russian language, he told his men, "I want each of you to pair off and double-check each other for operational readiness. Make sure your weapons are loaded and your breathing apparatuses are properly fastened. Don and clear to make sure you have a good seal."

After each of the men had stopped searching one another and he saw they were finished moving about, he called them to attention.

"Fall in," he yelled at them, and followed that command by, "Straighten up," which was a Russian command prompting them for the next command.

"Attention," he yelled, snapping the men into a tight standing position. Their rifles were in their right hands with the buttstock of each resting on the ground next to their right foot.

"Men, we are going into combat. The area we have been chosen to clear out has previously been isolated and cleared by Biocontrol units. There is an unidentified sickness in those buildings and it would do you well to keep your masks on. These Americans are trained well, but are hungry and desperate. They will make mistakes that you will not. Prepare yourself for glory."

The men began shouting from their position of attention.

"Kill, kill, kill."

Their yells were uniform and echoed through the quiet storefront buildings, reaching the ears of Nathan and the Recon Marines, who were just nesting down after a rapid deployment from the area that was being directly affected by the direct energy attack.

Jess was now waking up after her encounter with the weapon. "How long was I out?"

"Maybe an hour. I'm not sure," Nathan replied.

"What happened?"

"These guys said it was some kind of an energy weapon. The group was scattered when it went off. I couldn't see Denny, but I saw you, after I came to my senses."

"Where are we?"

"Not far from the shoot-out."

A Recon Marine, Lance Corporal Henderson, was looking out of one of the windows towards the direct energy weapon.

"We are going to have to set up an evac route. There's not enough of us to secure a decent perimeter."

Jess looked around the dimly lit room and counted four. "There's only four of us?"

"Yeah, those two," Nathan said, pointing at the two Marines that saved him, "and us."

"Not very good odds," she said.

"We may be better off than we suspect," Corporal Anders said.

"How's that?" Henderson asked.

"I'm sure there's more of us than four. We're just split up, right?"

"Right," Nathan clued in. "And if there's gunfire, backup might just stop by."

As if on cue, a massive firefight began outside.

Nathan, Jess, Henderson, and Anders listened for a moment. They could hear the distinct sounds of AK-47s being shot against America's preferred Colt-style rifles. The sounds were mixed with a variety of other distinct rifles.

"That's our crew," Nathan said.

"How do you know?" Henderson asked.

"Who else could pack a ragtag group of American fire-power together in one location?"

No sooner than Nathan had figured out who the attack was coming from, they heard the distinct sound of the direct energy weapon being fired off. The gunshots ceased and their joy seemed to melt away at the thought of what might have just happened. The anticipation in the room was high and they all feared the worst-case scenario.

Nathan jumped to his feet.

"No way," Anders said. "We can't go back out there."

Nathan did a quick assessment of what he had. Jess still had shaky motor skills, and that left three. It wasn't enough help to run out into the unknown environment against an enemy of unknown size with superweapons.

Nathan plopped back down onto the floor and waited for darkness.

DENNY AND MORGAN WEREN'T FAR FROM NATHAN'S position. Each of them had no idea where the other members of the group were. They would often hear the sounds of gunfire, reminiscent of the old West movies, except these weapons were more sophisticated and came in much higher calibers.

When Denny had awakened from his sleep, he didn't say a word to Morgan. He knew that Morgan had rendered him unconscious, and he was holding a grudge. It wasn't that he was angry with Morgan, he understood why he did what he did, but the frustration of being suckered in the back got under his skin.

It was now dark outside, but the sounds of shootings in the streets were still hyperactive.

Morgan, sensing that Denny was about to make his move, said, "Look, it's dark out there. It's what you've been waiting for, but you hear the sounds of gun fighting. What if they have night vision?"

"If they have night-vision capability, then I guess they have the advantage. Either way, I'm not going to die cowering in some lame building on my knees. If I die, it's going to be on my feet. Resisting!"

"Well, I hope you have a plan."

"Thanks for caring, Morg, but my plan is to survive. Aim small, miss small."

"Huh? Is that some kind of military lingo?"

Denny just looked at Morgan and wondered how any civilian could survive in hostile territory.

When Morgan saw that Denny was staring blankly at him, he said, "What?"

"Nothing. I'm just missing my veteran friends."

"You know, I get the feeling from you *veterans* that you think you're better than us *civilians*. In fact, when I hear you guys talking, you call us *civilians* as if it's a derogatory thing. Why is that?"

Denny knew that Morgan was picking a fight. The hook was baited and he was still frustrated with Morgan for knocking him out, so he took the bait.

"Morgan, you would probably be dead if not for the

veterans with combat experience or even training, for that matter."

"So it's true, you think you're better than us."

"It's not that we're better than you, we're just better equipped, all the way around."

"Better equipped? You can't even watch your back. I had to knock you out from behind because you're so gung ho that you can't think straight."

"Yeah, about that. I gave you my back because I trusted you. A weakness I won't demonstrate anymore."

Denny grabbed his pack from the corner and put it on his back.

"Thanks for watching over me, but if I can't trust you with my back, then I'm going to be heading out, alone."

"Fine. You *veterans* can get by just fine without us *civilians*. Good luck!" Morgan shouted.

"That's what I'm talking about. There's UN soldiers outside of these walls. They're looking for us, and you want to raise your voice. That's ignorant *civilian* stuff."

"Just go," Morgan said, trying to get the last word.

Denny was tired of all the talking. He wasn't a good debater and even worse at holding conversations. He was more of a thinker than anything. What he knew to be true was that Morgan had raised his voice one too many times, and that made him nervous that their position had been given away. When he had his backpack securely fastened on his shoulders, he double-checked his pocket to make sure his Karambit was still there.

He walked up to the door, pulled it open, and pulled his Karambit from his pocket.

Morgan walked up to him and Denny spotted him.

"What are you doing, Morg?"

"I'm not going to let a veteran die alone. You're taking a knife to a gunfight. Not so smart for a veteran."

"I'm not going to die."

"You don't know that. Death comes to us all."

"Now you're sounding like a veteran. We may be rubbing off on you."

Denny turned back to the door.

Morgan's view was obstructed by Denny, who was standing in the doorway.

When Denny was fully facing outward, six UN soldiers in Biocontrol suits stepped into view. The lead soldier pointed a Russian PK machine gun at him.

It all happened so fast that there was only reflex time. Denny ducked out of the way, exposing Morgan to the shooter. It wasn't a lack of care or even a lack of knowledge, it was a lack of time to coordinate the necessary motor skills to verbalize what Denny said too late.

"Incoming!" he yelled as he ducked to the side.

Morgan heard the call, but it was too late. A firestorm of 7.62 mm belt-fed projectiles went sailing through Morgan. Denny kicked the door closed and took cover in a darkened cubbyhole.

Morgan was now groping at his chest and trying to find Denny in the dark.

Denny was calling to Morgan, but the bullets were still being shot through the door. Denny could barely see Morgan, because of the light that was coming through the door. One of the UN soldiers had some kind of a back-mounted lighting system. To Denny, it was both a blessing and a curse. It gave away the soldier's position, but it also blinded and gave away his position. At the moment, the light was shining through the bullet holes in the door and putting light on Morgan, who was trying to take cover.

Denny called to him, but his calls were shrouded in the barrage.

"Denny, help."

"Morgan, come towards my voice."

"Denny, I'm all shot up."

"Morgan!"

The shots subsided, if but for a moment, giving Denny the opportunity he needed to save Morgan.

He ran over to Morgan and grabbed him by the back of the chest rig he was wearing and pulled him into the cubby.

"I can't breathe, Denny," Morgan gurgled.

"You're talking, that means you're breathing."

Denny knew Morgan was in bad shape. There were several bullet holes in his body and blood was streaming out beneath him.

Denny had Morgan resting on his lap, with his rifle pointing towards the door.

The door was kicked open by the UN soldiers that were on the other side and following them was another barrage of bullets. They came running into the room, but only one was shooting at Morgan and Denny. The gunshots seemed to be slowing as Denny took Morgan's rifle and shot at the lead soldier that had kicked the door open and ran in first.

The other soldiers were being shot at from outside of the

room. Denny was unsure if he had caught any bullets and was too consumed with adrenaline to stop and figure it out.

One by one, guns stopped shooting. The man that was firing on Morgan and Denny was dying on the floor.

"Don't shoot. I'm coming in," a familiar feminine voice said.

"They're all dead," she said as she stepped into the room, throwing the breathing apparatuses of the four UN troops Denny could not see onto the floor and into the lit area just outside of his cubbyhole where Denny was hiding.

The lady couldn't see who was in the room. She went back to the UN troop that had the lighting accessory on his pack and took it off. Carrying it back into the room, she used her left hand to guide the light, and her right hand to hold her pistol.

Denny was confident that Morgan was dead by now. He had his left hand over his chest feeling for a rising chest, but there was nothing. Keeping Morgan's weapon trained on the light that was approaching him, he felt Morgan's carotid artery. Morgan was dead.

The light peeked around the corner of the room and lit up Denny's face.

His left hand now up to block the piercing light, he said, "If you're here to kill me, get it over with. I'm hungry."

"Denny?" the woman said.

Setting the light down onto the floor, it now shone upon the white ceiling, reflecting enough light into the area for Denny to see the lady who had just saved his life.

"Tori?"

CHAPTER 9

Bicentennial Park, Indiana

RORY PRICE HAD MADE the decision to stay behind. The trek from southern Illinois to northwest Indiana was a long one, but all the talk of deviating off of the current mission objective and into South Dakota was not in his plans. He was missing his wife and daughter severely, and it now seemed in vain that he had traveled this far to save Americans from certain annihilation at the hands of tyrannical domestic and foreign enemies. He kept hearing rumors of a classified mission and the thought of unknown objectives didn't sit right with him.

Charles Buchanan and John James had left the afternoon before, for their mission to South Dakota. Rory was sitting against a pine tree, in the frigid northern air breeze, reading his Bible and searching for direction through a silent prayer.

He often found that God never spoke to him in a loud audible voice, but with soft impressions that always seemed to line up with the teachings of his Bible. This morning was no different, except he was cold and found it hard to focus on any one thing, like prayer or reading.

As he sat against that pine tree, he thought of home, the old ways, and the simple life. That train of thought took him to a life in captivity, a life without freedoms that he wasn't willing to just lay down and forget about. His next thought was of the people, like Jess, who had been captured by UN forces and rounded up like cattle. Most of them were not as fortunate as Jess. They weren't rescued by resistance fighters or let go by a change of heart, but they were sent north, into the unknown, into unthinkable possibilities.

Rory came to his decision.

With a deep breath and a loud sigh, he stood up and pulled out the compass that one of Buchanan's Marines had given him.

Rory was assigned by Buchanan to be the chaplain of the group. It was an honor he gratefully accepted. The Marines came to like and to trust Rory as a capable fighter and man of God—two descriptions some had problems reconciling. The issue was as clear as night and day to Rory. He even gave a Bible study to the Marines he was with on one of the Ten Commandments, *"Thou shalt not kill."* He took them to the original Hebrew word for *kill*, which is *ratsach*, and explained how the true definition of the word is not as broad as the English definition. In Hebrew, the commandment is best rendered *"Thou shalt not murder."* The killing that was going on wasn't murder if done in self-defense. Rory's Bible study relieved quite a bit of anxiety for the men who had a heavy conscience. Rory explained to them that Jesus never would have requested his disciples to have swords for anything other than self-defense. His Bible studies touched many people, and one of them saw fit to give Chaplain Rory Price a token. The token was the compass. To Rory, it was more than a gift that pointed north, but, like the Bible, if he stayed true to its direction, it would lead him in the right direction.

The same Marine that gave him the compass showed him how to use it with a map. He opened the map he was given and laid it upon the ground. Using rocks to hold down the four corners, he did as he was taught. He laid the compass flat upon the map, being careful to line up the straight edge of the compass with the north-facing arrow of the map. Then he rotated the map until the compasses arrow was facing magnetic north. Then Rory located the GN and made adjustments. Using his straight edge, he drew a line from his position, in Bicentennial Park, to Goose Island, Chicago. With that reading, he adjusted the dial, and began his trek to Chicago, Illinois.

Camp Parks Army Reserve Forces, Dublin, California

Sergeant Briggs, along with the men and women of his Army Reserves unit, had gathered several hard drives laden with terabytes of data. Unfortunately, the small North Korean EMP attack rendered every electronic gizmo in California useless. It wasn't that the data on the hard drives were corrupted, it was the fact that they couldn't find a working computer.

Camp Parks had running water and electricity, until it was discovered that the Reservists weren't responding to the orders issued by President Adalyn Baker during the first days of the Flip. Most of the Reservists left to join up with the UN command when they figured out they would be numbered with the resistance and have to go without a supply of life-saving water and food. Years before the Flip, California was suffering from liberal takeover of natural water supplies. The politicians continually wrote legislation allowing upwards of seventy percent of California's natural water supplies to run off the mountains and into the deltas to save the fish. Sergeant Briggs didn't find any humor in the fact that most of those politicians were now without water or, worse, dead. Like most other elected officials, they were rounded up and reintegrated with *the people*, where they found their final resting place somewhere other than a cemetery of their choosing.

"What else do we have?" Sergeant Briggs asked Specialist Felicia Edwards.

"Instruction manuals for Door Marking, Relocation Protocol, Consumer Intake—the list goes on and on."

"Is there anything on the power outage?"

"Nothing. It's like we were ghosted by a secret weapon."

"I'm starting to wonder if that's not the case."

"Seriously?"

"Think about it. Nothing electronic works. We huffed it back to the camp from the pen and nothing electronic between there and here was operable. What else could do that? I mean, if they killed the power, it wouldn't have affected the cars or our radios."

"Just when you think things can't get any worse, they drop a bomb. No pun intended."

"It wouldn't make sense to EMP yourself, though."

"My ex-husband was a geek about this kind of stuff. He spent so much money prepping for doomsday that he tended to neglect other financial matters. It's why we divorced. One time he made this cabinet thingy called a, uhh..." The word was escaping Felicia's memory.

"A Faraday cabinet?"

"That's it!" she said excitedly. "I was like, whatever!"

"If only you had been a believer."

"He lives, or lived, about a half hour from here. Maybe the stuff he kept in that cabinet can be of some use to us?"

Felicia saw James's face light up at the idea.

"That would be great, but I have one question. By a half hour you mean driving for a half hour?"

"Well, let's grab our rucks and get moving."

NATHAN, JESS, ANDERS, AND HENDERSON MADE IT safely out of the Biocontrol zone and back to the bivouac area where they had concealed their vehicles and equipment.

Nathan, remembering that Blake had exposed them to an unknown sickness that was ravaging the area, made the decision to stay isolated from the others until he was confident they were not contaminated. The last thing he wanted to do was to wipe out everybody with a bioweapon that they could not defend against.

It was now late morning and they were awakened by the

sounds of laughter. Nathan and Jess maintained their body heat by sharing the same sleeping bag. It was a tight fit, but southern Illinois winters were nothing to trifle with.

Nathan was lying still and listening to the Marines telling jokes and cutting each other down with insults. Nothing had changed since his time in service. The Marines were still a brotherhood, and while many non-Marines found it difficult to understand the esprit de corps, theirs was a brotherhood that bound them unto death.

Jess's head was nestled against Nathan's chest. The way they embraced one another as they slept was not only necessary to survival, but was heartwarming. Nathan couldn't see that Jess's eyes were open, but her embrace was enough for him to know she was awake.

"Did they wake you with their laughter?"

"No, I was already stirring a bit."

"Are you about ready to get organized? We have missing friends in that town."

"Yeah, I guess. How much did we lose last night?"

"You mean people and equipment?"

"No, weight! Of course people and equipment."

Nathan gave her a squeeze for being sarcastic. "I think we lost six HMMWVs and seventeen men. That's not counting the ones we were separated from. Denny's in there somewhere and we have to find him."

"We're going to have to go in together, yet separate, if we're to keep from exposing the others."

"I know. About that, how do you feel? Do you feel any different?"

"Not really," Jess said as she began pulling up and out of the sleeping bag.

Once Jess was exposed to the frigid morning air, she took in a deep breath and that shocked her lungs, causing her to cough.

Everybody that was apart from them stopped what they were doing to look at her.

"Relax, it's just a cough," she said.

About the time Ash saw that she was awake, he walked within ten feet of Nathan and Jess.

"Where's Denny?" he asked.

Nathan sat up to join Jess. "I don't know. Denny came to our aid yesterday and ended up getting hit with some kind of energy weapon that punched a hole through a brick storefront wall. It almost killed everybody. I was saved by a couple Recons and I grabbed Jess. I lost Denny in the rubble and the fog of combat."

"I never got to thank him for saving me."

"Yeah, well, if you were to find out what he had to do to save you, you might not be thanking him."

"Typical Denny stuff, eh?"

"For sure."

"I thought you guys might be hungry, so I brought you a couple MREs." Ash threw them to Nathan.

"Thanks, man. This is how I remember the Corps."

"How's that?" Jess asked.

"Waking up in frigid temperatures and eating frozen food that was prepared over a decade prior."

"I just lost my appetite."

Nathan smiled at her and stood up. He began packing his

belongings and taking inventory of everything he had. When he was done, he looked at the train track and noticed the train was gone. Calling over to one of the Marines, he asked, "What time did the train head out?"

"It headed out last night, sometime during all the shooting."

Nathan looked back at Jess and said, "There has to be a loading area or some kind of zone where they're putting people on that train."

"You're not thinking about going back in there, are you?"

"I already told you, Denny's still in there and I'm not leaving without him."

"I get so sick of all your *Semper Fi*."

"Are you coming?"

"Well, somebody's got to pull you out of the rubble. Might as well be me."

While they were packing their belongings, the others were watching them. None of them seemed to be doing anything that would give the appearance of a search and rescue mission. Nathan stopped long enough to look at them and asked, "Are any of you guys coming? We have men in there."

Ash stepped forward and said, "We were going to push through with the heavies. We just kind of figured that anybody else that was in there still was probably dead."

"Are you serious? We have all this meat and we're going to just *push through*?" Nathan yelled, pointing at all the Marines and national guardsmen.

"Listen," Ash said, "I heard the guys talking about what

was going on in that town. It's infected with something. Prolonged exposure could contaminate all of us."

Jess looked at Thor, who had just walked up to Ash and kneeled by his side.

"What about Thor?" she asked. "He's been walking freely around the camp, probably being petted by everybody. Have you had an eye on him this whole time? Is he carrying any contagion?"

Ash took his hand off of Thor's head.

"Look," Nathan said. "You guys push through and cause a distraction. That'll buy us time to search out Denny. We already lost Morgan and Blake. I'm not going to rest until I have my best friend back."

One of the Marine sergeants said, "Even at the price of jeopardizing the rest of us?"

"We don't leave anybody behind," Nathan yelled back at him. "If you guys can at least do that—push through, cause a distraction—we'll search the area and meet you on the other side."

"I'm all about tearing up those blue helmets. Let's do it."

"Great, give us a thirty-minute head start, since we're on foot, and start gunning through."

Nathan had never been accused of jeopardizing his men. He had to constantly remind himself that these men and women were volunteers and free Americans. Each one of them would die defending that freedom. It just made more sense for him to talk out the issues and differences of opinion until a common consensus was brought to the forefront. In this case, he reminded himself that these Marines, although left by Buchanan with a specific mission, were not his men.

Nathan wasn't a Marine Corps commander and couldn't force them to do anything, but made it seem reasonable to find common ground. That common ground was moving forward with as many people as possible. Nobody knew what was waiting for them on the other side of this town, but it had to be better than the open interstate. The UN had learned early on that flying over urban America was not a wise action. Many armaments had been confiscated by the resistance, some of which was antitank and air-defense weaponry. The risk outweighed the mission for the foreigners.

Nathan and Jess had taken an alternate route back to the area where they had last seen Denny. The railroad train, which ran south to north, was on a track that ran adjacent to Railroad Street. Using the cover of buildings, they made their way to a position where they could see the Federal Courthouse, which was being used as a junction for human trafficking. The railroad track made an intersection with East Main Street, which was the position where they had a third of a mile view west, towards what the locals called *the square*. The courthouse sat in the center of the square and was considered the seat of Franklin County. It was becoming painfully clear to Nathan and Jess that the UN occupation was bigger than they had anticipated.

From their position, where they were lying prone, they could see that a security fence had been erected with concertina wire above and below. The fence formed a rectangular shape around the center of Benton, engulfing East Washington and East Church streets, all the way west to South Du Quoin Street, where the fence's perimeter ended on its opposite end from their position near Railroad Street and East Main. Nathan and Jess could not see the end of the fence's structure, but knew it was immense. Their eyes could follow the security line a third of a mile to the courthouse, but beyond that, they had no idea that it continued on another half mile to Du Quoin Street.

They had to be careful not to give away their position. They were lying dangerously close to UN security guards who were working the eastern gate. Guards were patrolling the fence line from their positions on the ground. Nathan noticed there were no towers, but troops patrolled the rooftops.

"Coming this way wasn't a good idea," Nathan said.

"How could we have known?"

Jess was saddened by the people she saw being herded into the tail end of the train that had apparently been loading people through the night.

"Well, there's the train," she said.

"I think they've been loading the people into the cars as they round them up, then pull the train forward a bit to load more."

Nathan saw at least one loading area. They had constructed lateral fence lines that connected to the main security fence, but protruded outward towards makeshift loading docks.

"Look," Nathan said. "There's one of the areas they're herding people into and then loading them onto the train."

"Well, our boys in green will be coming through any minute now."

"When they do, we can't go inside the fence. Denny's not likely to be in there. He would never be taken alive."

"So which way we gonna head?"

"I think we should head northwest, along those buildings. The men on the rooftops will be distracted by our guys. Once we hit the other side of those buildings there, we should be good, providing no more superweapons are shot at us."

Nathan and Jess were startled when one of the rooftop UN guards suddenly began shouting in Russian. Their instincts told them to stand and run, and Jess had started to, but Nathan grabbed her by the shoulder and said, "Don't move."

The only word they could make out was "American," and the second word he shouted was not understandable. It soon came to their minds what he was yelling about when other guards came running to their position and were setting up a firing position made up of sandbags. The guards were frantically building it when the sound of HMMWVs and various other military vehicles came within earshot.

Nathan could hear the team rolling in like thunder and watched as the UN crews brought in their heavy anti-armor weapons. So far, Nathan couldn't spot the powerful direct energy weapon that had laid them to waste the day before. His hope that the weapon was still on the outside of the fence proved to be a bad wish when he saw it pulling up and facing towards the incoming Marines.

Nathan and Jess began to fear the worst.

"Oh no," Nathan whispered.

"We have to warn them," she said.

"There's no way to warn them, Jess. If we take off towards them, we'll be spotted and gunned down like wild boar."

"Then what?"

Nathan thought hard about what to do next. The thought of sacrificing himself entered his mind, but not only would he be giving his own life, but Jess's also, and Denny's, if he was still alive.

"We stay on mission," he said. "Let's go."

They stood up while the guards were distracted and took cover alongside the buildings that led them back to where they had last seen Denny.

Entering the building where the direct energy weapon had blasted a hole in the wall was frightening to them both.

Nathan and Jess began digging through the rubble.

Jess was tossing aside large chunks of wood when the other side of the room went quiet. Wondering why Nathan was no longer digging, she turned around and saw him holding Denny's rifle.

"Oh, Nathan, I'm so sorry!"

"He doesn't go anywhere without his rifle."

Nathan desperately continued to move through the rubble. He found no signs of anyone, living or dead.

"Nathan, we need to keep moving. We can't stay here."

Nathan kept tossing debris around as if he was either ignoring Jess or didn't hear her. Jess had to walk up to him and grab him by the arm.

"Nathan!"

"He was here, Jess. We were here, together. He came back for me and I left him."

"It didn't go down that simple, Nathan."

Jess could hear the shooting from the Marines blasting through the fences. Every minute or so, she heard the humming sound of the direct energy weapon just as it fired off another shock wave. Nathan was now standing still. This was the first time Jess had ever seen Nathan indecisive. She was now worried for him and their situation.

"Let's go," she said, tugging on his arm. She was too small framed to carry the weight or the strength necessary to pull Nathan out of the building. A simple tug away from her grasp was all he needed to break free of it.

"You go on ahead without me. I'm going to keep searching. He's got to be here somewhere."

"Denny didn't make it, Nathan."

"What did you just say?" Nathan turned to square off with her, as if challenging her to repeat the comment.

"You said it yourself," she said, stepping backwards. "You said he *never goes anywhere without his rifle.*"

"I didn't say he was dead, either."

"I know, neither did I," she said, stepping closer to him. "I said *he didn't make it.* Look, it's possible he was knocked out and taken prisoner while unconscious."

"I'm not arguing that possibility, Jess. That's why I have to stay and keep searching. If he's in there, I'm going to get him."

"By yourself? Because that's what it's going to be. The guys said they would pick us up on the other side, and that's if they even survive the counteroffensive that we saw them throwing together."

"If they tear up enough of that fence and put enough holes in those buildings, yeah, by myself. As crazy as it seems."

Jess grabbed Nathan around his waist and pulled him in close, planting a kiss on his lips.

"I love you, Mr. Roeh. I'll see you and Denny on the other side."

Jess wasn't referring to the fence. She was referring to the afterlife. She didn't believe Denny was still alive and thought Nathan was going on a suicide mission. She knew that there was nothing she'd be able to say that would talk him out of going into that battle-torn encampment to find Denny.

With a deep sigh, she planted her head on his chest and hugged him until she started to cry and then pushed him away, saying, "You better get yourself a plan together if you're going out there without the heavy guns support."

Jess walked away, stopping at the broken door frame to take one last look at Nathan, hoping that he would see her leaving and change his mind, but he just stepped off into the next room.

Nathan calmed his mind down enough to take a look at his ammunition and food supplies. Water wasn't a major threat to Nathan. The southern Illinois snowfall provided sufficient provision for that necessity. The problem was that he had one MRE that Ash had given him earlier, and only three magazines of ammo, totaling about sixty rounds.

He was still carrying Denny's rifle in his hands, so he dropped his pack and used some paracord to attach it vertically to the side so it wouldn't catch on doorframes as he walked through them. Once he double-checked his gear to make sure that everything was silenced, he left the building and headed back to where the Marines had slammed through the fence.

Two HMMWVs were destroyed in the center of the roadway with debris scattered all over. He could see bodies hanging out of the barely recognizable vehicles, and considered ammunition and food supplies. Looking up at the rooftops, he could see the guard that initially shouted to the others, warning of the incoming assault convoy.

Nathan slid by undetected into the building that had the guard on the roof. Finding the hatch was still open, he took his Ka-Bar from the sheath and climbed the ladder. The man on the roof was alone and preoccupied with what was going on to the north.

Nathan could still hear gunfire and, for a moment, considered making a hasty retreat to join them. It was his nature to stay with the pack, but Denny was more than a friend to Nathan, he was family.

The guard didn't even have his rifle ready; it was hanging from his shoulder. Nathan reached the ceiling, climbed through the hatch, and onto the roof. He could feel his heart pounding with adrenaline and almost feared the guard would hear it.

Surely with all the gunshots, it will just blend in, he thought.

As he started to walk towards the guard, the sounds of crunching snow eventually caught his attention. He turned around to see Nathan charging at him with a Ka-Bar in hand. The guard didn't have time to unsling his rifle, so he went into a defensive posture, putting his hands forward in an attempt to catch Nathan. Nathan parried the defensive maneuver by using his left hand to throw the guard's right shoulder to his right. When that happened, Nathan wasted no time sticking the UN guard in the abdomen with his knife. The soldier was wearing a shrapnel safety vest that protects against knives and sharp flying debris.

The soldier grabbed at the site where he was stabbed, but Nathan had already pulled the knife. With the soldier's hands down on his abdomen, Nathan's second stab went into the man's throat. Nathan held it there and followed the man down to the floor of the roof, maintaining control of the knife and bearing the weight of the man all the way down.

Nathan held his free hand over the man's mouth to silence him.

He then went through the man's belongings and found some Russian food rations. He placed them in his pack and left down the hatch and towards the Marines that he had spotted dead in the roadway.

Arriving at the HMMWVs, Nathan saw a mangled mess of vehicle parts. He saw one rifle with a magazine in the rifle's well, but couldn't pull it out. The blast of the direct energy weapon had somehow bent the magazine in such a fashion that he couldn't free it from the rifle. When he realized it wasn't coming out, he disassembled the base of the magazine and popped the spring out, which allowed the rounds to fall into his lap. After that, he tried to pull a Marine out of the HMMWV by his arm, but the arm wasn't attached and Nathan almost lost his balance, figuring he had to pull hard to free the body from the debris. Instead, he moved aside some parts of the vehicle that gave him a view of the magazine pouches on the Marine's chest rig. He found two magazines full of ammunition that would work with his rifle. Pocketing the magazines, he ran back to the inside of the building and looked out of the north-facing window towards the next building.

Nathan's plan was to move from cover to cover, taking out the rooftop guards before they had a chance to communicate. The next guard he could see was two buildings north of his location. When he had gathered a few mental notes and turned around to leave, he was struck in the face with the buttstock of a Bushmaster 30-06, rendering him unconscious.

CHAPTER 10

The District

EXECUTIVE COMMANDER MUHAIMIN had reassigned two UN Crowd Control regiments from vital missions in Midwestern America to a centralized rally point in Independence, Iowa, to address the issue of large masses of Marines gathered together in the Black Hills of South Dakota.

"Crowd Control" was the buzz word for "UN Infantry" when peace-keeping missions were the narrative, but Muhaimin was growing bored of the political correctness from the global chairs. He was already believing himself to be one of the greatest military minds in the world. He wasn't going to let a regiment of Marines undermine him or throw any further wrenches into the plans he had already laid the groundwork for. With new stresses coming from what he believed to be a Chinese attack on America, he was highly aggressive and his antisocial personality disorder always amplified his negative emotions. He could not afford a battle on two fronts, so he determined to deal with China later and focus on the immediate threat that presented itself currently on American soil.

As Muhaimin thought on these things, his phone rang. He reached into his coat pocket and removed his cell phone, paying careful attention to who was calling him on a secure line without an appointment.

"Captain Kianoush Delwadewala, one of the few people I look forward to hearing from. How was your trip back to the motherland?"

"Sir, you know how watchful the Iranian Homeland Security Forces have been. We have spared no expense of resources in aiding you with information and a watchful eye over your American project."

"Captain Delwadewala, you know I do not like it when you take the long way around. Cut to the part when you give me information I can use. I am a busy man."

"Sir, America was attacked by a high-tech North Korean electromagnetic weapon. We have nothing on record to show what it was exactly, but what we have been able to determine is that it was a low-altitude EMP missile-class weapon."

"Have you heard anything from the Koreans?"

"Kil Jong Ho has upped his anti-American rhetoric and touted his sovereignty as a superpower. He has said nothing that would lay responsibility on him. The UN doesn't know we have this information, but our monitoring shows the missile left the North Korean coastline and took a low-altitude trajectory directly to international waters just off the coast of America. The explosion detonated one thousand two hundred

miles off the western coast of Oregon and affected every state in about a two-thousand-mile radius."

"What was affected?"

"Everything electronic in the affected area has been rendered useless. The data feed we had from the Utah Data Center is gone. Operation Main Core is now a total loss. We have no way of locating the American resistance fighters, the FLIES drones are useless, and everything in western America is without power. Half of your UN forces are in the dark against the patriots. What technological edge we had on them is now gone."

"Thank you for calling, Captain Delwadewala. My Advanced Technological Weapons Systems czar has resigned his post. I once told you there may be a promotion in your future. I look forward to hearing your reply."

"Thank you for the offer, sir. It would be an honor to serve in that capacity, but I do feel that I can better serve your interests monitoring things from the motherland. The advanced weapons systems technology in America has been rendered incapacitated. The best weapon we now have against the patriots is the TITAN weapons system."

"Perhaps you are correct. Thank you again for calling."

Muhaimin disconnected his call with Delwadewala and put his cell phone away. He then walked into the White House Situation Room and spoke to a secretary.

"Connect me to the Rock Island Arsenal."

Coronado, California

Sergeant Briggs, Specialist Edwards, and the rest of the

platoon made their way to Edward's ex-husband's house. On approach, the Reservists could see that the hospitality of those who were still remaining in the Coronado area was lacking.

"This used to be a nice town," Sergeant Briggs said to Edwards, who was patrolling just to his right and to the rear.

Edwards saw a few gang members had come out of the abandoned houses, but they did not attack. Many were running from house to house, gathering larger numbers of people with each visit.

"This doesn't look like it's going to end in our favor if they keep growing in numbers," she replied.

"Private Price," Briggs called out.

"Here, Sergeant," the newest member of the team said as he came running up to Briggs.

"Do you still have that US flag?"

"Yeah, in my ruck."

"Raise the colors. I don't want these kids thinking we're anything other than US soldiers."

"You got it," he said as he dropped out of formation to dig through his ruck.

Price pulled out a three-by-five-foot US flag and couldn't find anything long enough to make a pole.

"Just bring it to the front. You and Smothers can hold it open and walk in front of the patrol," Edwards said.

Privates Price and Smothers ran to the front of the patrol and each carried a corner.

"Now we look like a marching band," Briggs said to Edwards.

"Maybe it'll give us a friendly appearance."

"Hopefully, keep your fingers crossed. How much further do we have to go, anyway?"

"Just about a mile."

On occasion, as was customary while on patrol, members would turn to do a check of their six to make sure nobody was behind them. One of the rear privates looked over his left shoulder and saw two armed gangsters coming out of a house. Feeling slightly intimidated, he didn't call out or say anything to any of the senior soldiers.

He watched them closely.

One of the gangsters was wearing a red-colored paisley handkerchief on his head. The other one was wearing the same pattern, but it was colored blue.

The two men joined up with the rear of the formation and fell into place, as if they were a part of the group. One by one, more gangsters came walking out of houses and joined the formation. Griggs and Edwards were seeing a ton of movement as well, but they were not checking their six. Completely oblivious to the change of circumstances, Briggs caught a reflective gaze from one of the large picture windows that was on a house. While remaining calm, Briggs continued forward as if nothing was wrong.

"Edwards?"

"Yeah?"

"Don't turn around just yet, but if you happen to get a glimpse at our six, you'll see that we've picked up a few members."

"Okay, by members, do you mean more soldiers? Because I doubt you mean more soldiers."

"No, as in Bloods and Crips, together in our formation.

"Should we light 'em up?"

"No, I'm not feeling that. It's more like they're expressing something."

"Yeah, unity. Bloods and Crips don't play nice with one another."

"They have a history of uniting when the cause arises. I never said anything to you about it, but if you look at my Army tattoo and look really close at the eagle's legs, you can see upside-down pitchforks. And, inside the globe, you'll see remnants of a five-pointed star."

Shocked at the comment, Edwards bounced her back, like she was hit in the face with a football. Catching herself, she took the chance to look to the rear and saw about thirty gang members, and the number was growing.

"So, you used to be a..."

Edwards left the sentence open ended so Briggs could fill in the blank.

"Blood. I was a member of the West Coast Blood set," Briggs said. "I was pretty much raised in the military. 'Brat' was what they called me. I had this rebellious stage where I wanted to go live with my mother. Mom and Dad divorced when I was very young. Apparently she didn't like the military life. After she died, I got caught up in gang activity."

Edwards looked over her shoulder more frequently than she ever did.

"Stop it," Briggs said. "You're making me nervous."

"So how'd you get out?"

"I started rebuilding relations with my dad. Eventually the guys would ask me why I wasn't throwing down anymore. I told them I was spending time with my dad and he didn't know I was a G. I never told them, or anybody, my real plans. I was getting out and trading in my reds for my greens. Nobody came looking for me, and I vanished when the Army sent me overseas and stationed me far away from home. It all worked out."

"So can you help get us out of this pickle?"

"Yeah, just don't react or do anything stupid. Keep the patrol moving forward and I'll drop out and talk to the Bloods leader."

Griggs dropped out of the formation and saw that the entire platoon was showing weakness by excessively looking behind them.

Griggs walked up to the man he believed to be the leader. On approach, Griggs could tell he found the right man.

"What it B like?" Griggs said.

The Blood leader looked at him and said, "Man, we got mad juice for you just now. You B up in here flying our colors with pride. Man, we're tired of hiding. We want our cities back, yo."

Griggs looked at the Crips leader and acknowledged him with a head nod. When he acknowledged him back, he returned his conversation to the Bloods' leader.

"Look, we just raided a FEMA compound of sorts. We were hoping to get some information from their databases but the lights went out. We're thinking EMP."

"Whatev, we got deez, don't we?" the man said, holding out his pistol.

"Yeah, I guess you're right, but we were hoping we could use our weapons on some blue helmets. It's just easier to find them with radios."

"We don't need those. Our people B around all over. You want blue helmets, we can show you blue helmets."

The Crips leader then spoke up.

"They be misrepresenting our colors, man."

"I guess what I need to know is, is there another FEMA camp in the area?"

"Not within a hundred miles. You can see we're not rollin' anymore. Ain't gonna happen," the Bloods leader said, getting frustrated. "We heard about some slave trains, though."

"Slave trains?" Griggs asked, his curiosity piqued.

"Yeah, the UN be pushing people onto trains and taking them east. Ain't nobody come back."

Edwards looked at Griggs and said, "We can always hit my ex's house later."

Griggs looked at the Bloods and asked, "Can you take us to the slave trains?"

Benton, Illinois

Nathan came to from his apparent blackout. He was cold and tied to a chair. His head was throbbing again, having just recovered from the direct energy weapon blast; he now had a migraine.

Nathan tried to move, but his arms were behind him. He could feel bits of rope and duct tape was being used to secure him. His worst fear was that he would eventually be caught alive by the UN and tortured into giving up information on everything and everyone he knew.

Nathan tried to move his legs, but he couldn't move them

either. His fingers were cold, but his toes were numb. There was a bitter coldness coming into the room from the outside that was freezing his digits. His immediate thoughts were on looking for a way to cut himself free. His chest rig was gone and he could not see his pack. Next, he looked about the room to see if he could identify any clues that would give up his captors. Nothing. All he could see was that he was in the center of a room.

"Oh good, you're awake," an unfamiliar voice said from behind him.

Nathan looked over and saw an unknown American walking out of a room behind him. "I hope you slept well."

"Well, I had a sleep aid. That helped a lot."

"Don't get smart with me, punk."

"Look, you suckered me unconscious and I'm tied to a chair. Forgive my grumpiness."

The man was older, in his fifties, and was wearing a few layers of clothing. His beard was long and grizzled. Nathan could smell him, even through all the layers of clothing.

"Why am I here? Who are you? You're not UN," Nathan asked.

"My name is Joseph Sutton."

"Never heard of you."

"I've heard of you."

"How so?"

"You came through my neighborhood, shooting things up. You wouldn't know me, but you've killed a few men on your wild rampages through southern Illinois. I think it's about time to pay the piper."

"I've shot through a lot of towns. Maybe you can be more

specific?"

"Marion. You're the punk that's connected to that girl that shot Cade in the head. I wasn't there, but I heard the gunshots and saw the injury."

"Look, let me go and I'll drink hot cocoa with you and share the whole story."

The man walked away to the back room and returned with a coffee mug.

"You mean this *hot cocoa?*" the man said as he began sipping the cocoa that he took from Nathan's MRE.

"I was saving that."

"Sorry, but I'm not sure an MRE is fitting for your last meal."

"So you're going to kill me, then?"

"I'm not. I'm just watching over you until the others get back."

"The others?"

"Yeah, they left for a bit. Not sure why."

As soon as Sutton had said that, the door opened and four people came walking into the room. The first three he didn't recognize. The fourth man was Cade Walker and his 30-06 Bushmaster rifle.

"Cade, thank God. Tell this guy I'm cool and get me out of here."

The other men looked at Cade and said, "How does he know your name?"

"I told you before. I used to ride with this guy and his men. When I saw how evil he was, I made the decision to leave him. When that happened, he had me killed; or so he thought."

Nathan didn't say anything further. He was under the assumption that Cade was saying what he had to in order to save him from the men.

One of the men looked at another and said, "I wish Donnie was here now. Then he could see that I was right. That chick we're after tried to kill Cade."

Nathan saw the bandage on Cade's head, but was reluctant to say anything about how it had happened. He wanted to believe Jess's story, but time would tell if she was right or paranoid.

"She tried to kill me, all right," Cade said. "She's been a thorn in the palm of my hand for months now."

Cade looked at the men and said, "Leave me alone for a few with our guest. We need to clear the air."

The men all left the room.

"Cade, what's all this about? Are you going to let me go?"

"Let you go? I've got you exactly where I want you."

"What are you talking about?"

"A few months ago, I had it made. I ran a cozy part of town with food and water."

"Yeah, so did I," Nathan interrupted.

"Don't ever interrupt me again."

Cade looked at Nathan in the eyes and Nathan saw only a blank stare. It was like his soul was missing.

Cade continued. "I had patrols that went out in search of resources, and my establishment was interrupted by an unwelcomed guest."

"Jessica," Nathan said.

"Where is she?" Cade asked in a calm yet disturbing manner.

"I don't know. We split up."

"That's not what I wanted to hear."

Cade pulled a bolt cutter out of his coat.

Nathan was gripped with fear for the first time in his life. He had been in many situations involving life and death. None of them made him susceptible to fear, but this was different. He was tied helplessly to a chair.

"Cade, you don't have to do this."

"That's what's cool, Nate. I know I don't *have to*, but I choose to. That's the beauty of freedom."

"Your freedom stops when it hinders mine!"

"That's your definition of freedom. Mine is a world where I'm calling the shots and you're listening, and right now, I'm giving you one more chance to tell me where Jess is."

"Cade..."

Nathan couldn't get the sentence out before Cade grabbed his left hand and forced Nathan's fist open. His hands were cold and weak. Nathan couldn't resist as he normally would have been able to. His cold fingers had no strength in them.

Cade held Nathan's hand flat against the chair and selected his pinky finger. He then bent it backwards to prevent Nathan from tucking it back into a fist. While he held his pinky back with one hand, he used his other hand to place the pinky in the bolt cutters. It took very little force to snip Nathan's pinky finger off at the first knuckle.

Nathan began screaming and violently shaking the chair.

The other men came running in and saw blood pouring out of Nathan's hand and onto the floor.

"What's going on here?" old man Sutton said.

"I told all of you to wait outside."

"You're not going to torture that man! If you do, I'm leaving with my car."

"You're not taking that car anywhere," Cade said.

He then walked up to Sutton and hit him in the neck with the bolt cutters, dropping him to his knees. Cade then punched Sutton and he died there on the cold floor.

One of the other three men came running up to Sutton and checked his pulse.

"You killed him, Cade!"

"It was an accident."

The man stood back up and looked at the others. They walked outside together and got into Sutton's car. When Cade heard the car start, he ran outside and pointed his rifle at the driver's side window. The driver, not seeing Cade, put the car in reverse and looked over his right shoulder to back out.

The man in the front passenger seat said, "He's pointing his gun at us."

As soon as the driver looked back forward, a shot rang out from Cade's rifle. The bullet struck the driver in the head and the car accelerated in reverse until it came to a stop in the building across the street. Cade turned and walked back into the area where Nathan was still bleeding.

"We better bandage that up so you don't bleed out on my floor."

Cade took the bandage off of his head and used Nathan's Ka-Bar to cut it into smaller pieces. He then wrapped Nathan's finger to help slow the bleeding.

"You have nine more fingers, Nate. That's twenty-seven more joints I can trim. Now, I'm asking nicely. Where's Jess?"

Nathan was breathing heavy when he said, "They're going to come looking for me."

"Oh yeah. I almost forgot."

Cade walked outside.

Nathan saw him walk past a couple windows and around the corner. When he came back in, he had a digital-camou-flaged bag. Fear was now gripping Nathan's heart as he recognized the bag. It was Ash's.

Nathan began to cry.

"Apparently, Ash grew tired of waiting on you. He left on his own to find you and Jess. He told me that he had one hoot of a firefight with the UN guys that were here. Before he died, he told me that they beat those blue helmets. I thought that was good news."

Cade unzipped the backpack and dumped the contents onto the floor.

Nathan stared in horror at Ash's head as it rolled out onto the uneven floorboards and into the corner of the room, where it came to a rest facing Nathan.

"No need to squirt, Nate. It's not like you haven't killed a few people. You gunned down my entire Southside Raiders party."

When Cade said those words, it was the same feeling one would have putting the final piece of a 50,000 word puzzle together. Everything made sense and he now had the broader picture, only the sense of achievement wasn't there.

Nathan's thoughts went back to Gorham when his sister was shot and bled out in his hands. He thought of Denny's sister and how she was burned alive. The fire that torched her was now burning inside of Nathan. He stared into Cade's eyes and he lost all sense of time and space. He felt only hate as adrenaline began shooting through his veins; he began hurling threats at Cade, completely forgetting that Cade was holding all the cards. His tunnel vision was narrowed as he stared into his eyes.

"Well, now. We can't be having you talking to me like that," Cade said, picking his rifle up out of the corner.

Walking up to Nathan, he pulled the bolt back, ejecting an empty shell to chamber a new one. He raised his rifle up to Nathan's head and placed it against his forehead.

"This is the part where we say our goodbyes."

Nathan was still full of rage and firmly pressed his forehead against the tip of the rifle, as if inviting Cade to pull the trigger and end his misery.

The shot rang out and blood splattered all over Nathan's face. Cade dropped dead, revealing two figures standing in the doorway. One was a female with a silver 1911 in hand.

"And stay down!" Tori said.

"Cunningham?"

"Hey, tiger. Heard you were bleeding," Tori said as she and Denny moved in to cut him free.

"Denny, I came looking for you."

"Don't worry about it, bro. I'm glad to see you're still alive."

Nathan stood up and hugged Denny and Tori.

"Cunningham, what are you doing here?"

"I've been chasing you for days. You tend to leave bullet holes and body counts wherever you go."

"There's so much to catch up on.'

"We can catch up later. It's good to see you again," Tori said, looking deep into Nathan's eyes.

Nathan's emotions were less like a man's and more like a roller coaster as he went from fear, to hate, to anger, and then into Tori's eye's, where he felt only a sense of passion. He had had a crush on Tori for a long time, but she was married to Richard and had two daughters with him. He knew his own boundaries and refused to cross them. He wanted to ask her a ton of questions, but like she said, they could catch up later.

"I found your rifle, Denny," Nathan said. "It must be in this back room."

Nathan walked into the back room and recovered everything that had been taken from him, minus the MRE that old man Sutton ate. Walking out, Nathan realized how bad the situation was that he had barely survived.

He handed Denny his rifle, stepped over Cade, and knelt down by Sutton.

"I think he was a good guy, just lied to," Nathan said, trying to keep Denny's eyes off of Ash's head.

"We heard a gunshot and then a loud crash," Denny said.

"We need to wrap that a little better," Tori said, grabbing the hand that Nathan had a pinky joint cut from.

Denny dropped his pack and removed a spool of gauze wrap. He took off the old wrap that Cade had applied, and replaced it with a clean wrap.

"That'll do for now," Denny added as he put away what was left of his gauze and grabbed his rifle and Cade's rifle from the floor.

Denny turned around to leave and Nathan said, "Wait!"

coming between him and Ash's head. "Let me get the door for you."

Tori saw what Nathan was doing and recognized Ash.

Before the Flip, the tightest members of the group were Nathan Roeh, Denny Ackers, Ash Dennings, Zig Sumner, Todd Smith, Stephen Gill, and Tori Cunningham. They were always the faithful participants in group meetings and training sessions. That's why when Tori and Stephen didn't show up at the Gorham rally point, it concerned Nathan so much. Life had been hectic since then and Nathan hadn't taken much time to dwell on their whereabouts. Sometimes he would wonder where they were and if they were still alive. Seeing Tori was both refreshing and heart sinking. He had growing feelings for Jess, but now there was Tori. When he saw where Tori and Denny were standing, he knew there was no way to shield them both from seeing Ash's head against the wall, but he thought he would give it a try and went for Denny.

Nathan went to pull the door open, stepping aside to reveal Ash's head.

"Denny, he died searching for me. Cade got to him before he found me."

"The ground's frozen," Tori said. "There's no way to bury him."

"He deserves a warrior's burial," Denny replied. "He was one of the best nonveteran group members we had. He made bad decisions, but he made good ones, too."

Denny looked up at Tori and said, "Remember Todd?"

"Yeah?"

"Todd died because of one of those bad decisions. Ash,

here, went out on a fool's errand, and Todd was shot when we went looking for him. I punched Ash in the face that day for what he had done."

"Denny, we've all made mistakes, good and bad. Let's check the perimeter and find his body. We'll burn him before we leave."

Nathan, Tori, and Denny left in search of Ash's body, but it was never recovered. That afternoon, they had a private memorial service for Morgan, Blake, and Ash.

By the time they had caught up with what was left of the Marines, much of the weapons, ammunition, and food supplies from the UN encampment were already loaded into the HMMWVs and the Deuces, which was military slang for two-ton trucks.

Jess saw Nathan and Denny walking towards them with a woman. When she saw Nathan was still alive and with Denny, she was overwhelmed with gladness. She took off running towards them.

Nathan saw her coming and was feeling an onset of awkwardness, which was sure to be the norm for some time to come. When she reached him, Nathan handed Denny his rifle and he caught her and did the usual spin-around-and-kiss routine, which had become their own custom.

"I feared the worst but hoped for the best," Jess told Nathan.

"We lost Ash and Morgan. We almost lost Denny, but Tori saved his hide. Tori, this is Jess. We met her back in Chester. Jess, this is Tori. She was a member of our Home Guard group. When she never showed up, I figured her for dead," Nathan said as he looked into Tori's eyes.

Jess read Nathan's emotional comment as he peered into Tori's eyes.

"After the Flip, Richard refused to come with me, so I stayed with him. He was killed with Charity in a house fire set by looters. Amelia was kidnapped and traded for liquor and later killed by a cannibal in the Belleville area."

Nobody knew how to respond to Tori's story of perseverance. What she had gone through was unimaginable horror to the group members. All Nathan could do was let go of Jess's hand and hug Tori.

Denny was also feeling the awkwardness of the situation, and he parted to assist the Marines and militiamen. The group spent the rest of the day warming up in the heated UN headquarters building and taking advantage of the generator. The train's engine was destroyed by a TOW missile, rendering it useless, and the prisoners that had been loaded in it were set free. Many of them were sharply divided in opinion. Some were disgruntled because, despite the shackles, they believed they were going someplace safe to finish out their lives, but the others were happy to be freed because they had been taken at gunpoint and weren't buying the UN's story of relocation and government housing. Most of the people were starving, but were sent away because there simply wasn't enough food to save them all.

The generators were portable, but ran on fuel, another resource that was hard to come by. Fortunately for the group, there were loads of fuel, food, and water on some of the rear cars of the train. They loaded what they could and rationed out what was left to the people they had freed.

CHAPTER 11

Gary, Indiana

PASTOR RORY PRICE was less than ten miles from East Chicago and the Illinois border. By chance, he stumbled into a group of travelers that gave him a ride to his current location. Albeit, he was given several warnings not to travel in this area alone, he took the warnings into consideration and departed on foot towards what he hoped to be Buchanan's primary destination. He wasn't sure of what he was looking for, but Buchanan's task had changed from Goose Island to South Dakota, and Rory wasn't up to the task of traveling so far from home. Looking back, Rory was starting to miss the company and wondered if he had made the right choice. Regardless, he now found himself at the cusp of a life-altering time in history.

Looking around at his environment, Rory knew he had a long road ahead of him. He was now standing in front of what appeared to be an old college or academy of sorts. The windows were broken and the doors were open. He thought for a second about going inside to get out of the cold just long enough to collect his thoughts.

Gary, Indiana, was once a town of 80,000 people, but now it looked like a ghost town. Choosing not to enter the building, he walked north along its east wall until he came to Roosevelt Park and saw a Lutheran church building across the street. Rory wasn't a Lutheran, but he knew the building was just a place of worship. As he walked closer to it, he saw signs in the yard with Persian writing on them. He recognized the language from his Bible college days. He couldn't read a word of it, but knew it was a warning.

Decades before the Flip, Muslims were marking Christian churches with symbols that communicated to other Muslims the need to destroy the building or to kill its members. This symbol was one of those. He noticed that the windows were busted and pews from the inside were sitting in the yard. He raised his rifle to the high ready position and proceeded to move towards the building. It was a large two-story building and had two steeples.

If nothing else, I can get a better view from one of those, he thought.

Rory entered the chapel and made his way to the spiral staircase that took him to the top of the steeple. From the top, he looked north and saw Lake Michigan and a great deal of smoke plumes. The smoke plumes were alarming simply because there were so many of them. The smoke plumes were stemming from smokestacks, and where smokestacks are, there are factories. Rory reasoned that the factories were being operated by manpower. The biggest question stirring in his mind was *Are these factories being operated by federal employees, slave labor, or UN personnel?* Secondly, he wondered, *What are the factories manufacturing?*

The wind shifted and Rory smelled burning hair. The odor was pungent enough to leave the steeple and descend the staircase. He exited the back door and saw a pile of human remains that were burnt to a crisp. They had been there for some time and the pile wasn't releasing the pungent odor that he had smelled from the top of the steeple. This was a different smell, more like old decomposing flesh. Closer examination revealed that these people were probably Christians, likely captured, killed, and burned by jihadist Muslims.

Rory said a quick prayer for himself and started heading north until he had traveled about two miles and came to a thirteen-story building. It had the best vantage point of anything in the area, so he had determined to climb the emergency exit stairs until he reached the roof. From this vantage point, he was able to see the factories and the smokestacks with great detail. In addition, there were trains rolling in and out of the area. He had never seen so many trains in one place. From his position, he could not see people, but he saw larger moving and stationary objects. He saw a great number of shipping containers being brought in on barges to the same location where the trains were bringing in their shipments.

Putting two and two together, Rory was beginning to understand the enormity of what he was seeing. The trains and barges were acting almost in unison as they came into the port and dropped off what he believed to be people. The trains had been coming in from the south to converge at this location, while the barges appeared to be coming down the banks of Lake Michigan to drop off their shipments of shipping containers. Rory was not a geography major, but was fairly certain the Mississippi didn't tie into Lake Michigan. He reasoned that the only two plausible options were that internationals from the Great Lakes area were also shipping people south to this location or that the containers were empty and being shipped to the US from Canada.

Slave labor? he thought.

The questions were more sophisticated now than before. He was looking for a FEMA camp and found a large manufacturing plant with manpower, electricity, and transport.

What's going on here?

"Take it easy, mister, and you won't get hurt," a male voice said from behind him.

The voice startled Rory, causing him to spin around and grab for his rifle, which was still slung on his shoulder.

"I said *easy* mister," he warned again.

Rory saw a black male, about six-foot-two-inches tall, grizzled looking and in his forties.

"I'm taking it easy. You just startled me is all," Rory said with his hands rising slowly. "I don't have anything worthwhile."

"Why are you just assuming I'm going to take your stuff?" the man asked.

"That's kind of been the nature of the times."

"Why are you up here?"

"I was traveling from southern Illinois to Goose Island, and I thought I could get a vantage point from up here."

"Why you want Goose Island?"

"I was traveling with a few companions and the plan was

to free the people from the UN internment camps, but the plan went south, and now I'm alone."

"Ain't nobody getting into Goose Island. It's a fortress."

"We will."

"Who's *we?*"

"I'm sure they'll be heading back, at some point. When they do, Goose Island will fall."

The man studied Rory for a moment then lowered his rifle. "Are you hungry?"

"Actually, yeah, I'm pretty hungry. I've been saving what little I have."

"My name is Markus. I have some friends downstairs. They said they spotted you from the ground level. I tracked you up here."

Markus walked over by Rory.

Rory extended his hand and said, "My name is Rory."

"Glad to meet you, Rory. I see you found the old steel-works," Markus said, pointing to the smoke plumes.

"What's going on over there?"

"You don't want to know."

"Please, enlighten me."

"It's a crematorium."

Rory was clearly shocked by the answer. "A crematorium?"

"Yeah. We don't have all the answers, but we believe some of the shipments are dead bodies and other shipments are, well, live cremations."

"Live cremations, as in *burned alive?*"

"Exactly. After the Flip, we started seeing these trains from the south and barges from the Kankakee and Illinois

Rivers converging to this location. We tracked them from the time they were captured until they reached the crematorium. They marched live Americans from those shipping containers and trains into those buildings that are nothing more than giant superheated ovens."

"This doesn't make any sense. What about the FEMA camps?"

"The camps are where they keep *the elect*."

"The elect?"

"Yeah, the chosen ones. There's a few they keep alive because they stand a better chance at being more productive or useful for what the UN calls *Relocation Protocol*."

"I've heard of the protocol. So, the whole spill they are telling the people is that they are being relocated, but they are actually separating the better educated and productive members of society from the sick and needy, only to take them there?"

"That's right. We think it's deeper than that, but that's what we know so far."

"This is worse than I could have imagined."

"Hey, look, you said you were hungry. This topic will make you lose your appetite. C'mon. Follow me."

Markus started to walk away and looked back over his shoulder to see Rory talking to himself.

"Are you talking to yourself?"

"Oh, ha-ha, no, I'm saying a prayer."

"Are you a religious man?"

"I was a pastor before the Flip. Now I'm doing what I can."

"We could use a chaplain, if you're approved by the board."

"The board?"

"We have a community here. We keep a low profile and move from place to place to avoid being captured."

"I see. I'd like to meet your community, but like I said before, I'm on a mission."

"Well, when you finish your prayer, come down to the tenth floor. I'll tell them you're coming. We'll be expecting you."

"Thank you, Markus."

Rory stayed on the roof, taking in all that he had learned from Markus. He felt like throwing up, but there was something in the way the world had changed that had changed him. He was starting to feel more calloused than he had ever felt, and that feeling of callousness wasn't a soothing feeling for him. He felt that it made him feel distant from his humanity. The more he thought on it, the more he realized that it wasn't making him less human, but it was making him more primal. It was the feeling of primality that made him uncomfortable. He was reconciling the primality with his Christianity by reciting Bible scriptures in his mind. He was very well versed in scripture and positive that his view of self-defense was completely scriptural.

Jesus had his disciples carrying swords, he thought, and, *The correct rendering of THOU SHALT NOT KILL is THOU SHALT NOT MURDER.*

A host of other relevant scriptures were combed through in his mind until he was able to justify the future, and necessary, killing of the genocidal madmen that were plaguing his country. He stood up straight and went down through the hatch of the roof and to the tenth floor.

The entire tenth floor had all the windows boarded up with wood or furniture. It was like walking through skid row with multiple residents at every door, filling the rooms and covering the floors with sleeping spaces.

From what he could tell, these people were packing light, in case they had to leave again.

Slowly walking down the hallway, the smell of human waste was sometimes overwhelming. He found himself covering his nose, but remembered he was a guest and did not wish to offend them. When he thought to do so, he would uncover his nose and try breathing through his mouth. This worked, for the most part, but sometimes he felt he could taste the odors.

Markus saw him walking down the hallway and waved to him, catching Rory's attention. Rory turned towards him and followed him to the end of the hall.

Markus opened a door and stepped aside so Rory could walk in first.

Rory was nervous about walking into a strange room first, so he said, "No, you go first, I insist."

"No problem, just trying to be cordial."

Markus walked in first and Rory followed.

Rory walked into the room and saw a few nicely dressed individuals. Sitting at an elongated table were twelve men and women. They weren't dressed like the people in the hall-ways, and the room didn't have a bad odor.

"Rory, I would like you to meet our board."

Rory took a quick glance around the table and saw that

each one of them had a name plate in front of them. Reasoning to himself, he knew that these name plates weren't manufactured for them after the Flip, so either these people were important before the Flip or the names weren't real. He reserved his thoughts to himself and chose not to address the matter.

"Hello, I'm Rory. I'm so glad to meet you."

Markus looked at the board and said, "This here is Rory; he's a pastor."

There was one person at the table that did the speaking after the introduction. His name plate was engraved as *Thomas Burgess.*

"Pastor Rory, do you have a last name?"

"Yes, sir. It's Price, Rory Price."

"Pastor Price, we would like to know more about your work as a pastor."

"Okay, let's see, I was called to preach more than two decades ago and went to Bible College in Indiana. After obtaining my bachelor's in Theology, I did some home missions work and eventually settled down and started pastoring in Murphysboro, Illinois."

"Really? We see you have a rifle. What's your view on killing?"

"Well, I was just thinking on that topic a few minutes ago, actually. I believe killing and murdering to be two separate acts. One is done in self-defense or in defense of something greater than yourself, where virtue is at the fore-front as a guidepost for matters of right and wrong. I believe a person's conscience is also a key point. If killing for the purpose of self-preservation offends your conscience, then you have a right to die with a clear conscience."

"That's an interesting point of view. So, to summarize, you believe *killing*, when done for self-preservation, is all right and not necessarily considered *murder*?"

"That's correct, sir. Even Jesus let his disciples carry swords and, at one point, told them to go into town to buy some."

"What about the scripture where that one disciple cut off the ear of a Roman soldier?"

"Jesus knew Peter had a sword. The sword wasn't for hunting, it was for self-defense. Times were tough. When he cut off the ear of the Roman centurion, Jesus told him to put away the sword because he was interfering with the plan of the cross. He had already told Peter the design for New Testament salvation. He told him he was going to die and rise again on the third day. But Peter was zealous and sometimes his brawn overrode his brains."

"I see. So if I asked you to kill for the sake of the greater good, you would do it?"

"I'm not inclined to do anything you say, sir. I'm not sure what this meeting is about, but I will kill where killing is necessary to insure the survival of myself, my family, and my country, so help me God!"

Thomas turned to the lady on his right and whispered in her ear. She then turned back to face Thomas and nodded her head yes at him.

Thomas looked at Markus and said, "Mr. Hopkins, would you see Pastor Price out of the room while we discuss things for just a moment?"

"Sure."

Markus opened the door and he and Rory stepped out.

"What's this about, Markus?"

"We have been looking for a pastor for some time. With the jihadists running about rural Chicago, we've been unable to find one. They've all been captured, killed, and burned. Some have had it even worse than that."

"I'm on a mission already, Markus. I'm not sure I'm up to the task."

"Let's wait on the board and see what they have to say. You can make your decision then."

Within minutes the door opened back up and Thomas Burgess invited them back into the room.

Thomas sat down and then looked back at Rory and said, "Pastor Price, we would be honored if you would stay here and be a part of our community. We could really use a spiritual advisor on our board."

Rory was thinking fast for a proper answer to the offer at hand. He didn't know these people and they could be the very best of humanity or, in a worst-case scenario, the worst of humanity. He had to think quickly in order to buy himself some time.

Rory looked at Thomas and said, "Sir, it's an honor to be asked to do such a thing, but it's customary that I pray about every decision I make."

"I respect that reply. Take all the time you need and know that we are here to assist in the betterment of our society."

"Thank you for seeing me. Have a good day, ladies and gentlemen."

Markus escorted him out of the room and down to the main lobby area.

"Where are you taking me now?"

"I would like to show you around our little community."

Rory followed Markus out of the building and to an area of town that was a couple blocks down the road. Looking up into the buildings, Rory could see armed guards standing in the rooms as they were looking out.

"What's going on here?"

"This is how we survive, Rory. I'm taking you to my home. You can meet my family."

Rory was receiving mixed vibes from the whole experience. Something seemed a little off-kilter, but he couldn't quite put his finger on it.

Markus led him into a three-story building, past a few armed guards, and into a room.

Standing in the middle of a dining room area was a woman.

"Honey, I'd like you to meet my new friend Rory."

The compliment of being called a friend was heartwarming to him, but the awkwardness of walking into a strange room where a wife was caught off guard took precedence over the comment.

"Hello, ma'am, it's a pleasure to meet you."

A young girl came out of the kitchen and snuggled up to the woman.

"This is my wife, Kara, and my daughter, Elise."

"Hello," Kara said as she pulled Elise in close.

"Don't worry about Rory. He's a pastor. He's going to pray about being our new minister."

"New minister?" Rory asked. The comment caught his attention.

Kara answered, "Our last minister caught a guilty conscience."

"That's enough, Kara," Markus said, interrupting her to silence her information sharing.

Rory was catching bits and pieces of a puzzle that he was working desperately to solve, and the whole time he was feeling uncomfortable in his own skin. He was driven by both a desire to survive and a desire to know the truth.

Choosing not to press the matter of the guilty-conscience comment, he took a moment to hear a humming sound that sounded like electricity.

"Do I hear electrical power?" he asked.

"Yes, yes, we have generators and food in the fridge. We don't have running water yet, but we're working on that one still."

"Food in the fridge?"

"Oh yes, I was going to feed you. Sorry that I was side-tracked by our visit to the board. Honey," he said, looking to Kara, "could you put some meat on for our new guest?"

"You've got meat?"

"All will be revealed in time. Relax yourself. It's probably been a long while since you've eaten this good."

Just Outside of Black Hills Ordnance Depot, Edgemont, South Dakota

It had been a two-day trip for General John James, Admiral Belt McKanty, Lieutenant Colonel Charles

Buchanan, Gunnery Sergeant Franks, Captain Kurt Riley, Sergeant First Class Benjamin Reynolds, and many others. They had mapped the terrain and roads out before they left Valparaiso, Indiana, and counted on a fifteen- to seventeen-hour trip if they went nonstop and traded out drivers. Along the way, they had only stopped to refuel and to empty their bladders.

The group was now closing in on their destination and they were eager to see if the secret Marine Corps regiment was up to par.

General James looked over at Lieutenant Colonel Buchanan and said, "Charles, tell the men we're pulling over one last time. We're going to make sure our gear's together so we can at least look professional when we pull into the depot."

"Roger that, John."

James and Buchanan were in the back seat of the third HMMWV. The driver was a lance corporal named Leroy Bennett, and his front-seat passenger was Gunnery Sergeant Franks.

There had been a lot of hoopla over using first names now that the apocalypse had come. The commandant insisted on being more relaxed with some things, but maintaining strict discipline in other areas. He didn't see any harm with a change in name protocol; and while Buchanan was initially uneasy with it, he eventually opened up to using first names. Gunny, on the other hand, had shared his first and middle name far more than any other. When asked what his name was, he would reply, "My first name is Gunnery, my middle name is

Sergeant, and my last name is Franks. My close friends call me Gunny, for short." With that being said, Gunny only had a couple close friends, and they were the people calling on him. To all others, his name was Gunnery Sergeant Franks.

Buchanan patted Franks on the shoulder and said, "Did you copy what John said?"

"Yes, sir."

Franks grabbed the mic that was sitting near his feet and called out to the rest of the convoy.

"Attention Romeo Lima," he said, referring to Operation Returning Liberty, "This is Echo Seven Foxtrot. We are nearing Alpha Oscar," referring to the area of operation, "so break out your moon floss and toothpaste. We're going to empty ourselves and look sharp going in. Over."

Buchanan looked at Franks and said, "Did you have to say moon floss on the radio?"

"Probably not, sir. But I figured with all the lax chatter, I might catch a break to be myself again."

"You'll get your chance real soon. All this travel isn't doing well for honing poor combat skills."

The convoy came to a stop and the Marines, militiamen, and civilians that were traveling alongside the general stepped out and found themselves private spots where they could use their moon floss. Moon floss was the term the Marines used for toilet paper. It had become a popular term years prior to the Flip.

Within a few minutes, Gunny was yelling at everybody to fall in, a military term for *get into formation*.

Once again, the civilian militiamen were standing in their

formation and trying their best to mimic the military men and veterans.

When everybody was in their place, Buchanan took his position in front of all the units and waited on James to address the men. They were considering their environment an active war zone, so they did not salute one another, although any person watching from afar could see who was in charge by who was giving the orders.

James walked up to Buchanan and said, "Let's look at everybody casually and not make much of a scene. Some of these men are under oath, but all of them are volunteers and at liberty to leave at any time."

"Yes, sir."

Both men began looking over the units. Buchanan asked his officers and senior enlisted to help them. Within a few minutes they were done and loading back up into the convoy.

Colonel Edward Hensworth, and Lieutenant Colonels Cody Barker, Zachary Barnes, Jack Wright, Bobby Cox, and David Howard were notified that a very large convoy of US military vehicles and civilian POVs (privately owned vehicles) was entering into their area of operation. Hensworth gave the command and the lieutenant colonels issued orders to set up a security perimeter.

The Army depot was massive in size. Given the size alone, there was no way to secure the entire perimeter with a regiment. The colonel had set up a specific perimeter that was manageable for the size of his regiment. When the word came for them to secure it, they sprang into action and took control of the zone.

There was nothing coming into or leaving the area they had secured without authorization. Seeing the regiment was secretly placed there, only one person knew of its whereabouts, and that was Commandant John James.

Looking forward into the horizon, the men could see several CH-53E Super Stallion helicopters lifting into the air and taking control of the perimeter. Two of the choppers took an attack position, one with its port side to the convoy and the other with its starboard side to the convoy. It probably wasn't enough firepower to stop them, given the fact they were heavily armed with antitank weaponry and heavy guns, but it was enough to make the statement that this area was under strict control.

The area was not fenced in and was open on all sides. The front of their convoy was approached by several Marines in battle fatigues. They walked towards the lead vehicle as they came to a stop. The Marines checked the first vehicle and gave them clearance. The second vehicle in the convoy was then approached by the Marines. It was given the same clearance and entered the depot. The Marines then approached the HMMWV and the Marine recognized the commandant.

"Sir, we've been anxiously awaiting your arrival."

"Thank you, Marine, I'm glad to be here."

"Sir, are the rest of these vehicles with you?"

"Yes, they are. They've come a long way and they're good men and patriots."

"Yes, sir. You're clear," the Marine said with gladness as

he waved the rest of the vehicles into the depot's security perimeter.

Arsenal Island, formerly known as Rock Island Arsenal

Roughly four hundred high-ranked enlisted UN soldiers worked at Arsenal Island. For years, the formal name had been bounced back and forth from Rock Island Arsenal to Arsenal Island. When Muhaimin had come into possession of the State of Illinois, he went with Arsenal Island, because he figured it brought anonymity to the munitions manufacturer.

They had recently received a call from Muhaimin demanding a census of the island and a list of military-manufactured equipment and munitions. The list gave him logistics and ground superiority that he never knew he had. Along with this new set of capabilities came a reassurance of certain victory against a growing patriot resistance.

Muhaimin had almost no sea support. The French and the Iranians had a small navy, and the Russians were using their navy to secure new lands in Eastern Europe. Russia had been a growing threat since the turn of the millennia. Their donation of troops to the UN was a sideshow distraction to relieve the pressure that the UN was putting on them regarding the occupation of Ukraine and other hostile territorial takeovers. With almost no support coming in from sea, Muhaimin was glad to receive the list of logistical support that was being manufactured in America.

Among the manufactured items being produced at

Arsenal Island were MREs (meals ready-to-eat), Colt-style service rifles and 5.56 mm NATO ammunition, M225B Black Voids (2028 model tanks with gun-howitzers and heavy machine gun turrets), grenade launchers, shrapnel vests, and helmets.

With his troop size shrinking, Muhaimin had been spread thin. On one front, he had the resistance fighters, who were scattered and lacking leadership to form an effective resistance. Because he had initially underestimated the patriots, he was now brought to his current problem of being spread thin. He had found himself trying to reorganize his manpower so he could wipe out large gatherings of military resistance, like the group he had identified using the Main Core program.

On another front, he found he had apparently made a new enemy with North Korea. He could not afford going to war with another country, especially now that China would probably back the North Koreans. It was his ego that had brought the North Korean attack to American shores, wiping out every piece of electronic superiority that he had over the Americans living on the West Coast. If China was to find out that it was Muhaimin that had orchestrated the death of Councilor Pao, it would bring a new set of problems and circumstances for the already troubled executive commander.

With these thoughts in mind, Muhaimin entered the White House Situation Room, where he had requested a meeting with the UN Council regarding the current status of America and the progress he was making. His goals were not the same as the UN's, but he was smart enough to know that he had to sell to them what it was that they were wanting to hear. The bottom line to Muhaimin was that he needed more troops.

"Gentlemen, so good to see you again," he said as he looked up at the hologram. "It saddens me to hear of the loss of Ambassador Pao."

Ambassador Makarovich was always the second most outspoken member of the council, after Pao. He was the first to respond to Muhaimin.

"General Muhaimin—" he started to say before he was interrupted.

"It's Executive Commander Muhaimin," he said, correcting the ambassador.

"Right, Executive Commander Muhaimin, since you are so very good at creating positions of power, perhaps you can explain to us why it is you need more UN troops?"

Muhaimin played coy about the attack on America. He knew exactly what country attacked him, but wasn't willing to reveal his abuse of power with the Iranian Homeland Security intelligence.

"Gentlemen, America's West Coast was attacked with some type of electromagnetic weapon, rendering me without contact to all troops in operation west of South Dakota. This means that the Main Core program and the Utah Data Center are useless."

Idin Afsadi, the Iranian ambassador to the UN, asked Muhaimin, "Are you being successful in other areas of the operation? Are you securing more ground and isolating these pockets of resistance so that we can move forward with Agenda 21?"

"The short answer is yes. We have a great number of

isolated pockets of resistance, but putting that aside, we have relocated several million, but keep in mind that the US population was over three hundred million, and ten percent of those are veterans. In addition, roughly one million active-duty military personnel are actively aiding in the resistance. It's true that they are scattered and leaderless, but effective nonetheless."

"Iran's military analyst has advised me that the US Navy had a sizeable fleet in the Pacific. It is now my understanding that what we thought to be a problem with the EMP attack may have actually worked in our favor. Executive Commander Muhaimin, you have never operated with advanced technological systems, and you have been successful. Why do you feel so attached to these systems, and can you return to your roots as a guerilla fighter and use your primitive skills to defeat the American resistance?"

The statement just made by Afsadi was true. Muhaimin found himself in retrospection wondering why he had allowed himself to become as the Americans were. He had always hated the US for their reliance on technology and fossil fuels. He believed the US to be the great Satan and had somehow allowed that spirit to affect himself. Now he was finding that the very shoes of the people he hated were on his own feet.

"You're correct, Ambassador Afsadi. I do not need to rely upon technology, but I do need troop strength. I am asking the council to send more troops to aid in this operation. Further use of advanced weapon systems are not needed or being requested."

Ambassador Makarovich interrupted by saying, "Request

denied. You have the full might of the United Nations locked down in this operation. There are urgent matters elsewhere that need our supervision and you are taking up our time. Good day, General Muhaimin."

Makarovich disconnected the signal to the White House Situation Room. As Muhaimin stood there looking at the blank spot in space where the hologram had once lit up the room, he was irate at the disrespect he was shown by Makarovich, especially the way he spoke the last word and slapped him in the face with terminating the signal.

Everybody in the room dared not to look at him and they continued to work as if they heard and saw nothing. The silence was interrupted by the sound of a federal employee typing on a keyboard. Muhaimin snapped out of his blank stare into space and pulled out his pistol. Walking out of the room, the employees heard two gunshots, but nobody dared to move to see what had happened outside of the door.

When Muhaimin had walked away, several UN guards came running from around the corner to the sound of the gunshots, and saw two dead Russian UN soldiers lying outside of the White House Situation Room.

CHAPTER 12

Mount Vernon, Illinois, 240 miles south of Chicago

THERE WAS a big to-do over going through Mount Vernon. Like Benton, Mount Vernon was a larger southern Illinois town and the seat of its county. It had already been discovered that the UN liked to make use of the capitol buildings and/or the county courthouses. After barely surviving their previous encounter with the TITAN I direct energy weapon system, most of the men were livid about the possibility of cutting through another UN-controlled zone. The benefit of their last encounter was that they were able to free several thousand Americans from certain death, most of whom they could not care for and bring along. There weren't enough supplies or vehicles, even with the UN vehicles they had just seized, to accommodate them.

By the time they reached the outer city limits, they could tell that something was amiss. The UN activity levels were down and no UN vehicles could be spotted anywhere. Aside from a couple destroyed personnel carriers, it looked as if they had packed up and left.

The group proceeded with caution as they slowly rolled into the town.

Jess could tell that Nathan was preoccupied with something on his mind. Ever since Tori was found, he had seemed a little off. Tori and Denny were riding together in a separate HMMWV while Jess and Nathan were in another. She knew he had gone through a lot with his encounter with Cade, having lost a fingertip while being tortured, but also saw a different Nathan than she was used to. She couldn't tell if his mental preoccupation was back in that torture room or if his mind was on Tori. Either way, she kept trying to probe him for information, but he just kept giving her the runaround. She wasn't feeling the same connection with him that she had before. It was almost as if his life spark was fizzling out.

"Hey, I'm talking to you," she said, nudging him. She had just made two attempts at asking him if he thought the UN had evacuated.

Nathan snapped out of his daydream. He was back in Gorham, alone with Tori, walking on the Mississippi River when Jess captured his attention.

"Huh, what?"

"Do you think they evacuated? It's possible they have left."

"Can we stop here and check it out on foot?" Nathan asked Sergeant Banks.

"Makes good sense to me," he replied.

The convoy came to a stop. The antitank infantry and heavy gunners stayed in their turrets while many of the infantry Marines and militiamen walked in on foot.

"The whole town is ghosted out," Sergeant Banks said.

Looking ahead, Jess saw a fence similar to the one in Benton.

"Check it out," she said, pointing down the street.

"Denny, you have binos, don't you?"

"No, they got busted up in Benton."

"We don't need binos," Banks said. "We have TOWs," he continued by motioning on to one of the Marine lance corporals to go get a TOW mounted up.

Within a couple minutes, several Marine TOW gunners were setting up a TOW in the middle of the street so they could look through the high-magnification lenses and see detailed information.

"We're up," one of them said.

"Can I look?" Nathan asked.

"Yeah, go ahead." Sergeant Banks gave permission.

Nathan stepped behind the TOW and looked through the day-sight tracker.

"Wow, it's been a long time since I've looked through one of these."

"What do you see?" Tori asked, touching Nathan on the back.

Jess saw the touch and saw his change in demeanor when she was around.

"Well, I see the fence, but there's no sign of life anywhere."

Each of them took their turn looking through the TOW system.

"That's enough, guys," Sergeant Banks interrupted. "We have to use our system sparingly because we only have a couple of these left."

Jess walked up to Nathan and planted a kiss on his cheek. "It's okay, babe. I'll get you one next Christmas."

"We need to keep moving," Nathan said, averting a potential conflict. He was feeling emotional conflict between his feelings for Jess and Tori, but the last thing he wanted was for them to have conflict between one another.

Denny had been feeling an attraction towards Tori since she first arrived. They had been spending most of their time together, and he was under the assumption that it was a mutual attraction. Nathan had Jess, and now Tori had finally rejoined the group, this time without a husband. He only thought it plausible that he and Tori might have some kind of relationship. He had seen the way she touched Nathan and the response it got from Jess. Not willing to interfere with what Nathan might do, he chose to pull back, as he usually did, and see how it played out. He would never think of interfering with Nathan's feelings for Tori, if he still had them.

The group had packed up the TOW equipment and started on foot towards the fenced structure. The closer they got, the more they could see that it was indeed abandoned, but even more horrifying was the sight of several hundred dead Americans.

"It's obvious what happened here," Banks whispered. "I'm not sure where they went, but I'm betting their train never arrived."

Nathan picked up on what Banks was saying. The train they had destroyed in Benton was a prisoner transport, complete with hand and leg shackles. Its destination was most likely Chicago, FEMA's Region V compound, and it was supposed to pick up Americans at this Human Handling Center and transport them northward, to the destination point. When the train never came, they dispatched the people on sight.

There were entire families lying dead, covered lightly in snow. The temperature was below freezing, keeping the smell and the act of decomposition at bay. It seemed almost impossible, to the men who were familiar with Mount Vernon, that it was emptied out and now void of life.

The men stayed on high alert and maintained a tight 360-degree area of observation. When one of the combat engineers cut the bolt on the fence, they heard a shout from atop a building. Every person with a gun pointed it in the direction of the voice. It was a foreign language and was mixed with English.

Sergeant Banks gave the hand signal for everyone to spread out and get low. Everyone took cover and kept their weapons trained on the building, where they continued to hear a voice. A squad of Marines, Nathan, and Denny approached the building. They carefully looked down the walls of every corner and could not see a ladder up, so they breached the front door of the building and made their way to the hatch, where they found the ladder. They carefully climbed up the ladder and onto the roof, finding an Iranian UN soldier with his hands in the air and his rifle on the snowy rooftop.

The Marines kept him at gunpoint and gave him commands to get down. As the man was lowering himself, Denny moved forward and kicked the man's rifle away from his reach. Nathan picked it up and immediately noticed that it was a Colt-style M4 rifle, American manufactured.

"Do you speak English?" Banks asked.

"Me speaks English small," he replied.

"Where did you get this gun?" Nathan asked him.

"They give it me."

Nathan took the magazine out of the magazine well and inspected the bolt. The chamber was empty, as was the magazine. He ran his good pinky into the chamber of the barrel and discovered that it was caked with carbon, indicating he had been firing his gun and, most likely, all of his ammunition.

"Check this out." Nathan showed his pinky to Banks.

"Do you think he shot them up?" Banks asked.

"I think he helped. I doubt he scared off his buddies by emptying his rifle into the air."

"Did you kill those people?" Banks asked the Iranian, now noticeably scared.

When he didn't answer the question, Nathan raised his voice a little and asked the same question. "Did you shoot those people?"

Nathan was being animated with his question. He pointed the empty rifle at the man as he asked, and jerked the rifle back and forth to aid in demonstration of his question. The man did not answer, whether out of confusion, fear, or refusal.

"Let me say it this way," Nathan barked as he took one of

the magazines from his pouch and slapped it into the M4, charging the bolt to the rear and letting it go to make it a ready-to-fire weapon. Nathan pointed it at the man and said, "Did you kill those people?"

"Please no shoot," he replied. "Wife and family."

Nathan thought of his sister, Katie, while Denny's thoughts shifted to his sister, Heather. Both were killed months earlier in a raid on their southern Illinois homestead.

Banks used Nathan's pause to place his hand on the handguard of the M4 and push it down.

"Maybe we can use him," he told Nathan. "He's got to know something. He was probably left behind by accident or something. He may know where they've gone or what they're planning."

Nathan took the magazine from the rifle and ejected the round. Once he had collected the ejected round, he put it back in the magazine and into his pouch.

"If we take him downstairs, we'll have to protect him. There are men down there that want UN blood. I'll deal with Jess, she's a little bitter toward these guys and might act hastily to put a bullet in his head."

"That goes for Tori, too," Denny added. "She's beast mode."

Three of the Marines led the way down the hatch, followed by the Iranian, and the rest came down after him.

Tori saw the POW first.

"No way," she exclaimed and briskly walked toward the Iranian, pulling her shiny 1911 from its place and pointing it at the man's head, as if prepared to execute him.

"Whoa, whoa, whoa," Sergeant Banks shouted as he moved towards Tori.

The commotion caused Jess to look in that direction, who had a similar response.

She pulled out her Walther P22 pistol, charging after the man from the opposite angle as Tori. Jess was standing at about thirty degrees of angle to the man's front and Tori was standing at about one hundred fifty degrees of angle.

Banks found himself flailing his arms at both of them, knowing full well that he wouldn't be able to stop a bullet, let alone two bullets.

Both Jess and Tori would have shot the man if not for the others that were moving in from behind him. Nathan, Denny, and the rest of the Marines had completed their descent and caught up to Banks and the Iranian POW.

"Easy, girls," Nathan called out.

Denny ran up to Tori and gently brought her arm down. Nathan wasn't as gentle with Jess as Denny was with Tori. He pushed her gun down and spun her into him, embracing her. It wasn't until after he was holding Jess that he realized the moment had been deescalated and Tori was watching him as he held Jess.

Tori put the gun away and said, "I'm good."

Jess pulled away from Nathan and pointed at the POW. "Please explain what's going on here? Blue helmets are a disease, and we are the cure."

"Nobody's arguing that, Jess, but Sergeant Banks has a good idea."

Nathan gave a head nod to Banks as if to have him explain his idea.

"If we kill this turd, we waste a good bullet," he said, looking at Jess. "Maybe two," he said as he turned towards Tori. "But if we spare him, it's likely we can pull some good information out of him."

"Like, where's everyone gone?" Denny added.

"Can we waterboard him?" Tori interjected into the conversation.

"With a canteen? Not likely, but anything aside from killing him. We need the information."

Tori and Jess looked at each other and for once were feeling a sense of kindred spirit. The two of them gently smirked at each other.

"Fine," Jess said, putting away her Walther pistol. "But me and Tori get to interrogate him," she insisted.

Banks looked at Nathan and Denny.

Denny gave Banks a shoulder shrug, and Nathan said, "It'll be fine," reassuring Sergeant Banks that they wouldn't kill the Iranian at the first opportunity.

"All right, but I'm going to have a lance colonel make sure you don't get carried away." A *lance colonel* was Marine lingo for a lance corporal who always tries to take control of situations if he is not the senior enlisted Marine.

"Done," Tori answered.

"Lance Corporal Jones," Banks called out.

Jones came walking up from the rear of the group. "What's up?"

"Jess and Tori here are going to interrogate this prisoner. Your job is to make sure they don't kill him or wound him in such a way that could lead to said death."

"Got it," he said, happy to have an assignment.

Tori smirked at the Iranian and walked up to him while Banks zip-tied his hands behind him.

She grabbed him and walked away. Jess followed them and smiled at Nathan as she went.

"I hope we don't come to regret this," Nathan whispered to Denny.

Tori, Jess, and Jones took the POW to a train car that was sitting on the track. There were two or three of them sitting there alone, with no engine or caboose in sight. They stepped up into the car and pulled the door almost closed, leaving about one foot of opened door space.

Gary, Indiana

"What do you think?" Markus asked Rory, who had a blank look on his face. "About the meat?"

Markus had his wife grill up some meat from the fridge. They sat together and talked about memories of the old ways. Memories from before the Flip. Rory's mind went elsewhere when that conversation died down.

"Oh, sorry, I was thinking about that crematorium place."

"Ah, well, we're not too interested in going there, are we?"

"I don't know. I came with a large group of men and we were going to Goose Island, but then they were sidetracked. That's how I ended up here."

"So you've seen a lot of violence and understand that we live in a very different America than we used to."

"Of course. I just want Americans to have their freedoms back. That's what I fight for."

"But until that day comes, you're prepared to do what you have to do to survive, right?"

Sensing that Markus was taking this conversation somewhere, he addressed his question. "Where are you taking this?"

"Come with me. I probably shouldn't be showing you this yet, but I think you're going to fit in."

Markus stood up and walked towards the front door.

Rory followed him.

Both of them had left their rifles standing in the corner, behind the door. When they had picked up their guns, they headed back outside.

"Where are you taking me?"

"I'm going to show you how we survive, Rory. I've heard enough from you to know you've got a good heart, but will also do what you have to in order to survive another day. And that other day is the day you will see America restored, but you have to live that long first."

Markus came to a place in the center of town. He pointed up to the building where they had met the board on the tenth floor.

"You see those guards in the windows there?"

"Yeah, I missed them before."

"They saw you, that's how I found out about you. They were actually waiting for me when I was talking to you on the roof. We always try to recruit before we move people in."

"I'm a bit confused, Markus."

"What I told you before about moving from place to place was just a story we tell people that we're trying to get to know."

"Okay."

"Those guys in the windows keep the people on the tenth floor safe."

"Okay, no problems there."

"But they also maintain a watchful eye on the streets. If they see somebody, an emissary, like myself, is sent out to meet them and to assess for asset."

Markus could see that Rory was having a hard time following his story.

"Rory, if we think they can be an asset, we introduce them to the board. If the board agrees, they are let in. If not, then they stay on the tenth floor."

"Wait a minute, I thought the tenth floor was *the community*."

"No, the community is everybody but the people on the tenth floor, excluding the board. They are kept there for strategic purposes."

"Markus, please cut to the chase, because I'm getting lost in what you're trying to say."

"Follow me." Markus motioned to Rory with his hands.

Markus led him to the bottom floor of a butcher's shop.

"This is where we process our meat."

"About that, where are you getting your supply of meat?"

"From the tenth floor, Rory. Don't you understand?"

Rory started dry heaving and then vomited at the feet of Markus. When he was done, he wiped his mouth and said, "We're done, Markus."

"You can't leave, Rory."

"Watch me," he said in a challenging tone.

"You're our new shepherd, Pastor Rory. We need you here."

"I'm not staying here. You're sick, they're sick, you're all sick people."

"You're only saying that because you don't understand just yet. Give it a couple more days."

"No, you don't understand. I'm not a murderer and I'm not a cannibal."

"No, you're a survivor, Rory. Those people on the tenth floor will be wasted in that crematorium. They have a use here. We keep them safe up there, and we tell them that we're looking for placement homes. When they leave with us, they die quick, Rory. It's not murder when it's done for survival. That's what you said. Kill where killing is necessary to insure survival. Those are your words, Rory."

"You're sick and you've perverted my message, Markus."

"Run, Rory. They will come looking for you. If you resist, you won't make it to the tenth floor. You'll be on tonight's menu."

Rory took off running towards Lake Michigan and he didn't look back. His heart was pounding and his veins were full of adrenaline. He couldn't feel his face, his fingers, or his feet. He was beginning to lose the motor skills necessary to keep moving forward.

Rory was never trained for these kind of conditions. He wasn't prepared for traveling alone or for the survivor's mentality. The loss of blood flow to his limbs was from a naturally occurring physiological effect caused by the extremely stressful situation that he had found himself in. His blood was drawn in to protect his vital organs. When this happened, there was a lack of blood flow to his extremities. This caused a lack of feeling and control of his legs. Rory was starting to feel shaky and figured the sensations were caused by low blood sugar. When he was out of sight, he found a place to sit and dig through his bag in search of anything with sugar in it. His search for a sugary treat was in vain. No sooner than he sat down, he realized that he had left his bag at Markus's house.

Rory stayed hidden for a couple hours, as he was hoping to wait out their search for him. He'd already heard a couple different search parties roaming the streets. Traveling on the streets of this city was going to be easy, in Rory's mind. The streets were bogged down with automobiles that had been stopped due to FEMA checkpoints, and later by UN checkpoints. Rory's plan was to move down the street from car to car, hiding under them and inside them wherever he could, until he was far enough out of this area to stand up straight again.

He had initiated his plan of movement and wasn't but a few vehicles away when a dog began to bark at him. His fear was that this dog was going to give away his position. He thought in earnest for a way to silence the dog without shooting it. Rory stuck his finger down his own throat and began trying to induce vomiting. Puking was easy for him. He was still nauseous from the news that he had unknowingly eaten human flesh. With one attempt, Rory vomited the flesh and threw the chunks at the dog. This effort worked on the starving animal. It stopped barking instantly and it cautiously moved towards the flesh and began eating it.

Rory kept a low profile and continued moving along the

roadway. He did so until he felt he was well out of the zone of Markus's operation.

Rory next found himself nearing Interstate 90, where he feared heavily occupied zones of UN troops, checkpoints, and exchanges. He was dangerously close to the crematorium, where he could clearly see the plumes of factory smoke. He had lost some elevation since his previous glimpse over the interstate walls, so he could no longer see the train yard and factory buildings.

Taking a moment to sit and relax, he leaned against an old abandoned building and was close enough to the ground to see a thin coat of ash gently blowing along the surface of the sidewalks and roadways. He looked at his hands and saw that some of this ash was now on his palms. Rory jumped back to his feet, realizing that ashes from the crematorium were settling on the city. Dusting the rear of his pants off, he could see that the fine particles of ash were more than gently blowing along the surface of the city streets and sidewalks, but he was covered in a fine layer of the ash that he could not feel. Until now, he hadn't taken the time to examine the color of his skin or the cleanliness of his clothes. He frantically began dusting the human remains from his clothes and body. He found himself patting his jeans, only to see small plumes of the fine substance blowing back into the breeze.

The faint sound of several automobiles caught his ear. It was the familiar sound of US military vehicles. The roads were congested, so Rory knew they had to be making slow progress. He walked towards the sound of the vehicles, hoping to meet with the servicemen and to share his experiences with Lieutenant Charles Buchanan. The closer he moved to the sound of the vehicles, the more people he began to see moving out of the projects and towards the vehicles. Not knowing the intentions of the people, he didn't know if he should slow his pace or speed it up.

The vehicles were now in view and he could see that they were Army vehicles. Once he had confirmed the presence of the Army, he felt comfortable picking up his pace. Rory was within a hundred yards of the convoy when a mob of people came charging like mad bulls from the buildings on the south side of the convoy. The convoy opened fire on the people, causing Rory to stop and watch in horror. A rocket came flying out of one of the upper-story windows and impacted the lead vehicle. It was an enormous explosion that sent several of the nearby mob flying in the opposite direction, away from the vehicles. Some of them caught fire and ran around screaming until they fell and stopped moving. The convoy continued to fire into the mob until they finally stopped the assault on the convoy and fled back into the projects.

The second vehicle in the convoy was now the lead vehicle and pushed the fiery wreckage until the path was clear for himself and those behind him to continue on. They were now nearing Rory's position.

When the convoy was feet away from him, he laid his rifle onto the ground and raised his hands into the air.

"Take me with you. I'm a friendly," he shouted. "I have military friends. I have high-ranking Marine friends and mission objectives. Please, take me with you."

One by one, each vehicle in the convoy passed him by.

Many of the drivers and gunners looked at him, but showed no sign of interest or compassion.

He felt in his heart that God was speaking to him in that moment, telling him to say, *"I am about the Lord's work."*

With only two vehicles left in the convoy, Rory followed after the impression he felt in his heart.

"Please, I am about the work of the Lord."

The last convoy stopped next to him. An Army private first class was driving the vehicle and a Specialist was in the gunner's turret, but it was the passenger in the front seat that said, "Are you a preacher or something?"

The soldier was wearing a Kevlar helmet with a captain insignia. His face was bearded and his cheekbones were dirty, not unlike everybody else that had no running water.

"I am, and I was separated from a group of Marines that were on an important mission."

"Get in, preacher, we are on an important mission and we need God on our side. I'm Captain Lewis Richards."

San Diego, California

The Bloods and Crips gangs took Sergeant Griggs to San Diego, where the reports were that the trains were taking American slaves and heading somewhere east.

The constant sound of gunfire was apparent from where they were poised near San Diego Bay. Americans were fighting back against the UN invaders, who had very little support technologically. Everything electronic or electrical in San Diego was rendered useless. There were no sounds of trains, no sounds of vehicles, no sounds of ships coming and going in and out of the bay. The only sounds these days were the sounds of people's screams before and after a gunshot. San Diego was clearly a war zone, where the enemy wasn't a politician or a different color of skin, but wore a blue helmet and spoke in French, Russian, or Persian.

"I guess it be no good showing you the slave trains if they not be moving," the Bloods leader said.

Just then a group of UN soldiers were seen a few hundred meters up the road. Griggs gave the command to his unit to take cover.

The Bloods leader looked at the Crips leader and said, "You ready to roll?"

"Man, you know I be ready to roll."

The several dozen gang members jumped out of the group and took off running towards the UN soldiers.

Griggs looked at Edwards and said, "Well, I guess that's our cue."

Griggs's unit of soldiers advanced towards the UN soldiers, who had donned riot shields and rifles. Unlike the gangsters, his men and women were advancing forward using the buildings as cover.

The Bloods and Crips opened fire on the UN soldiers. Their bullets were flying wildly towards the foreign invaders, but otherwise showing little results.

"They're outside of the range of those pistols," Edwards said.

"Yeah, let's show them some support."

Griggs went prone, along with many others, and set their sights to the proper elevation. There was very little wind where they were prone, but on the road, where the buildings gave way to roadways, the wind was blowing faster.

Griggs launched the first shot and couldn't see the impact.

"I think you shot left."

Griggs guessed some windage calculations, setting his aim more to the right. He shot another round and dropped a UN soldier.

"Set your elevation to three hundred yards and go six clicks right for windage," he told his unit.

The soldiers started dropping the UN soldiers, enough so that they began to flee. The gangsters gave chase and followed them into a side road where they lost seven men to the UN invaders before they finally closed in on them enough to execute what was left.

Griggs stood up and looked around.

"All clear," Griggs shouted.

One of the soldiers spotted a UN MCC (mobile command center) sitting along the roadway. "Hey, guys, check that out."

"It's useless," another said.

"Yeah, but maybe there's some logbooks or something we can use," Edwards suggested.

"Let's look and see."

The group made their way to the MCC and did a breach-style clearing to make sure it wasn't occupied. Griggs stepped in and started rummaging through the drawers, looking for logs. Edwards was near him, doing the same.

"Hey, check it out," she said, showing him a clipboard

with several pieces of paper attached. "These guys are morons."

"What did you find?"

She handed him the clipboard and right behind the cover sheet was a list of virtually every UN-occupied zone with the twelve FEMA regions of the United States and the frequencies they were using to communicate. More surprising was the list of names they were filed under.

"Bioengineering and Research, Sheridan, Oregon?" Griggs read out loud. "Bioengineering and Research, Metropolitan, San Diego? Bioengineering Research and Development, High Desert State, Nevada? What is all this?"

"All those places used to be federal penitentiaries. Sounds like they're being used for more sinister purposes now."

Griggs continued to thumb through the alphabetical list of places and their frequencies, from A to Z. When he was done, he looked back at the second page of the clipboard and saw *Arsenal Island, Illinois, Region V*.

"None of this is good news, Eddie."

Eddie was Griggs's pet name for Edwards when they weren't in uniform. She caught the discrepancy and corrected him.

"Edwards."

"Sorry, my mind is elsewhere. You ever feel absolute zeal and at the same time absolute helplessness?"

"Not until now."

"What can we do? I'm out of ideas."

"Well, we can start by taking those freqs back to my ex's house. Maybe he shielded his radios from that EMP thing."

"Let's go."

Black Hills Ordnance Depot, Edgemont, South Dakota

General John James's HMMWV came to a stop and he stepped out and waited on his entourage of officers and high-ranking enlisted Marines to meet with him before heading up to meet Hensworth. After a couple of minutes, he was joined by Admiral Belt McKanty and the others. Together they walked up to the makeshift parade deck area and the commandant was greeted by Colonel Hensworth.

"General John James, it is such an honor to see you again."

"Likewise, Colonel. I see you have kept things tidy and organized, just the way I like it."

"Yes, sir. I hope the perimeter security wasn't much of a burden."

"I was glad to see it, Colonel."

James stepped aside and said, "I would like you to meet my friends Admiral Belt McKanty, Lieutenant Colonel Charles Buchanan, Gunnery Sergeant Franks, Captain Kurt Riley, and Sergeant First Class Benjamin Reynolds."

Hensworth shook all of their hands and said, "Gentlemen, without any further hesitation, I would like to invite you into the chow hall."

They all looked at each other with half smiles and grins.

"Colonel, we would love to sit down and eat."

The colonel led the entire group into a separate bunker

where tables were neatly aligned and dressed for banquet-style food.

"Gentleman," the colonel said, "we don't have free-range chickens or cattle here, but we have canned goods that I have saved for this very occasion."

Gunnery Sergeant Franks insisted that the officers eat first. He knew they had much talking to do and there were many details and much information to share. It was generally James's style to let the enlisted eat first, but in this case, there was much to discuss.

When the officers had gone through the serving line, they took their plates to a table that was apart from the others. Only James, McKanty, Hensworth, Buchanan, Riley, Barker, Barnes, Wright, Cox, and Howard were allowed to sit at the special table. The information that was about to be shared was confidential and not intended for the ears of just any military personnel.

John James took a drink and looked across the table.

"Gentlemen, Marines and Sergeant First Class Reynolds, I'm glad you all have made it this far. Admiral McKanty and I have spent the last few months traveling through adverse conditions, from the District to where we now sit at the Black Hills Army Depot, South Dakota.

"We've suffered losses along the way, meeting new friends and tasting what America had become. My newest friend, Charles Buchanan, has endured even harder times, traversing from Illinois to northern Indiana and now to South Dakota. Most of you have endured similarly these last few months.

"We have all tasted the brutal reality of this *new America* we now find ourselves in. Truth is, I saw this coming a long time before it became reality. Belt and I were the longest-serving Joint Chiefs, so it stands to reason we are very close friends.

"I brought my concerns to Belt, who shared the same feelings I did, and we constructed a plan to lay the groundwork for a reinstitution of constitutionality. President Adalyn Baker, just as her predecessors failed to do, held no one accountable for the government's wasteful spending. I exploited this vulnerability and reactivated the 21st Marine Corps Regiment. I funneled funds into the unit, under the guise of FEMA structuring, and was able to ship military gear, weapons, air support, and Marines into the undisclosed location.

"While this was happening, President Baker continued to support UN legislation geared towards globalizing the United States currency and laws. She would often call on the Joint Chiefs of Staff for security-based questions and strategic placement of FEMA headquarters and the conversion of federal penitentiaries into FEMA internment and relocation housing compounds.

"In these classified meetings, we often objected to the president's notion that we should be involved in the international community, in any degree. She often rebuked us, giving us clear instruction to oversee her plans for involvement in the new world order.

"The plan was to have the UN enter the US through the Gulf of Mexico, utilizing the Mississippi River to reach the Midwest, Canada to reach the northern states, the Pacific Ocean to reach the western states, and the Atlantic Ocean to reach the eastern states. With this plan, the UN could peacefully enter the US under cover of martial law, to set up control zones and eventually set up control points for the relocation of American citizens from the cities to the processing centers, otherwise called Human Handling Centers. Basically, every state prison would function as a receiving and shipping center. In larger rural communities, control zones would be managed where people would be relocated.

"To the president, hunger would be a powerful motivator to move people from the cities. Invoking the executive orders that her predecessors had set up before her made her task easy."

Hensworth raised his hand to ask a question.

"Yes, Colonel?"

"Sir, I'm having a hard time believing that there's enough space in all the state prisons and federal prisons combined to accommodate the US population, even adding in makeshift processing centers."

"You're correct, Colonel. There's not enough space. Enter *Relocation Protocol*. The best and brightest of Americans would be interned at special wings of these compounds. If they cooperate, their families would be allowed to stay with them. If they resisted, then they were to be sent to Chicago's crematorium, a converted steelworks plant sitting on Lake Michigan's southern shore, where they would disappear.

"There were other meetings regarding biological research and development. Much of it was over my head, but I clearly remember talks of inoculating Americans with sickness to control fertility. The research was also supposed to involve injections that isolate favorable genes in humans, allowing for a more genetically superior selection process, but the serum had the opposite effect, it was breaking down human immune systems instead. The last I heard, there was an outbreak of smallpox and other nasty diseases. Fifty percent of all FEMA-controlled compounds were fitted with Bioengineering and Research facilities. These buildings were supposed to be given to scientists capable of performing ongoing research. We left before further results were shared with the Joint Chiefs."

"That's quite a bit to take in," the colonel said.

"And completely believable," Lieutenant Colonel Barnes said. "Our own government has been spoon-feeding Americans this stuff for years, and they never saw the ramifications of what might come to pass."

"Mandated immunizations, government housing, cell phones, energy assistance, and debt forgiveness. It all fed into the larger narrative that the government was prepping American dependence upon larger government," Lieutenant Colonel Cox said.

"The bottom line, gentlemen, is the government became too big for its britches. It was allowed to expand and to have control over every aspect of daily living, because too many Americans became dependent upon free stuff, and when that free stuff was taken away, the government used it to control the masses. A bigger government became the solution, and what's bigger than federal government?" James asked.

"Global government," Buchanan answered.

"You're as sharp as a tack, Charles. The answer became global government. The only people who saw the greater narrative were the American constitutionalists, who were villainized as Bible-thumping, gun-toting, liberty-fighting patriots."

"So here we are. A regiment and a half of Marines, a few hundred militia, and some Army. Our army may be larger than that of most countries, but is it enough to start an offensive against a global community?" Hensworth said, as if asking rhetorically.

"Honestly, I didn't dream this up on the backs of our military support. I was reading my history books, researching the Revolutionary War, when it came to me."

The table saw that the general's facial expression changed. James was having a hard time trying to put into words what he was trying to say. He knew Hensworth's comment about the global community was true, and he also understood that peace was won through superior might, but the answer he found hard to speak out loud was the truth that America could only be strong when the everyday American said, *"Enough is enough"* and rose to the challenge.

James took a few moments to organize his thoughts into words that could sell.

"Buchanan braved over fifteen hundred miles with a few Marines and a militia. I escaped from the District with the help of patriots. I had to have a few eye-opening experiences before I could see this truth, but America was built on the backs of everyday Americans who were willing to say enough is enough. History will show you, gentlemen, that only about three percent are willing to take this stand. A quote that won't leave my mind...a quote that I go to sleep thinking about, if my memory serves me correctly, was spoken by a

British captain in 1763. His name escapes me, but the quote was, '*Hammer the Americans hard enough and you will forge the best weapon in the world.*'"

James ended his motivational speech with that quote, and it raised the hair on the back of each of their necks.

"Gentlemen, all they need to start that fire is a spark. Freedom is a burning fire inside of every American. Once that flame starts, nobody can control it."

"I'm in," Hensworth said.

"I'm in," Buchanan added.

Around the table, the comment was repeated until each and every officer had committed themselves to the cause. When it came back around to James, he added, "In the words of Patrick Henry, '*Give me liberty or give me death.*'"

Abandoned UN Control Point, Mount Vernon, Illinois

Very little sunlight was entering the doorway of the train car. Jess, Tori, and Jones had shackled the Iranian man to the wall of the car. The way the transport car was designed allowed for the prisoner to be stretched, hands over head and legs spread. This made escape all the more difficult. His arms and legs were spread more than shoulder width apart. There was a center restraint system installed, but no straps were present. Lance Corporal Jones had removed his belt and secured the hips of the thin Iranian man to the restraint bar that was running horizontally along the length of the wall. Unable to thrust his hips, lower his arms, or kick his legs, the man was at the mercy of his captors.

"I bet you're going to speak perfect English now," Tori whispered in his ear. It was loud enough for Jones and Jess to hear, but the reason for the whisper was to set the mood, not to keep people from hearing her.

"I speak English. Please don't hurt me."

Jones left their side and went to the back end of the train car and sat down with his back resting against the wall.

Jess pulled a knife out of her boot and poked it just to the left of the man's eye.

"You don't need your eyes to speak English, blue man."

"Please don't hurt me. I will talk."

"Where did your friends go, blue man?"

"I no understand."

Jess put more pressure on the knife and leaned in to provide for a thrust of the knife should he not comply with her request.

"Wait a second, Jess," Tori interrupted. "You're doing it all wrong."

"Oh, and you've interrogated people before?"

"Interrogated? Really? Is that what we're calling this? Let's not be coy, here. This man has information we need and we're going to torture him until he feeds it to us."

"Fine, you torture him, then."

Jess tossed her knife to Tori, but Tori didn't catch it. She just let it hit her chest and fall to the floor. She had to dodge her feet to avoid being stabbed by it.

"Easy, girlfriend. I have my own methods."

Tori reached into her pocket and pulled out some chunks of tissue paper. She proceeded to tear off little pieces and shove them into her ears.

"What are you doing?" Jess asked.

Tori pulled out her shiny 1911. "Meet Bubba."

"So now we're gonna shoot him?"

"Precisely," Tori said, pointing her gun at the Iranian and pulling the trigger.

Jones jumped up and Jess ran out of the train car. Jones followed after her, jumping out of the car and holding his ears. The gunshot was so loud that both of their heads were ringing.

When Jess and Jones came to their senses, they looked back to see many of the Marines, including Nathan and Denny, running to their location.

Tori was now standing next to the Iranian man with her gun pointed at his head. She was screaming in his ear, "Now you're going to tell us where the rest of the UN soldiers went or I'm going to blow your pathetic blue head off."

Nathan noticed the man was bleeding from his leg where Tori had shot him.

The man was answering her question out of fear and pain.

"They were reassigned by the executive commander to report to Independence, Iowa."

"Why were they reassigned?"

"The executive commander has received word of a large gathering of resistance fighters in South Dakota. They are to rally in Independence to form an assault strategy."

"Where's the rest of Americans that were here?"

"The trains left with what they could, and when the next train didn't arrive, we were ordered to get rid of the excess."

"Who's this executive commander you speak of?"

The man didn't answer, so Tori shot his other leg. The man was now almost completely hanging by his wrists.

Screaming, the man said, "Please stop shooting me."

"I'll stop shooting you when you start answering my questions."

The group was standing outside of the train car, watching and hearing everything.

Jess was still rubbing her ears when she leaned into Nathan and said, "I don't know if I love her or hate her."

The Iranian man said, "If I talk to you about him, he'll kill me."

Tori laughed at his comment. "Can't you see? I'm going to kill you if you don't."

"His name is Abdul Muhaimin. His reach is long, he hears everything, and I'm sure he sees you coming."

Tori pressed the gun to his head even harder, causing him to cry out.

"I'm telling you what you want."

"What else can you tell me about Abdallah Mammon?"

"It's Abdul Muhaimin. He was a captain in the Iranian Jihadist Wars. He won many awards to be promoted to general of the UN forces in America. When the US president died, he announced himself executive commander of America and UN forces in America."

"The president is dead?" Sergeant Banks asked.

"Did he say the president is dead?" Nathan shouted to Tori.

"Yeah, he said she was dead. Now he's going to tell us how she died."

"I don't know how she died. Nobody knows and nobody asks."

"What are your long-term orders?"

"To move all citizens from these US cities to the trains and barges, for transport to the Human Handling Centers. From there, they are separated into categories."

"And what categories are those?"

"Vital and invasive."

"Elaborate."

"Vital citizens are interned until Relocation Protocols are initiated."

"And what of the invasive citizens?"

The man was beginning to feel faint and was having difficulty speaking. Tori caught on to this and unshackled the man's first wrist, letting him dangle by one arm while she unshackled the second. The man fell to the floor and Tori jumped off the train. She walked over to Jess and said, "Your turn."

Jess rolled her eyes at Tori.

Nathan looked at Denny and said, "Can you patch him up? He's got more to tell us. Maybe he'll open up more later, seeing how we were so nice."

"Sure thing, boss."

Nathan hadn't heard that from Denny for a while and it reminded him of more peaceful days.

Sergeant Banks looked at Nathan and said, "That was a lot of information. We need to sit down and talk about it."

"What's to talk about? The president is dead, the United States has been invaded by the UN, and our people are being called *invasive* and shipped to certain death."

"You forgot the part about the UN forces being reassigned to Independence, Iowa, for some kind of support."

"That means Illinois isn't going to have as much opposition," Jess said.

Nathan, returning a look to her, said, "They left him behind; they're sure to have more spies lying around."

"I think they left him accidentally," Banks said.

"How can you tell?"

"Well, would they really leave him with no ammo? I bet they took off without a roll call."

"I got something even better out of all that," Tori said. "If the UN is pulling all their manpower to Independence, Iowa, then there must be a sizeable resistance there."

"We haven't heard a peep out of the UN communications systems we have; otherwise, we might have heard what's going on," Nathan said.

"Perhaps that's because they've changed their tactics, and we don't know what they are, but I bet he does," Banks said, pointing to the Iranian man.

Denny hollered down from the train car. "He's going to need some blood."

"What type?" Nathan asked.

Denny searched for the man's ID or service tags, in search of his blood type. "I can't find anything." Denny thought for a moment and tried to remember his training. "He's going to need O negative."

Banks turned around and started shouting, "Do any of you have O negative blood?"

Most of the Marines were shaking their head no.

"Okay, then, it's hardball. Let's see those tags. Take your tags out and hold them up."

Banks walked around to each Marine and inspected their dog tags. When he came up to Lance Corporal Jones, he saw O negative on his tags.

"I'm not willing to donate to a blue hat."

"This isn't about saving him, Jones, it's about saving us. It's about saving America. He's got information we need."

"Fine." Jones started rolling up his sleeve.

Digging into his medical pack, Denny found that he only had one field blood-transfusion kit. Rethinking his plan, he asked, "I only have one of these, Nathan, are we sure we want to waste it on him?"

"I can't think of a nobler reason than to save priceless and life-saving information for the American people."

Denny had Jones relax on the edge of the train car door while he tied a tourniquet around his upper arm. Using the blood-transfer device and the blood-pack unit, he collected 450ml of blood from Jones and tried to give it to the Iranian man, but he was cold and Denny couldn't find a vein.

"I need a couple of you up here to help me heat him up. He's cold."

Everybody stood around looking at each other, hoping that somebody else would volunteer. Tori finally broke the silence, "Okay, I'll do it, but only if I get to be the one to render him *invasive* when we're done with him."

"Done," Banks agreed.

Tori climbed up into the train car and kicked Denny out.

"Sorry, Den, but this is our private time and you don't get to peek."

Tori closed the door and undressed the man. She was disgusted to do so, but it was a matter of survival and saving a dying man. After she had exposed his skin, she bared hers next to his to share her body heat. After a few moments, Denny checked in on him and Tori. He caught her rolling off of him and turned his head away.

"That should be good enough, Tori. Sorry, I should have knocked."

"I'm just glad it's over."

Denny opened the door the rest of the way to let in more light. Then made his second attempt at finding a vein; after a few pokes, he was given blood.

The man's legs were already patched up. Fortunately, the shots were clean and the bullets didn't sever any arteries.

By the time the Iranian man had awakened from his sleep, the group had attached one of their portable generators to a small insulated building and warmed the interior. With the man's vitals now under control, he found himself lying on the floor next to Tori. His hands were zip-tied and his legs were throbbing.

"Good morning," she said.

"I was hoping this was all a bad dream."

"It's a nightmare, dude. We weren't done chatting. I thought it was rude when you dozed off on me."

"I really don't know too much."

"That's funny, because I remember you acting like you could barely speak any English at all, and then suddenly, BANG, you can speak perfect English, albeit a little accented, but still..."

"If you promise not to kill me, I'll tell you whatever you want."

"Can you hold that thought?"

Tori stood up and walked out of the room.

A minute later, Jess walked into the room and sat next to the man. "Okay, now what's the deal?"

"If you promise not to kill me, I'll tell you whatever you want."

"I can live with that. Start talking."

"What do you want to know?"

"Just start talking."

"My name is Nasrallah Gulestan. I have three children and a wife. I serve in the Iranian army and was assigned UN duty. I just do what I'm told, okay?"

"Okay, so tell me what you were told."

"We receive shipments of Americans, supplies, and fencing projects. We set up temporary handling centers and put more Americans on each train until they are full. They are then shipped north. I don't know where they take them, but I do know there are duty stations north of here that keep special Americans, and another duty station that...that..."

"That what?"

The man was afraid to reveal the last part of his comment, but when Jess pressured him to speak, he gave in.

"That processes them."

"Processes how?"

"UN Biocontrol Units inoculate them. Some of them resist the inoculation, and the others, not so much. Most of these people are sick before they get to the stations."

"What are you inoculating them with?"

"I don't know. We get our shipments with tags on the boxes from FEMA Bioengineering and Research. We do what we are told. I'm just taking orders. I'm a military man."

"One more question. Do you think it's right to invade another country, capture its people, inject them with unknown substances, watch them get sick and then kill them?"

Jess wired the question in a way the man was not suspecting. She picked up on his verb *processes* and figured they were killing the sick in some fashion. To be sure, and to have him admit to it, meant she had to approach it from another angle.

"I am not allowed to disagree," he answered, skirting the response Jess was looking for.

Jess took out her knife and the man began to squirm and kick, but the pain was so much that he could barely resist.

"Take it easy. I promised not to kill you."

She cut the rank from his collar and the UN name strip from his jacket.

"Now you can agree or disagree. I've removed you from the bonds of UN and Iranian control. This is America, and in America you can say whatever you want."

The man looked sternly at her, thinking she was the weaker of the two interrogators, and said, "I am Iranian, not American, I have been killing Americans since I was a small boy. I do want to live, but I cannot betray my country by telling you I disagree."

Jess stood up and Tori walked into the room. When the man saw Tori, he began to squirm like he did when Jess had the knife.

"I have a request," Tori said. "Tell us how to access the UN communications network. We used to listen in, but they've done something different so that we can't hear radio traffic."

"They are cycling a list of frequencies," the man said with a shaky voice.

"What are the frequencies?"

"I don't know, only the officers carry them."

"Well then, you're of no further use to us."

Tori pulled her pistol up and said, "You've met Bubba, haven't you?"

"You promised me you wouldn't kill me."

"No, she promised she wouldn't kill you, but I was promised I could kill you. *Comprende?*"

The man started to speak, but Tori put a bullet through his mouth as he opened it.

Jess and Tori walked out of the room together.

The group was waiting outside and everybody was standing up after hearing the gunshot.

"What did you find out?" Banks asked.

"They've been inoculating Americans with some kind of juice that either makes them sick or has no effect. From what we could tell, they are somehow killing the people that get sick from the inoculation, but doing something else with the people that have immunities against it," Jess replied.

"What about the radio comm?"

Tori interjected, "They've been cycling through a list of designated frequencies and only the officers carry that list."

Nathan started walking towards his HMMWV. Stopping short of it, he turned around and asked, "How are we supposed to get an officer when we don't know where they've gone?"

"Chicago," Jess said.

"She's right," Nathan responded, looking over toward Banks. "If there's a Human Handling Center north of us, it's Chicago. It's our destination anyway. I'm betting there's UN officers overseeing the FEMA employees."

"Get that generator packed and start mounting up. We're wasting time," Banks yelled out.

Everybody scurried to a vehicle. A few men ran over to the generator and loaded it into one of the five-ton trucks. After the group was sorted, they headed north, using Interstate 57, being under the assumption the interstates may very well be opened up, due to a recalling of UN soldiers. The highways were vulnerable to teams of brigands, but if the interstate was accessible, this would make for a quicker trip north.

CHAPTER 13

Gary, Indiana

"So tell me about yourself, Mr. uh..." Captain Richards asked, trying to get a name from Rory.

"Forgive my rudeness. I'm Rory Price. I was a Pentecostal pastor before the Flip; now I'm just doing what I can."

"Where did you preach at?"

"I pastored in Murphysboro, a small town in southern Illinois."

"No kidding? I have relatives down there, not too far from Murphy."

"Oh yeah, where at?"

"Grand Tower, it's a little town on the Mississippi. Even smaller than Murphy."

"Are you serious? I was just in Gorham a few months ago with some friends."

"Who are your friends?"

"You probably wouldn't know them. Our friendship was

brief. I was under the yoke of a sick man just before the UN began to establish a heavy presence. This guy named Denny and a few others found their way into my home and got me out of that town. Then I met his best friend Nathan and Nathan's girlfriend, Jess. I met so many good people."

"Nathan Roeh is the name of my family that's from Grand Tower. He's my nephew on my sister's side."

"That sounds familiar to me. Was he in the Marines?"

"Yes, a few years prior to the Flip. He was an Internet coder or something like that."

"I think we have the same guy here, Captain."

"Wow, it's a small world, Rory. You can't tell it these days, with the invasion and all. Makes things larger than life. What was Nathan doing when you saw him last?"

"He was headed this way to the FEMA Region V headquarters in pursuit of liberating American prisoners. I've learned so much since then."

"Listen, Rory. We're heading into battle. We captured several bits of intelligence from the blue hats. From what we can tell, they are mounting up a heavy force against a US military unit in South Dakota. We've been listening to their comms and communicating with other US military units around the Midwest. We are going to join the fight and hopefully win a decisive battle, maybe even a war. We have the home-court advantage."

"The Marines I was with were heading in that direction. They were shady about what was going on, though. I was with a Marine lieutenant colonel, Charles Buchanan, when he met the commandant of the Marine Corps just a couple days ago."

"Commandant? Are you sure?"

"Absolutely. We spent the day with him. Authoritative and stern—I liked that about him."

"The commandant of the Marine Corps is like the equivalent of the Army Chief of Staff. He's a member of the Joint Chiefs of the United States. This is big news."

"How so?"

"It tells me that the Joint Chiefs are no longer commissioned as presidential advisors. It's likely they stepped down or were fired. It provides hope for a strong unified front. We just need the opportunity to form the front."

The convoy was moving west when Rory saw the Illinois state limits sign. It wasn't until they found themselves in South Holland that they ran into roadblocks and street signs directing them to the nearest Human Handling Center. Many of the street signs said MARTIAL LAW IS NOW IN EFFECT, and other signs directed RFID-chipped citizens to report to loading docks. Most of the street signs led them to makeshift train stations that were erected alongside the train tracks.

The convoy seemed to be ignoring the warning signs and continued on the street that was labeled UN VEHICLES ONLY.

"I've got a bad feeling about this, Captain. Don't you think we should delineate off this road and onto another road that's not so heavily labeled UN?"

"Relax, Rory. Most of the streets we've seen labeled UN have been abandoned."

No sooner than Captain Richards had said that, a rocket

struck the first vehicle in the convoy. Rory was gripped with panic as he ducked his head and took cover.

Captain Richards picked up the mic on his radio and commanded the convoy to mow through.

The second vehicle in the convoy became the lead vehicle, and blasted through the wreckage just like they had done in Gary, Indiana.

"What's going on?" Rory asked in a panic.

"Seems you were right, preacher. If we make it out of this alive, I'm going to field promote you to chaplain."

"If we get out of this alive?"

"Yeah, we're being chased by UN APCs now."

"What's an APC?"

"Armored personnel carrier. They're bad news. Like mini tanks. Those bad boys are fitted with .50-caliber guns. We need to take up an offensive position or we'll get eaten up."

Richards held the mic up to his mouth again and said, "Take an offensive position up there behind those buildings. I want my Javelins to nail them when they break the threshold. We can't mess this up, boys. Make it work."

The convoy split up into two teams when they reached the end of the road and took cover on the opposite side of the buildings. A few men jumped out and placed Javelins on their shoulders. Javelins were fire-and-forget-type rockets that were launched from the shoulders of military personnel.

When the APCs broke the threshold of the buildings, they opened fire on the HMMWVs with their .50-caliber guns.

The Army soldiers also attacked using their Javelins. The rockets launched into the air, taking a skyward trajectory, until they came down onto their intended targets and impacted onto the APCs, blowing them to bits. The men cheered, but the celebration was short lived.

Many of the men slowed their cheers and took the time to look around, seeing they had lost at least seven more brothers to a UN attack. The loss of Americans always seemed to strengthen their resolve. Captain Richards felt like calling his men into formation, but the place was a battle zone and enemy UN personnel could be anywhere, perhaps even reinforcements.

Richards felt that some things just couldn't be put into words. His notion to speak to his men was piled into the back of his mind with so many other things that needed to be done and said. The words would come later, but for now, all he could say was, "Collect the fallen, then mount up. We're still on mission, gents."

Rory had never had a rocket shot into a convoy he was riding in. The experience was surreal, to say the least. Words escaped him as he aided the soldiers in the collection of their fallen brothers, his fallen brothers, the men of vision for a liberty that they would never experience again.

Rory felt the same strengthening resolve to see this through unto whatever end may come. *Their deaths must never be in vain,* he thought.

Black Hills Army Depot, South Dakota

Sergeant Rick Hammel, communications specialist, came running into the bunker where James was having his meeting with the brave and committed officers of the newly reactivated 21st Marine Corps Regiment.

"Gentlemen, I'm sorry to interrupt, but I have something to say of urgent importance."

Hammel was breathing heavily, as if he had just completed a two-mile run, and it may very well have taken that much endurance to run with the radio equipment he now had on his back.

"Go ahead, Sergeant, speak," the commandant commanded.

"I've managed to pick up a frequency that FEMA and the UN ground forces share to relay information back and forth. They're headed this way with an extremely sizeable force, and their intentions are not to take prisoners."

"They must have followed you here," Hensworth said.

"They didn't follow," Hammel said. "They had some kind of tracking system called Main Core."

James locked eyes with Buchanan. "This is exactly what I was talking to you about. We've all been rigged with GPS implants and everything FEMA wants to know about us can be found in these devices. The Main Core program is the culmination of the old Red Tape Program. They must have E-Tech that allows them to trace our location."

"Well, what are we waiting for?" Buchanan replied. "Let's hit the dirt."

"There's a town not ten miles from here. We can meet them with some old-school urban guerilla combat," Hensworth suggested.

"What's their location, Sergeant?" James asked.

"Their location was not established over the radio, but their rally point is Independence, Iowa."

"Independence, Iowa?" Wright said with a half smirk.

"It's like they're using our patriotism as a weapon against us," Barnes said.

"Do we have a time stamp on Independence, or are we going to have to guess it?" James asked, trying to keep the questions together and on the same track.

"There was no mention of any time frame whatsoever, sir. We're flying blind as far as time stamps go."

"Stay with us, Sergeant. I want you here if anything else comes over that frequency. Hensworth, I want the air support tucked away in that town you mentioned. Refresh my memory, what do we have in way of artillery?"

"Thirty howitzers."

"I'm expecting these dirtbags to play hardball. They're not operating under the Geneva Convention standard of warfare and neither are we. They're going to come at us hard and they're going to break all the rules. Buchanan, I'm making you a full bird, effective immediately. Each of you will command a battalion. Buchanan, exactly what did you bring?"

"Weapons 2/24, a company of Engineers, a company of Recons, and some hard corps militia."

"Can you run seven companies?"

"I'll storm the gates of hell with seven companies."

"That's what I like to hear. I'm giving you 3/25 India, Kilo, Lima, and Weapons. That's two weapons companies under your command and the support they need to lay down some hurt."

James looked across the table at the other colonels and said, "That leaves a battalion of Marines with armor and air support for each of you. Let's make this a dirty war, gentlemen. Buchanan, you're authorized to shoot ground troops with .50 cals and whatever heavy guns you feel like shooting at them. Do you understand?"

"Roger that, sir. We're no longer fluffing pillows or riding the rainbow train."

Buchanan had picked up on the fact that the commandant was back in military mode, no longer calling him by his first name. He was more comfortable in fight mode than he was otherwise. For a moment, Buchanan gave thought to his old friends from Gorham. So much had happened since then. He took a second to hope that Nathan and the rest of the Posse was safe and found themselves still on mission. Buchanan had told Nathan that he would rally with them in Chicago, but a more pressing matter needed his attention. It was the game-changing moment when he had received a transmission from John James.

Independence, Iowa, 17:56 Hours

Independence was on full lockdown and cleared of all civilian population, by orders of Executive Commander Abdul Muhaimin. Every road was blockaded and had UN checkpoints coming into and leaving the city. It was almost 18:00 hours in Iowa when the last of the reallocated UN ground forces came rolling through the checkpoints.

Captain Rashoutan Siroosi, of the Advanced Weapons Systems Company, had arrived a little behind schedule, causing Captain Alexander Zacharov to confront him regarding the topic of insolence.

"Captain Siroosi, how is it you came to command an advanced weapons company when you can't even make it to a rally point on time?"

"Relax, Russian, the executive commander will be here soon. As long as we arrive before he does, there's no worry."

Zacharov knew that being called Russian was intended to be derogatory. The Russians had always had a high sense of pride and certainly did not like being ridiculed because of it. Siroosi held his peace and commanded his unit to post itself and to look presentable for the executive commander.

Within the next hour, Muhaimin was looking out of the window of the helicopter and down onto the two regiments of ground forces that were moving into formation. He felt strong seeing a regiment of UN strength at his disposal, and was fully confident that two regiments of his men could defeat, humiliate, and dishearten the resistance. He needed this moment to be an example of his strength over the Americans so that no nation would dare resist his authority. Not only did he want the world to know he was capable of great feats, but also that he was not to be trifled with. He understood that should he lose, it would be the beginning of the end for his ambitions. This is why, not only was he matching his strength against the size of the Marine Corps Regiment in South Dakota, but he was doubling it to insure certain victory and to immortalize himself in the annals of history with the likes of Napoleon Bonaparte, Attila the Hun, Genghis Khan, and Sun Tzu.

Colonel Artan Mota and Colonel Vala Baghnalia were

standing at the front of the two-regiment formation. Mota was commander over all units assigned to Fema Region VII, while Baghnalia was the commander over all units assigned to FEMA Region V.

Muhaimin landed and was met by both commanders. He was happy to see the two Iranian commanders he had appointed over his Midwest regions.

In his native Persian language, he said, "I've had about all I can take from the Russian pigs. After we finish this little task, we're going to purge them from command ranks. I don't want any direct contact with any of them."

"Yes, sir," they replied.

Looking out upon the formation, he could see Russian captains standing at command point in front of the companies.

"Colonel Baghnalia."

"Yes, Executive Commander?"

"I need a good spot to hold a meeting."

"I think that school building would be an excellent spot, sir."

"So do I."

"Colonel Mota."

"Yes, Executive Commander."

"Hold an emergency meeting, at 19:00 hours, with all the officers and command their presence."

"Yes, sir."

Mota began to walk away.

"And, Colonel," Muhaimin said, stopping Mota in his tracks. "Make sure nobody misses the meeting."

"Yes, Executive Commander."

Just a few minutes before 19:00 hours, the Russian and Iranian commanders over companies of the Midwestern FEMA Regions came walking into the school building. The men were directed to check their weapons in at the door and then they were walked to the gymnasium, where they sat on the bleachers in a tight formation.

Colonels Mota and Baghnalia entered the gym and stood in front of the group. A squad of Iranian riflemen came in after them and secured the doors, then marched over behind the colonels and stood in a row with their rifles at port arms.

"Gentlemen, the executive commander commands that you pledge your allegiance to him as the supreme power of the land and the fist of Allah. If you are willing to make this pledge, stand and repeat after me."

Many stood out of fear, but of those who didn't were two Russian captains. Alexander Zacharov and Erik Babatyev of the Russian UN assignments to the US.

Mota gave the command and the squad of riflemen ran to the front and took the two Russians out of formation and placed them on their knees in front of the bleachers.

"Are there any other Russians who do not wish to swear their allegiance to the fist of Allah?"

The room was quiet.

"We do not have time, in these days, to worry about our allegiances. If you are not with the executive commander, then you are against him."

Mota looked at the riflemen and nodded. The men executed the two Russian captains and their blood flowed from their lifeless bodies towards the bleachers and eventually ran underneath them.

Those who remained recited their allegiance and affirmed commitment to the cause of their executive commander. They were free to leave and rejoin the executive commander in the classroom he had selected. After all the officers had taken their seats, Muhaimin began his speech.

"Tomorrow will be the dawn of a new era. The patriot resistance seems to be gathering enough leadership to reform its military. A regiment-sized unit of Marines has been gathering in South Dakota, where they are making plans to retake these lands. Your job is to insure their annihilation and to suck the life out of their patriot cause. I want their ambitions of freedom and liberty to die with them. I want the news of their demise to reach the borders of every rural area and every city where hope can still be found. There's no need for hope, just like there's no use to run or fight. This is my will; see it through."

Muhaimin turned and walked out.

CHAPTER 14

Champaign, Illinois, 100 miles south of Chicago

SERGEANT BANKS WAS LEADING the convoy north on I-57. The group had made it to the northern parts of Champaign without incident, until the driver of one of the HMMWVs happened to look into one of his side mirrors and saw a stream of cars and trucks pulling out onto the I-57 north exit.

"Guys, we have a pool of incoming POVs."

The passenger grabbed his mic and announced to the convoy, "We have incoming."

Everybody that heard the radio traffic was looking over their shoulders, trying to get a view of what was behind them. Others were confused at the comment and were looking skyward for an incoming air attack.

The gunners mounted their turrets, taking positions behind their heavy guns. They were traveling 50 mph, making a TOW weapon attack improbable. The .50-caliber machine guns were locked and loaded. Each gunner was waiting for a command or for the unidentified convoy to make the first move.

"I need a SITREP, back there," Banks said on his radio.

"Thirty Victors, zero weapons, maintaining consistent cruise speed."

That bit of information told Banks that there were thirty vehicles that appeared to be unarmed, not taking an aggressive posture.

"They have a Bravo Hotel Mike Charlie Uniform," the voice relayed back to Banks, informing him of a UN Mobile Command Unit.

"Pull over and take an offensive position," Banks commanded on the mic.

The lead vehicle slowed and did a U-turn, which prompted every vehicle to follow into a tactically offensive position. With the heavy guns pointed at the convoy, which had slowed to a near stop, the men and women of the POV convoy slowly stepped out of their vehicles with their hands in the air.

"Don't shoot," some of them shouted.

The Marines waited for commands from Banks, who watched them closely as they were stepping out of their vehicles.

"We're on the same side," one of them shouted.

"Secure these people," Banks shouted.

When Nathan, Denny, Jess, and Tori caught wind of what was going on, they stepped out of their HUMMWVs and pointed their rifles at the men and women.

"Don't shoot," they shouted once more.

"Get on the ground," Nathan commanded.

Denny, Banks, Nathan, and other Marines joined in on forcing the people to the ground at gunpoint.

"Who are you? Why are you following us?" Banks questioned.

Nathan studied them closely and recognized their patches and their demeanor.

"It's cool, Sergeant. They're with us."

"Do you know these people?"

"Not *these people*, but I know of them and what they stand for. Frankly, if they've survived this long, they might come in handy. They're members of a three-percenters group."

"Like a militia group?"

"That's it."

"We're with you guys. We're on the same team," a man on the ground said.

"Okay, get up," Banks said and motioned to the Marines to lower their weapons.

"We've been fighting against some blue hats for weeks. Then they just left," the man said.

"What's your name?" Nathan asked.

"Troy, what's yours?"

"I'm Nathan. This is Denny, Tori, Jess, and those guys have name tags."

"Glad to meet you guys. So are you on mission? We'd like to join."

"Yes," Banks answered. "What do you have over there?" he asked, pointing to the mobile command unit.

"We captured it from one of the blue-hat skirmishes."

"What kind of intel did you manage to secure?" Nathan

asked.

"We've got some good stuff. It was a good capture. Until recently, the UN traffic was all English. Now it sounds like Persian. I'm guessing they're starting to see that they can't communicate without us capturing their radio traffic. Before they went Persian, we overheard information suggesting that US forces were capturing key strategic power grid points."

Everybody in the group was looking around at each other in awe and dismay.

Troy saw their faces and continued his monologue. "It's true. This MCU has picked up communications from all over the US. From what we have gathered, the western states are not only without power, but their electronics are down, their cars are down, nothing with an electronic signal works."

"Would they have nuked the West Coast?" Nathan asked rhetorically, looking at Banks.

"Wait," Tori said. "Did you say we were nuked?"

"Not necessarily," Denny interrupted. "A nuclear attack would fry anything electrical, but we don't have to head straight for the worst-case scenario. They could have seen that we were beating them on every front. Maybe they employed an EMP-style attack?" he suggested.

"I'm voting that they nuked us," Jess said.

"Why would they nuke us, Jess? They want this land inhabitable. That's why they're here. Don't you remember all the hubbub about the global community and the Agenda 21 initiative?"

"I thought Agenda 21 was hocus-pocus," Banks said.

"I'm sorry to interrupt, guys, but we've been listening to a great deal of communications. There's no indication that we were nuked. The West Coast, from what we've heard, is inhabitable. It's just like their electronics went out. We were thinking EMP, too," he said.

Denny nudged Jess as if to say told you so.

Troy continued, "They were driving around inside the area. No signs of a nuclear attack anywhere. Even the FEMA compounds and the UN control points were without power. Oh yeah, and an outbreak of some kind."

"Outbreak?"

"People are getting sick and they're starting to quarantine areas around some of the FEMA compounds."

"And the hits keep coming," Nathan quipped. "Well, we're on our way to Chicago. We're supposed to meet a friend with more firepower. I don't have a problem with you coming along with us, as long as Banks is cool with it, too. As you can see, we already have several POVs tagging along."

Banks appreciated the inclusion. He knew Nathan had been running the show for most of their trip from Gorham. "I'm good with it. So, you say they're speaking Iranian now?"

"Yeah."

"We should've kept the skinny guy," Banks said.

"You made a deal with me," Tori said. "How was I supposed to know he'd ever come in handy?"

"Okay, we just need to get another translator."

Troy grabbed his own face and said, "Man, I don't know why we didn't think of this earlier."

"What?"

"We left a wounded Iranian blue hat back in town."

The group all looked at each other and smiled big.

"Well," Nathan said, "go get him."

DECADES BEFORE THE FLIP, *the federal government had been buying up American soil, even though Article 1 Section 8 of the US Constitution limited this to ten square miles for the purpose of needful federal things such as forts, dock-yards, and buildings. The amount of land owned by the government was alarming. At any time, these lands could have been posted and controlled by the government, where events unfolded outside of the American eye and away from public knowledge. This image shows all land owned by the federal government (seen in gray), as of 2005. The current federal land mass is even larger:*

As of mid-2015, US presidents have issued 18,450 executive orders, bypassing congress, to force their will upon the people, even though this power was not enumerated among the powers listed in the US Constitution under Article 2 Section 2, but on the contrary stated in Article 1 Section 1 that congress had all legislative powers.

For years, the CIA, FBI, NSA, DHS, and other government organizations had been collecting and storing data, belonging to Americans, without probable cause and without warrants, despite the fourth amendment of the Bill of Rights. The amount of data collected daily was so much that the government had to build a multibillion dollar domestic surveillance center to store it. The address is N 11600 W, Saratoga Springs, UT.

These seemingly worriless events had yet to touch the bellies of the American people. The gradual decline of American rights were so incremental that it was not felt as a whole. It would have seemed that America was at peace knowing that the government was taking care of them and presumed the welfare of the people were at the forefront, but the truth is this:

The bigger the government gets, the less liberty the people will enjoy. When the government grows so large that is has control over every aspect of individual liberty, then it ceases to be freedom, and becomes privilege, a temporary benefit issued to the people as a license.

WANT MORE? GET BOOK THREE - ENDGAME

L. Douglas Hogan is a USMC veteran with over twenty years in public service. Among these are four years in the US Marines (three years as a USMC antitank infantryman, one year as a Marksmanship instructor), ten years as a part-time police officer and sheriff's deputy, and twenty plus years working in state government doing security work and supervision. He has been married almost thirty years, has two children, and is faithful to his church, where he resides in southern Illinois.

IN MEMORIAM
ALVIN E. DICKEY
1940-2015
SEMPER FI

Made in the USA
Middletown, DE
23 October 2020